TOOTHLESS GRINS AND HIS FATHER'S SINS

THE TOOTH FAIRY CHRONICLES

BOOK SEVEN

VICTORIA ROCUS

Serenade Publishing

www.serenadepublishing.com

For all the wonderful readers who have traveled with me on Rosie and Declan's loving adventure while cheering them along as you went, this final one's for you. "Go raibh mile maith agat (Have a million good things)."

ALSO BY VICTORIA ROCUS

The Tooth Fairy Chronicles

Tooth Decay With A Side Of Fae

Toothaches And Wedding Cakes

Baby Tooth And Tangled Roots

Wisdom Tooth And The Awful Truth

Toothpicks And Wicked Tricks

Missing Teeth And What Lies Beneath

Toothless Grins And His Father's Sins

GLOSSARY AND PRONUNCIATION OF ANCIENT OTHERWORLD GAELIC

Ádh goidte – (AH god-cha) "Stolen luck" based on the ancient Otherworldly belief that "luck" was finite and could be stolen from another person

Ádh mór – (AH-mure) good luck

Áilleacht – (AW-l'yacht) beauty

Amharc Scáth – (OW-erk skah) "Shadow Viewing" is a magical skill that allows the practitioner to be in two places at one time.

Anam – (AH-num) soul

An Galar Amú, - (un GA-lur uh-MOO) "The Wasting Disease" is a blood- centered, cancer-style Otherworldly disease similar to Mundane leukemia. Rosie's mother succumbed to this disease.

Aoibheann – (Ay-veen) a feminine name meaning "radiant beauty," the name of *Crann Bethadh's* head housekeeper.

Balor's Súil Olc - (Bal-orr soo-il ol-ukh) a curse meant to bring ill luck; refers to a legendary enemy of the Fae

Beacha siúinéir – (Bakh-ah shoe-in-air) carpenter bee

Beltane –(BYAL-tuhn-uh) an ancient pagan festival celebrated on May 1ˢᵗ to mark the beginning of summer, the height of spring, and the fertility of the land and its people.

Bhrocaire – (vro-KER-uh) a dog belonging to the terrier family

Blasanna beaga – (Bla-san uh-BYEG-uh) "little tastes" or appetizers

Bronntanas – (BRUN-tun-as) a gift

Caladbolg – (Kalla-bolog) an ancient magical sword given to The Black Knight to wield justice.

Caille – (KAH-lyeh) veil

Ciann Ti – (KEE-an tee) head of a household

Caoineadh Mathair ar son na Marbh – (KWEEN-uh MAH-her air son na MAR-uv) a litany of grief sung by a mother at the death of her child

Cloch Chroí – (Cloch -Kree) "Heart Stone" is a community housed in a monastery-type building for the training and guidance of Druid noviciates

Cófra – (KOH-fra) a cupboard

Contúirteach – (Kuhn-TOR-tchuk) dangerous

Crann Bethadh – (Crown -Ba-ha) the Fae "Tree of Life," an oak tree of immense proportions that houses The Morrigan, Queen Maeve of *I Idir*, and the Royal Family. Sometimes called "The Raven's Nest."

Cuach an Fhithich – (Kwach an Hih-hee) "Raven's Hollow" is the name of the estate belonging to House *Badh* which claims The Morrigan as a family member; the location of the estate is nearby to *Crann Bethadh*, the Royal Seat of *I Idir*.

Cú Chulainn – (Koo HULL-un) legendary warrior hero from Celtic mythology and long-time consort to the Queen

Deirdre – (DEER-druh) a Gaelic feminine name that means "sorrowful" or "broken-hearted"

Draoi a Rugadh – (Dree-ee rug uhak) "Wizard Born"

Draoithe – (dree-ha) Druids

Draoi truagh – (dree troo-ah) – "wicked sorcerer"

Droch ádh – (drock-aw) bad luck

Eimer – (EE-mer) a feminine name meaning "swift" or "quick"

Fáilteachas an Tí – (FAWL-cha-chus un tee) a Fae philosophy that anyone entering a home by invite of the host is to be treated with respect and free of fear from any bodily or magical harm; a proper Fae host will always see to a guest's comfort with suitable seating and offered refreshments

Fear Gorta – (far Gor-tah) the ancient Celtic spirit of famine and ill luck

Féchín – (FEH-heen) a masculine name meaning "little raven"

Francach – (FRON-akh) a rat

Gan luach scáthanna – (gun lu-akh skah-han-nah) translates to "worthless shadows," meaning figments of one's over-active imagination

Grá Ma Shaol – (graw moh hweel) translates to "Love of my Life," a title Declan uses for Rosie

I Idir - (ē ēdar) "In Between"- the Fae kingdom in the Other-world ruled by Queen Maeve, The Morrigan, goddess of war and destruction

Iníon – (in-yeen) daughter

Isolach – (EES-lac) cellar

Láidir – (Loyd-er) strength

Leanaí – (la-NAH-ee) child or baby

Liatharóid bata – (lee-ah-ROH-id bah-tuh) translates to "stick ball;" an Otherworldly game similar to croquet

Litha – (LEE-tha) a pagan sabbat celebrating the Summer Solstice and the longest day of the year with festivities centered on abundance and the joy of life

Mallachtaí – (mah-lukh-tee) curses

Mná-síghe – (mnah-shee) a group of keening Fae women; Banshees

Moccus – (Mok-us) an ancient Celtic god similar to the Roman Mercury

Mo Shiorghra - (MO-hear-gra) "Eternal Love" or "One and Only"

Mo Rós Beag Dealgach – (moh rohs byeg dyalg-okh) translates to "My Thorny Little Rose," a title Declan gives to Rosie

Na Sean Bhealaí – (nah shanvay-lee) "The Old Ways" of the Fae folk

Nead an Fhithigh Dhorcha – (nyad un hih-hee dor-kha) "The Nest of the Dark Raven Throne"

Oisin – (USH-seen) a masculine name meaning "little deer;" the name of Declan's missing half-brother

Piseóga – (PISH-og-uh) a spell-casted charm or amulet

Púca – (Poo-kuh) a race of household fairy folk associated with rural living

Reilig – (REH-lik) sacred burial ground or cemetery

Riail na Banríona – (ree-yal nuh bun-ree-uh-na) "The Queen's Rule;" a law of *I Idir* that allows the Queen the ability to over-rule a decision or law decided upon by the Ruling Council; the Queen's right to have the final word

Riail na Dtrí – (ree-yal nuh tree) "The Rule of Three;" an Otherworldly tenet stating that any magic sent into the world, either positive or negative, will return to the sender three-fold; the idea that magic always carries a price

Saighdiúirí (SYE-doo-ir) soldiers

Seamair – (SHAM-er) clover; sometimes referring to the Gaelic word for shamrock

Sedd Myrdynn – (SATH MYR-thin) a Welsh phrase meaning "Seat of Merlin:" property that is spell casted to connect directly to the magic of the current Merlin; the wards surrounding it prevent any magical or physical trespassing

Sióga Glasa – (she-ogue glah-suh) Green Faires; a race of Fae entirely wiped out by the Formorians, with the only survivor being a child named Rowana

Sláinte – (slahn-cha) translates to "health," and is used as a cheer while lifting a toast or consuming an alcoholic beverage

Snaidhm Sciath Cheilteach – (SNI-im SHKEE-a KEL-tak) the Celtic Shield Knot for protection against bad luck or evil intent

Solas mo Chroí – (SOL-us muh KREE) "Light" or "Center" of My Heart; an endearment Declan uses for Rosie

Solas sióg – (sol-as sh-o-g) "fairy light;" small balls of light energy created by *Sidhe* with high levels of magical skill

Spiorad cráite – (spyur-ud krah-cha) a wandering spirit who hasn't moved on to the Afterlife

Súil olc – (SOO-il OHL-k) translates to the "evil eye," a malevolent spell causing bad luck or ill intent: the Fae use a series of finger gestures to ward against becoming a victim of it

Taibhse (tavh-sheh) a ghost

Teaghlach – (chye-loch) family

Tinneas – (TIN-ness) an illness or sickness

Tir na nÓg – (TEER nah NOHG) a mythical island of light, beauty and eternal youth

Torc fiáin – (torc fee-ayn) wild boar

Trócaire Naofa – (TROCK-uh-ruh Nee-fuh) "Sacred Mercy," a tenet of Fae sacred law in which a *Tuatha de Danann Sidhe* can ask for a quick merciful death by instant beheading rather than suffer a long and painful recovery only to eventually be sentenced to death once again

Ulchabhán – (UL-khuh-wawn) an owl

GLOSSARY AND PRONUNCIATION OF OTHERWORLD NORDBOERNE WORDS

Dökkálfar – (DOK-kahl-fahr) the "Dark Elves" of Asgard; thought to have more magical skill than their "Light Elf" counterparts

Faðir – (FAH-theer) father

Freyja – (FRAY-uh) – an important goddess in the Norse pantheon; similar in nature to the Fae Morrigan

Groenn Dalr – (gro-en dahl-r) "Green Valley," a bustling city in Asgard closest to *I Idir*

Hefnd – (hemt) *Dökkálfar* sacred law allowing for vengeance against one's enemies including death

Hlidskjalf – (HLITH-skyahlf) Odin's famous throne that allows him to see all parts of Asgard at one time

Jotun – (Jow-tn) Dark Elven ritual magic often requiring blood sacrifice to *Freyja*; this type of magic often includes elemental manipulation, shapeshifting, illusions, soul travel, and immense strength

Seiokonor - (swek-uh-nor) Master Sorcerer of *Jotun* magic

Sveinur – (Svay-ner) Apprentice of *Jotun* magic under the tutorage of a *Seiokonor*

Taufr – (tow-fr) an amulet or talisman used in *Jotun* magic

GLOSSARY AND PRONOUNCIATION OF MODERN MUNDANE POLISH WORDS

Bigos – (bee-gowz) a traditional Polish stew made with sauerkraut, pork and sausage; other meats like venison and beef can be substituted

Borscht – (Boar-sht) a soup made with beets often served with boiled potatoes

Kawiarnia – (kah-V'YAR-nyah) a café or small diner

Kolacyki –(kow-WACH-key) a small cookie style pastry usually with a fruit, cheese, or poppy seed filling

Plaki ziemniaczane – (PLAHT-skee zhyem-nyah-CHAH-neh) a fried pancake made from grated potatoes and onions

Pierogi –(puh-row-gee) a small boiled dumpling stuffed with a variety of fillings such as potato, cabbage, meat, sweetened farmer's cheese or fruit

Tarnów – (taar-now) a large city in southeastern Poland near *Zilipie*

Zilipie –(zah-LEE-pye) a small town in southeastern Poland noted for its colorfully painted cottages

GLOSSARY AND PRONUNCIATION OF MODERN MUNDANE TURKISH WORDS

Bichura –(Bee-ju-ra) a Turkish house sprite that offers protection to women and the household, though they are often easily angered

Bourek –(buh-REK) a Turkish style eggroll filled with chopped beef and cheese, along with aromatic spices and herbs like cinnamon and parsley, and deep-fried

Djinn –(jin) a race of Turkish magical practitioners, often confused in mythology with Christian angels; they can appear in both human and animal form and have been known to possess humans, though Mundane myths wrongly have them offering wishes

Qaf –(qf) a primeval mountain range where the natural and supernatural world meet, and home to the djinn; like *I Idir*, it contains a Border Veil between the Mundane and the Otherworld, but one that is much more difficult to cross

Myrkiborg – (MEERK-ee-borg) "Dark Fortress"

Rúin fealltach – (ROON FAL-tukh) traitorous secrets

"What you leave behind is not what is engraved in stone monuments, but what is woven into the lives of others."

— Pericles

TOOTHLESS 1

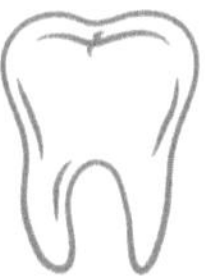

CREATING DARK MAGIC
18 MONTHS LATER

THE *SVEINUR* (young apprentice) laid the eighth dead rat upon the pile of stacked wood, its hairless, scaly tail hanging outward in the same manner as the other seven. The creature's beady, round eye reflected the light from the flickering lantern giving the appearance that the *francach* (rat) was cursing him with Balor's *Súil Olc* (Balor's Evil Eye), and the boy couldn't help but shudder in spite of the *taufr* (amulet) of protection he wore around his neck. While he found the large rats that roamed the wharves near his home wholly vile, the *sveinur* detested the necessary killing involved in the *Jotun* (dark Elven magic) ritual. Still, if he could draw the same level of magic using these repulsive rodents, it was a far better choice than the cats and dogs his *Seiokonor* (Master Sorcerer) had first suggested. It took more sewer rats to satisfy *Freyja* (Nordboerne goddess) than the larger animals, but in the apprentice's mind, it was the option that was easiest on his conscience.

This thought brought to mind the memory of his own *madra* (dog), and he wondered with a heavy heart how the animal fared without him. The boy did not like to think of the last time he had seen the *bhrocaire* (terrier), the look of betrayal in his companion's eyes as he had been locked in that kennel, the frantic, shrill barking that the *sveinur* could still hear in his head every night as he swung in his hammock. Still, it made no difference. No matter the boy's feelings about it, the *madra* was better off without him. This was no life he wanted to inflict on his oldest *cara* (friend). The animal was far better off where he was, surrounded by folk who lovingly cared for him.

Brushing away his childish musings, the student practitioner pulled the linen bag from the pocket of his jacket and sprinkled the contents on top of the pyre of rats. He could already smell the pungent tang of dried mare's dung and rooster blood, mixed with the sweet, spicy overlay of the fresh yarrow and the green hint of the crushed daisy petals the goddess called her own. Once lit, the acrid, magical smoke would fill his nose and mouth, eventually letting the *Jotun* of his people consume his soul.

With the *reið* (physical tools or paraphernalia of ritual *Jotun* magic) all in its proper place, the apprentice drew a circle around himself with a piece of red chalk, then called up *solas sióg* ("fairy light") to his fingers. In the beginning, the *Sidhe* magic that made up half of his soul warred with the *Jotun* sorcery of his Elven heritage. However, it wasn't long before the dark rose up against the light in both elements, winding the two energies into one powerful force. It took only a simple flick of his wrist to send the ball of heat towards the magical pyre, setting the whole configuration on fire.

The wood that formed the spell's base was damp, specifically scavenged from the crumbling wharves to produce an abundance of the desired smoke. It took several tedious minutes for the soggy wood to react to the flame, allowing the boy too much time to wallow in the self-loathing and doubt that sometimes crept its way into his mind. Thus, by the time the flames finally began their consumption of the rats, allowing the smoke to rise up and pour into the circle, the young sorcerer practically wept in relief. It wasn't long before he felt none of the thoughts that offered only sadness and pain. It was only within the circle of smoke that he was truly free, feeling only the pulse of dark energy in his veins, a blessed gift from the dark goddess herself.

TOOTHLESS 2

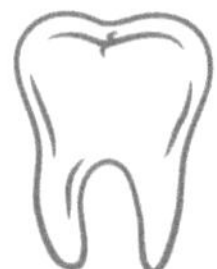

FOR THE FITZPATRICKS IT'S TRAGIC

ACCORDING to statistics on the US government website, 2,300 children disappeared every day. Though mainstream media tended to highlight only cases involving abduction, according to this same source, only 3% were actually kidnapped by strangers, with another 10% purposely taken by a non-custodial parent or family member. That left the other 87% with the generic title of "runaway," a moniker that hardly evoked the grief and pain left behind in the wake of their disappearance.

I know all of this because, in the aftermath of *Oisin's* vanishing, I'd spent hours and hours online searching world-wide databases of missing and exploited children in the hope that I'd find some clue that would help us find him. This was my main focus for nearly a month after my husband's brother left us, the endless scrolling through faces of lost children, each one someone's lost daughter or son, brother or sister, niece or nephew. Most nights I wept in front of my laptop, until one evening early into the Mundane new year, my Eternal Mate gently took the computer from my hands and closed it. "'Tis enough sufferin', *Stór mo Chroí.* Ya' will not find his face among these par' *leanaí.* I love ya' too much ta' let ya' keep chasing *gan luach scáthanna* (worthless shadows)." Despite my angry railing at him in good ole' Rosie fashion, deep down, I knew he was right. The internet search was just something I was using to make myself feel useful, as if I were doing "something" instead of just sitting around in high anxiety mode. To my mind, the search for my brother-in-law was moving far too slow, with too much talking and planning and too little action. As the weeks went by, one after another, it appeared that the urgency by The Throne to help us find *Oisín* had lost momentum, and I worried that at some point, the Powers That Be would give up the search all together now that the boy had passed into his 14th year, marking his as an adult in the eyes of *Sidhe* law and culture.

It was like the teenager had vanished into thin air, and when I use the word "vanish" to describe *Oisín's* Halloween disappearance, I mean it in the literal sense. Only minutes after we'd determined that the boy was with his biological father, the whole group of us headed back to the road where Lady Roxanne had found my son. Against my better judgement, Dylan was brought along to try and help locate the spot where *Oisín* had taken him after their round of trick or treating. I could not understand why with having the great Merlin and his son in our midst, we needed to rely on the shaky testimony of my traumatized five-year-old. It made no sense at all to me.

However, as both Merlins had expected and I hadn't understood, any and all traces of residual magical energy had been carefully "cleared out," undoubtedly by the *Jotun* practicing Callum Fitzpatrick. Thus, we were forced to rely on the Mundane style method of physical "tracking," using footprints, broken branches, crushed vegetation, and unusual scents to look for him. Dylan, atop his father's shoulders and hanging on for dear life, was able to point out a massive white oak he thought he remembered, mostly due to the obscenities spray painted on the trunk of it. He was also able to recall which path his teenage uncle had taken adjacent to that tree, leading us to a clearing that had a few physical signs indicating it had recently been inhabited; mainly the cooling remnants of the fire Dylan had mentioned. Unfortunately, there was absolutely nothing else found there that could help direct us to where the boy might have been taken.

That proclamation coming from the head of *I Idir's* security didn't stop my husband from going back to that spot near the Salem-Beverly Bridge every day for weeks afterward, in fox form, with the hope of finding something someone had missed, some miniscule clue as to where we should look next.

Poor Declan wore his guilt over *Oisin's* disappearance like a full body cast; a heavy, cumbersome suit of fortitude and self-sacrifice that kept anyone from getting too close to the feelings of acute blame he held inside. Because of the Bond, I knew better. I fully felt every shred of regret and shame he carried over his half-brother leaving the comfort of his loving family for the empty promises of his blackened soul father. "I pushed him too hard, Love," he'd say in those early moments when he was still willing to share any words on the topic. "Ya' were right. I shad' have tried harder ta' understand how much his early years had shaped his thinkin'. Instead, I just drew bigger lines in the sand, gave him more ultimatums. I might as well have pushed the boy inta' our sire's arms myself."

It did no good to tell him that he wasn't to blame or that this might be the path *Oisin* had to walk. Words only held power if the recipient was willing to listen to them with an open heart. I was the same way. Going over and over in my head every conversation and interaction I'd had with the boy in the days leading up to that awful night. What could I have said differently? Done differently to change the way that day had unfolded? All of the "would haves, could haves, and should haves" filled the empty spaces of my mind when it wasn't taken over with the daily grind of everyday living.

That's the thing about grief. After the initial shock it brings to your life, you end up gathering it all up and stuffing it into a mental "kit bag" of sorts, carrying it around like a backpack full of stones you don't want to carry but somehow can't seem to take off. *Oisin's* departure from our family left a big empty hole. It was noticeable from the empty chair at the table, to bedrooms in both Salem and *I Idir* that sat empty and quiet, as well as in the eyes of his dog, *Seamus*, who padded the halls of *Dun Siorai* in sad frustration. All of us were affected, especially Dylan, who after that fateful night and the few days that followed, now adamantly refused to ever talk about his *uncail* or any of the events that formed that terrible *Samhain*.

TOOTHLESS 3

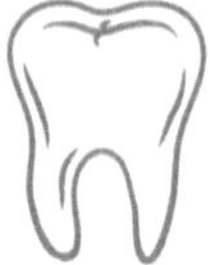

TROUBLE AT THE BORDER

EVEN WITH TEMPERATURES NEAR FREEZING, the smell of the decomposing corpses made his stomach roll. The fact that he even noticed the stink of the dead stood as testament that he'd been away from active duty far too long. Ten years ago, he would have simply ignored the putrid smell as he went about his business. There was no doubt about it. Life beyond The Job had made him soft, and if he couldn't regain his edge, people were going to die. People he'd made the mistake of caring about.

The Black Knight forced himself to swallow the mouthful of Mundane coffee, daring his gut to revolt, while he looked over the map detailing the magical border between the two worlds. Pinpointed were the specific areas the Mundanes were breaching the Veil in growing numbers. Unlike the Otherworldly folk, who could magically jump to an exact location in the other dimension, the few genetically altered humans wanting to cross the metaphysical divide could only land at the very spot where one reality physically meshed into another. Unfortunately for the Fae, that portal, for lack of a better word, intruded onto the border of the Kingdom of *I Idir*, making the unwanted intruders mainly the problem of The Morrigan.

There had been tales of humans accidentally crossing The *Caille* (Veil) for hundreds of years, creating the stuff of human legends and myths. But in the last two decades or so, there had been an uptick in purposeful efforts by the Mundanes in achieving this crossing; usually at the secret direction of their governments, and with scientifically made genetic alterations to their human DNA that allowed for passage through to the other side of The Veil. Unfortunately, once they passed through without enough Fae physiology, they began to quickly suffer a breakdown in their pulmonary systems causing excess fluid to build in their lungs, followed by heart failure and, eventually, death.

Except for the one intruder with the bullet in his forehead, this was the cause of death for the rest of the decaying bodies in the corner of the tent, all of them succumbing to pulmonary edema while they slowly and painfully suffocated. And if the gray pallor and clammy skin was any indication, the prisoner currently being forced into the tent would soon be joining his associates.

"I found him hidin' near the east grid, ma' Lord," the young Fae lieutenant explained. "He seemed alive enough ta' still talk, so I brought him here."

"Excellent work, McGeary," the Knight replied. "I'll interrogate him myself. Why don't you grab a few minutes in the mess tent before you head back out."

"*Go raibh maith agat, Ginearálta* (Thank you, General)," the kid replied with a snappy salute, pushing his prisoner roughly into a wooden chair. The *Sidhe* male appeared to be not much more than seventeen, flushed with Fae pride and excitement over his successful capture.

It had been a long time since the Fae of *I Idir* had been forced to take up weapons against an enemy. The Morrigan had brought peace and stability to her kingdom for several hundred years, and though the *Sidhe* folk of *I Idr* still trained their young in the traditional military arts, there had been little need for active troops. Thus, with the Fae inborn predilection for competitive fighting with ancient weapons, the Black Knight had no trouble mustering a small army to patrol the Veil border, recruiting both male and female *saighdiúirí* (soldiers) from every House in the Ruling Council; all of them already trained and ready to defend their homeland against the bold Mundanes.

The General addressed the prisoner. "Let's start with a simple question. What's your name and who sent you? If I had to guess, I'd say you're from somewhere in the Eastern European block."

The man glared in between labored breaths, then spit on the ground in defiance. Taking a chance, the Black Knight spoke in perfect Russian. *"Let's not fuck around. You are sure as shit in the process of dying and nothing can change that. Every minute that you sit here, your lungs are filling with fluid. Pretty soon, no oxygen will get through at all and you'll suffocate. Slowly, painfully, as you gasp for air like a fish out of water. I can end it for you a whole lot faster, my friend, if you just tell me what I want to know. What country do you represent?"*

The Russian spit again, looking at the General with blood shot eyes raging with hatred and answered back in the same language. *"You can go to fucking hell, you mixed-blood freak. We know who you are. You are a traitor to your own kind. And when the 'Cleansing' comes, you will be the first to die. You and the rest of that Raven Bitch's line. The suffering my people face when we cross the Veil is only a taste of the pain in store for you pointy-eared monsters."* The dying man tried to choke out a laugh that quickly turned to strangled coughing. *"You'll...see...soon... enough,"* he gasped, retching out each word.

The Black Knight considered the Russian's warning. This was the third time in the past three weeks one of these marauders had mentioned a "cleansing" of sorts. As of yet, his network in the Mundane world had been unable to gather any more intelligence on the topic. Still, it didn't bode well. Ethnic cleansing had been used to systematically eradicate whole races of people within human kind going back to ancient times. It wasn't a new concept, but not one the Fae had faced recently. Not since the *Formorians* had wiped out the *Sióga Glasa* (Green Fairies), almost seventeen years ago. His foster daughter, "Rowana," had been the only survivor, the last of her kind.

If this was what the Russians were working on, then it could only mean other Mundane countries were involved. When it came to annihilating the Fae and gaining control of the Otherworld, several of them were a united front. He needed information ASAP. They didn't have the luxury of waiting any longer. He needed to put the plan of action he'd been forced up until now to put on hold simply because of bad timing and political connections. There was no more time to give.

The Russian invader was now to the point of deep wheezing. He wouldn't be alive much longer. *"Last chance to take the easy way out, comrade,"* Beck said, holding up *Caladbolg* for the man to see. The spy's eyes widened at the ancient broad sword, but said nothing as he turned his head away, too weak to do much else. *"As you wish,"* the 27th Merlin replied. He snapped his fingers and a large full-length mirror appeared in front of the Russian. *"So, you can watch yourself* die," he explained in Russian. *"The mirror will also record your final agonizing moments so we can let your family know what became of you and anyone else who attempts to cross this Veil."* Then, the Black Knight of *I Idir* turned his back and walked out of the tent, leaving the gasping man to die alone.

TOOTHLESS 4

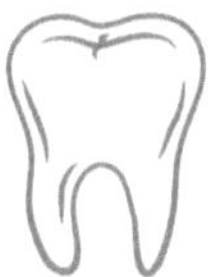

THE BLACK KNIGHT'S ORDER

"You know how I feel about these last-minute jumps, Declan," I complained as I tugged harder on the cords of my front-lacing corset, hoping to make it tighter. "Especially in the middle of the work week like this. It's already tomorrow evening there, for Pete's sake! Doing this always screws up my Circadian Rhythm. I'm not sure why this 'hush-hush, secret meeting' couldn't have waited for a few more weeks until we returned to *I Idir* for the summer."

"Aye, Love. Ya' have told me this same thing. Multiple times," the Love of my Life replies, not bothering to hide the husbandly annoyance in his voice. "But as I have explained ta' ya', the Black Knight has called this an 'emergency meeting.' He has stated it is imperative that we are all made aware of information that has come to light from the Veil border. I am told that even Herself will be in attendance."

"Oh goody. That makes it even worse. She makes everything so much more...intense," I say, then stop to wait for familiar tinkling of bells in my head. When there is silence, I continue. "Do you think this has anything to do with *Oisin?*"

His Lordship shrugged. "'Tis the truth when I tell ya' I donna' have a single clue as ta' what Beck's newest "emergency" is about. I would think if it only concerned the boy's disappearance, he would have just come to speak with us alone. Whatever this is, it concerns a grand number of people. My whole team has been commanded to attend, though as far as I ken' tell, you are one of the few Ladies to have been included."

"Lucky me," I answer, strengthening my shield and trying hard not to show the anxiety I felt over that statement.

"Ya' shad' take it as an honor that the Queen includes us both in her inner circle, Lass. Her Majesty is vera' particular about who she selects as a *rúnchara* (confidant). Not many hold that honor."

Secretly, I think to myself that the so-called 'honor" is a double-edged sword I could have lived without. Despite full shields, I hear those annoying tinkling of bells that signal Herself is listening in and is amused by my sarcasm. Buttons to banjos, as my friend Mel always says. You would think after nearly seven years that damn spell would have dissipated. Just goes to show you how powerful The Morrigan actually is. My not-so-private thoughts are interrupted by my husband's intense scrutiny of my appearance. "What?" I ask. "This gown isn't fancy enough for *Crann Bethadh?*"

"No. The dress is as lovely as always, but it hangs on ya' like it is two sizes too big. Have ya' lost more weight, Love?" he questions, a frowny crease forming in the middle of his forehead.

It's my turn to shrug. "I'm not sure. I haven't weighed myself for a while. Not since my annual physical last summer."

"Perhaps ya' should schedule something with Robyn ta' see why ya' are shrinkin' befar' ma' eyes," he counters.

"I feel fine, Sweetie. Really. It's just with all of this…stuff going on with *Oisin* and the trouble at the Veil Border, I don't seem to have much of an appetite." Honestly, I'm telling the absolute truth. Food doesn't hold my interest like it once did. I find my desire to spend time in the kitchen cooking, a past-time I dearly loved, at an all-time low, with my ordering carry-out to be delivered more and more these days. I'd been writing my change of attitude off as a reaction to the turmoil in my life, though the physician in me has some other "concerns."

It is those "concerns" that have my husband's attention as well. He is fully aware that my mother was nearly forty, the same age as I currently am, when she began to show signs of *An Galar Amú*, "The Wasting Disease," similar in symptoms to Mundane leukemia. It affects about 18% of people with Fae genetic markers, and is thought to be caused by damage to Otherworldly blood cell structure brought on by frequent trips through the Veil. Why it affects some people more than others is still a mystery Dr. Brannigan is working on. Despite making some positive progress with a combination treatment of high-level magic and physical blood transfusions from a healthy donor, the disease still takes the lives of about 86% of folks diagnosed with *An Galar Amú*.

I'm not up for a big discussion about the things that float around in the back of my mind. Not when I already have a command performance at The Raven's Nest staring me straight in the face. "Truly, Sweetie. I think it's just stress. *Oisin's* running away from us really packed an emotional wallop for me." The Tax Man doesn't look the least appeased so I add, "If it makes you feel better, I'll call Robyn's office and schedule an appointment here in Salem before we leave for the summer session in *I Idir*."

In return, I am enveloped in my *Mo Shiorghra's* familiar arms. "I appreciate that, Love," he murmurs into my hair. "Ya' ar probably right about it just bein' stress, but it would make yar' par' husband feel better hearin' it from the Doc himself."

* * *

As instructed, we jump from our home in Salem on a Wednesday afternoon directly to a Thursday evening in the main foyer of *Crann Bethadh*. We are met by a small contingent of Troll Guards and *Aoibheann*, who guides us to the Queen's personal parlor, a space I've never been invited to, and a clue to how "exclusive" this meeting really is. As I've mentioned before, *Crann Bethadh*, the Royal Seat, is housed in the Fae "Tree of Life," which is one hundred percent an actual gigantic, living tree with roots, leaves, branches, and so on. Once you wrap your head around that concept, you can stand in awe at the absolute beauty housed in the rooms that make up the inside of the immense estate.

Though I spent a few weeks housed in *Crann Bethadh's* guest quarters after my supposed "arrest" for the murder of Marcy Kilcrabtree, I was basically confined to those handful of rooms, and not free to explore. I've also spent time in the grand ballroom and the Ruling Council Chambers in my role as Lady *Nuada,* and I've visited the *Banphrionsa* and Black Knight in their family quarters, as well as attending some events in the opulent guest parlor. However, I have never been privy to any of The Morrigan's personal space. Thus, upon first entering the room I try not to look like an "Inner Circle amateur" with wide eyes and my mouth hanging open.

The room itself is round in shape and capped by a huge towering dome, an architectural concept I can't begin to explain inside a freaking tree. The ceiling of the dome is painted to resemble the night sky and damned if the "stars" aren't literally twinkling. In my head I hear my husband. *"'Tis remarkable, is it not? It changes throughout the day and night ta' mirror the actual sky. I was here once while a summer storm raged outside. One could see flashes of lighting between the painted clouds."*

Infatuated by the ceiling, I almost miss the floor to ceiling curved glass windows that make up nearly all the "walls" of the space, giving one the appearance of standing outdoors while still being inside. The furniture in the room is limited to a few scattered chairs and low divans, coupled with side tables, all exquisitely carved with various raven figures, and a free standing open-sided fireplace of sorts in the very center of the room, currently without flame because of the mild spring temperatures. I suppose the minimalist concept is specifically designed to keep your attention drawn to the natural view surrounding you from top and bottom, and to the elaborate throne-like chair that dominates every piece of furniture in the open space of the room.

Declan notices me gaping at the chair and says to my mind, *"It has its own name, ya' know 'Nead an Fhithigh Dhor-cha...'The Nest of the Dark Raven.' 'Tis why Crann Bethadh is sometimes called 'The Raven's Nest.' It refers ta' this specific chair. They say it was built for The Morrigan nearly a thousand years ago by a grove of ancient Draoithe* (Druids) *using magical energy gathered from Tir na nÓg. There is nothing else as powerful as it in the Otherworld, not even the famous throne of the Jade Emperor or Odin's Hlidskjalf."*

Though I have had nearly seven years to come to terms with the crazy path the Universe has set me upon, my half-Mundane-half tooth fairy self has never felt more...well... inadequate among these *Tuatha de Danann* movers and shak-ers. Perhaps that's why I'm caught off guard, giving a little startled jump when a sarcastically familiar voice behind me says, "Lady *Nuada*…what a surprise to see you here. I thought this was a meeting intended for Her Majesty's best and brightest."

TOOTHLESS 5

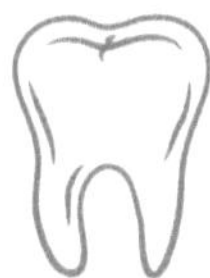

KEEPING in mind where I am, I take the protocol-correct, higher ground. "Lady *Mac Badh,* so nice to see you too. How fares House *Badh's* newest heir?"

"My son is every *mathair's* dream, Lady Sister. Wee *Féchín* (Little Raven) has gained nearly six pounds and sleeps through the night," she gloats. "And such a head of hair he has! Why…I imagine it won't be long until we will need to start braiding it," she adds with a smug smile. "And I am sure you've hard that my Lord and I have taken the Eternal Bond. We are vera' blessed to be so much in love."

It's obvious my sister-in-law throws in both comments simply to get my goat. Up until now, Declan and I had been the only Ruling Class couple that had undergone the Eternal Bond Ritual. No doubt, neither my sister-in-law or her ever-competive mate could let that stand. However, the two of them did appear to be a match made in *Dubnos* (Otherworld hell). I've come to believe that the Universe had a really strange sense of humor especially where human relation-ships were concerned.

Her other snarky comment about her baby's hair was directed towards my Ronin, who at 20 months, still has only a sparse head of ginger curls, taking, as he does, after my side of the family in all things but his *Sidhe* heritage. Because we've spent most of the past eight months in Salem for the Mundane school year, this is the first time I've seen Meghan since we returned to *Dun Sirai* for the Solstice sabbat in December. I'd be lying if I said I had missed her "shining personality" and cutting repartee.

"Congratulations on both pieces of news, Lady *Mac Badh*. You and your Lord must be very happy," I comment blandly. This surely wasn't the place to be rude. "I'm so happy to hear Baby *Féchín* is healthy and happy. Blessed be."

Meghan's pregnancy and the birth of House *Badh*'s newest heir was, if we were being completely honest, a mixed bag of news. If nothing else, it was a solid reminder that even the best laid plans could be turned on their head by the will of the Universe. More to the point, it made a lot of people "vera, vera happy." It was a monumentally joyous occasion for House *Badh*, as they now had not only a male heir but a spare in line for House leadership, a ridiculous patriarchal requirement I always felt was odd under such a strong female monarchy. Undoubtedly, it was a blessing to the new parents who seemed gloriously happy, while it gave my mother-in-law something more to brag about as a *sean-mamháthair* (grandmother) to four *Tuatha de Dannan* grand-sons, as if she were personally responsible for the fecundity of House *Nuada*.

On the other hand, though he'd never dare to come right out and say it, I'd lay dollars to doughnuts that the Black Knight had not been exactly thrilled when he'd first heard the "happy news" that Lady *Mac Badh* was expecting. When

Oisin's disappearance did little to help lead The Throne to Callum Fitzpatrick, it was no secret that the Queen's Hand of Justice intended to use Declan's sister as "bait" to draw out her heinous father. That had been the plan all along, the reason Declan and I were "persuaded" to agree to the end of her sentenced exile. But before any tactical arrangements could be put in place, the *Mac Badhs* came forward with their big announcement, putting a temporary stop to any spy work The Throne had intended. There was no way in *Dubnos* the politically powerful House *Badh* was going to take any chance with their progeny, and even Her Majesty knew better than to push the topic.

This had all taken place nearly a month after that awful *Samhain* night, with *Féchín Dónall Mac Badh* being born at the end of last August. The new *mathair* had petitioned The Throne for the traditional six months post-partum before returning to her "spy duties," and had been granted it, her social and political standing not allowing for anything else. I have no doubt our fearless leader was not happy about any of this. "Beck" had no patience at all when his assets were unable to meet their duties, but was surely held in check to keep his opinions to himself by Her Majesty.

The fact that Meghan was here tonight, coupled with the fact that the six-month post-partum reprieve had come to an end a few weeks ago, clued me in on why we'd all been summoned to *Crann Bethadh*. After all this waiting, a new plan was in the works. Whether or not my Tax Man had any knowledge of what that might entail was a mystery. I don't even kid myself anymore. There's no guarantee Declan would have told me even if he had known something. His keeping secrets from me has been a bone of contention between us for nearly the entire seven years I've known him, and a bad habit I can't seem to break him of. Across the room, I observe him making the rounds, chatting with other members of his team, easy and confident in his role as Lord of House *Nuada.* I think to myself, how damn naive it was for me to ever think he'd abandon the responsibilities of his Fae destiny no matter how much he professed I was the center of it.

There is, however, no time for me to contemplate the inner workings of our relationship as the sound of tinkling bells in my head announces that our Royal Hostess is somewhere near. Even six and a half years after I allowed the goddess of war and destruction access to my head in order to save my husband from the clutches of the North Koreans, a channel still remained open between us. Though she directly spoke to me less often, Herself had no problem letting me know she could invade my privacy whenever she chose.

The Morrigan appeared in the room out of thin air. One moment her chair was empty, the next she was lounging in it, dressed entirely in black silk except for a heavy gold chain hanging from her neck on which hung a massive morganite pendant. Sitting in that ebony chair, carved raven wings making up the back, and claw-like appendages at the bottom of the front legs, one could easily imagine goddess and chair meshing into one and taking flight right out one of the many windows in the room. Honestly, I hoped that wouldn't happen tonight. I'd seen Herself shift from raven to goddess and back to winged bird and it was…well…terrifying. It had taken me a long time to get used to Declan shifting into his fox form, and even now, I preferred not to be around when he did it.

The rest of the room noticed the Queen's arrival as well, dropping casual conversation and moving into court protocol mode. As usual, the Lord Warrior and Royal Consort, *Cú Chulainn,* stood behind Her Majesty, while the Black Knight took his spot at her right. I inventoried the room, but didn't see the elder *Banphrionsa* in attendance, which was a bit disappointing as Maureen Beckett always seemed to make the dullest mandated events more palatable. It was also interesting to note that besides The Morrigan and myself, only three other female members of Beck's spy network were in attendance; Lady Meghan *Mac Badh*, Lady Roxanne Brannagan, and my mother-in-law, Lady *Siobhan* Donnely *Nuada*, who, as of late, had kept *"Nuada"* as part of her title, but who'd dropped the "Fitzpatrick" part in favor of her maiden name.

Because it was clear we were following high court conduct, none of the ladies took a seat until we were invited to. "Ladies, please make yourself comfortable," Her Majesty said with a wave of her hand. As I knew she would, Meghan immediately grabbed a seat on a small divan next to Lady Roxanne, who, as a Princess of Avalon, technically outranked us, though I never found Roxie, as she preferred to be called, one to put on airs. I figured by claiming that seat, my devious sister-in-law was attempting to make it appear that she was on equal footing with Doc Robyn's bride, which was rather silly because we all knew she wasn't.

However, it was the way the game was played in *I Idir*, the constant hustle for a "better seat at the social table." (As you might expect, I am terrible at that game, though as Beck had predicted, rumors regarding us being together in the forest during *Oíche Fiáin* had made me "popular," but not in the way one would prefer. Plus, the Black Knight was wrong about my Tax Man finding the situation and the subsequent rumors "amusing." His Lordship had not thought them funny at all, and had told the man so in true cranky Declan style.) And, as my luck usually held, my darling mother-in-law took a seat in a single chair nearest to the Queen, leaving me to park myself alone on another divan, an action that didn't go unnoticed by my husband who, in turn, gave his *mathair* his very best lordly "stink eye." Yup. Just a typical day at Court.

The men remained standing as was the custom when Her Majesty was present. Declan came and stood behind me, while the two other spouses did the same. The doors to the Queen's personal parlor opened, and in came *Aoibheann*, followed by her waitstaff with carts of refreshments. Most days, I'd be more than happy to partake in the delicacies of *Crann Bethadh's* amazing kitchen, but my currently-Mundane-body-clock knew it was Wednesday afternoon in Salem, my day-off, and I had a load of things to do before Dylan's little league game and Liam's piano lessons later in the afternoon. The last thing I wanted to do was waste time eating *blasanna beaga* ("little tastes"/appetizers) when we could just get down to the business at hand.

The second that thought formed in my brain, I instantly regretted it. *Fáilteachas an Tí* (Hospitality of the Home) was a die-hard cultural Fae tradition, a long-held philosophy that no matter what your social standing was, or how opulent or humble your home might be, one offered the best of the larder to one's guests. I didn't need to look up to know that the Raven Queen's eyes were on me, and when she said in a voice that sounded suspiciously sarcastic, "Come, everyone share the bounty of *Aoibheann's* lovely carts. We will talk while we eat so as to not waste anyone's 'precious' time," I knew, without a doubt, I had caught Herself's attention. And not in a good way.

TOOTHLESS 6

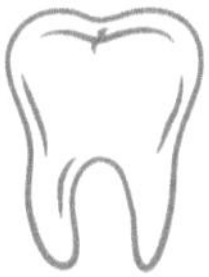

...AND SAVING FACE

I SELECTED a few tidbits off the passing cart and slide them onto my plate, keeping my eyes anywhere but in the direction of the Queen, who was quietly conversing with the two men at her side. I'd already received a retaliatory sharp poke to the temple, to which I replied with what I hope was a sincere-sounding apology. *"I'm sorry, Your Majesty. That was very rude of me. Especially after you were so gracious to offer us such a lovely array of delights. I do apologize."*

There is no reply, so I focus on nibbling at my "lovely delights." The whole situation makes me feel self-conscious and awkward as there is no one sitting next to me to talk to and Declan is involved in a conversation with Robyn. I consider trying to find a seat closer to my mother-in-law, but no doubt she'll just tell me that my joining her makes me look "desperate and weak." It's how *Siobhan* rolls. Across from me on the other divan, Roxie's plastered smile indicates she's politely bored over Meghan's chattering about her new son's feeding schedule and some dull plans to redecorate the music room at Raven's Hollow. It's why when the Black Knight calls for everyone's attention, I'm pretty sure I'm not the only one pleased to be released from this chit chat hell.

"I appreciate everyone's presence here tonight. I realize this comes in the middle of the week and many of you have pressing…duties in the mundane world." Beck looks directly at me when he says this and I try not to appear embarrassed. Jeesh. Apparently, I didn't get the memo about being selected to take the role of "scapegoat" tonight. "I wouldn't have called this meeting if I hadn't felt it was absolutely necessary," he continues. "I've just returned from the Veil Border, and as many of you are aware, the situation there has gotten increasingly volatile. Whereas only few months ago we were seeing an average of a dozen or so breeches a month, that number has doubled as a weekly tally, making average monthly totals closer to one hundred. Something has definitely changed on the Mundane side with their bio-tech research that's allowing more and more fully human terrorists to jump the divide between the dimensions."

A lord in the front of the room stepped forward, signaling his desire to speak. "I ken' confer that the Black Knight speaks the *contúirteach* (dangerous) truth. As ya' all are aware, the lands of House McCool sit in close proximity ta' the Veil line. Ma' men have captured four bastards in the past week attemptin' ta' hide in ma' south woods. They was half dead and strugglin' ta' breathe, but still put up a fierce fight rather than surrender. These Mundane *bastardai* (bastards) donna' go down easy."

Another man stood, a gentleman whose colors marked him as part of House *Badh*. "I concur the findins' of Lord McCool. I just completed ma' rotation at the Veil Border last Eventide. I be no expert on the health of the Mundane, but they do seem ta' be takin' longer to die from the effects of crossin' over."

I could hear murmurings of agreement throughout the room, side conversations staring like small fires amongst the invited guests. Up until now, the Queen had remained unmoved and silent, but the kibitzing among her rank and file apparently annoyed her enough to cause the solid, wooden wings that made up the back of her chair to loudly flutter. The room went instantly still, Herself having the reputation for less patience than even her imposing Hand of Justice. The Black Knight went on. "Your observations are correct. The Mundanes are taking longer to suffer the effects of the Otherworld than when they first started appearing. In the past, humans crossing over usually began showing pulmonary issues within four or five hours. This limited how far they could go once they crossed and what they could accomplish on our land. Now it seems it takes them eight to twelve hours to succumb, forcing us to use traditional means to take them down. So far, they haven't been able to cross with any weapons made of metal, which gives us the edge, being trained in the ancient arts. However, it would be naive to think that they aren't hard at work to even the balance. I myself have come across a Mundane opponent or two who handled a broad sword better than I would have thought in their modern age. They are crossing over better prepared, with fortitude, stamina, and misguided hatred for the Fae to carry them onward."

It was our cousin Duncan who next stepped forward to speak. "What is our plan to combat these monstrous fiends, ma' Lord. I am ready and able to serve as ma' Queen needs."

To the Mundane ear, Duncan's statement would sound like typical sycophant bullshit, but in the Otherworld, especially in the Court of the Raven Queen, Duncan's statement would be anticipated when coming from a House as prominent as ours. Herself's control over her Ruling Council was the reason she'd been able to stay in power for as long as she has, her Lords knowing exactly what she expected from each and every one of them.

"The Throne acknowledges your loyalty and service with gratitude, Duncan Fitzpatrick *Nuada*," the Black Knight replied. "You are correct. We do have a new plan in the works. As I mentioned earlier, I've just returned from the Veil Border. One of the marauders was apprehended alive by Lt. Aiden McGeary of House Lir," he says, throwing a bone of recognition to another prominent Ruling Council House. "I was thus able to interrogate the man before he succumbed to pulmonary edema. He wouldn't verify who he was working for, but he understood my Russian and answered back in the same way, so I'm willing to bet he was sent by the Kremlin. He spoke about something he called 'the cleansing,' how it would be deadly to the Fae. Obviously, something vile is in the works, along with this increased ability the Mundanes have created to stay longer in the Otherworld.

We no longer have the luxury of time to wait on any captured marauders giving us intel. We need to cut the head off the snake; someone who knows the inner workings of *I Idir* and is using this knowledge to help the Mundane governments in their attempt to overtake the Veil and invade the Otherworld."

A shiver ran down my back. I knew with certainty the Black Knight was talking about my husband's murderous *athair*. My husband knew it as well, and behind me, placed his hands on my shoulders to offer support, and I wondered if we'll ever be free of Callum Fitzpatrick.

Beck doesn't specifically mention my father-in-law by name, nor does he make mention of the still missing *Oisin*. Nonetheless, everything is made clear to the group by this so-called "new plan" in the works. "In the next few days, we will be sending Lady *Mac Badh* into the Mundane World to gather intelligence and report back to us. Once we have the information we need, we will start sending out small units of assets to locate and capture key figures and bring them to our Mundane holding cell where they can be further interrogated about this whole 'cleansing' fuckery."

All heads turn toward my sister-in-law who looks cool as a cucumber, obviously notified in advance of what would be said tonight. Her mate, on the other hand, looked anything but calm. His lips were formed into a tight line, and there was a deep furrow between his brows. I'm not a huge fan of *Cillian Mac Badh*. Personally, I find him to be arrogant and selfish, while barely containing the very real mean streak I know he's capable of sharing with others. Still, being a fated mate as well, I understand the angst he holds over sending his wife, the mother of his son, into a situation that has every possibility of going bad. My Tax Man would be beside himself with worry if the tables were turned. But as they are both cut from the same cloth, bred from birth to put the welfare of *I Idir* before anything else, neither man would object over the orders of The Throne.

Raising a glass that suddenly appears in her hand, the Queen speaks directly to her inner spy circle for the first time this evening. "I propose a toast to Lady *Mac Badh*." She waits for a short minute, letting the attendees pick up their glasses before continuing. "May her mission into the Mundane world uncover the *rúin fealltach* (treacherous secrets) that finally will come to light. Sláinte!"

Everyone in attendance drinks down the contents of their cups, and although the mood of the group is somberly positive, supportive of Meghan's upcoming quest, when I glance toward Herself, there's something in The Morrigan's expression that gives me concern, a vague sense of steel-like resolve that even her magic-born smile can't begin to hide.

TOOTHLESS 7

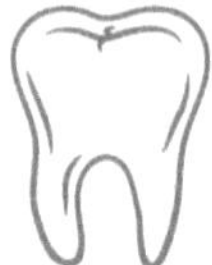

A GHOST IN THE HALLS

THE MOVE to *I Idir* for the summer months is always more complicated than going back to Salem in late August, mainly because the Beltane sabbat falls approximately ten days before the official end of the school year. This requires dual-dimension inhabitants like us to go to the Otherworld for the holiday then return to the Mundane only to have to jump back to *I Idir* a week and a half later. I suppose my complaining sounds a bit petty, given all the extra help I'm blessed to have. Still, the double crossing with its time change is physically taxing on my toddler, while even the two older boys show some level of crankiness related to the shifts in their sleeping patterns.

I'm aware that a handful of dual-citizenship families have tried on more than one occasion to petition the administration of *Cerridwen* Prep to change the school's calendar as to better meet their needs, but are always met with a polite but firm refusal, explaining that it was best to keep their schedule as close to the laws of the Massachusetts' public school system as possible. Thus, those of us who adhere to the spiritual and cultural tenets of "Wheel of the Year," we "Dualies," as we're sometimes called, spend more time preparing to attend the sabbat, as well as adjusting our body clocks afterward, than hours and minutes actually spent in the Otherworld.

That's not to say I don't enjoy the festival. It's a lovely celebration, full of hope and joyful revelry, and goodness knows, with all the Mundane problems currently at the Veil Border, we Fae folk could use any opportunity to destress and have some quality clan time together. On the other hand, as Lady of House *Nuada*, my hostess duties increase tenfold, and though I have a wonderful staff, it requires a lot of "hands on" attention by yours truly to host the holiday. For the past few years, Lady *Siobhan* has spent the sabbat with us at *Dun Siorai*, and as much as I hate to admit it, she's been a big help in making sure things run smoothly.

This year, however, she is staying at *Cuach an Fhithich* (Raven's Hollow) to "monitor the welfare" of her newest grandson while her daughter is "serving The Throne." I can't imagine *Siobhan* being there incites grateful praise from the child's *athair*, nor his parents, Lord and Lady *Badh*. Baby *Féchín* (Little Raven) has his own *scathach*, a very competent, athletic *Sidhe* by the name of *Eimer*, and staff and security twice as large as that of *Dun Siorai*. I'd lay odds her help wasn't requested by anyone residing at Raven's Hollow, but turning her away wasn't an option either. Lady *Siobhan* Donnely *Nuada* had, as the saying goes, friends in high places.

That left most of the planning and logistics to myself, Cook, and Master Tuck, who according to common rumor, were now officially a "couple." During the sabbat, there were several small estate gatherings throughout the day; a hearty open house breakfast, an elegant female-only tea party held after the May Pole dance, and a hearty luncheon for a handful of Declan's closest male friends and kin that took place after their annual Beltane hunt. All of these daytime festivities led up to a very large banquet style feast for eighty to a hundred attendees with the first course not even being served until 9:00 pm in the evening. It made for a very long day.

And, it was for that reason I was in the lower level of the estate rummaging around the storage rooms looking for a certain set of vintage crystal serving bowls that Cook had described as being shaped like spring tulip blossoms. My mind had immediately jumped to a floral themed table-scape design I had dreamt up in my head for the lady's tea party, and once the idea was solidly planted there, nothing else would do.

Normally, I'd send Master Tuck and a member of his staff down into the estate's lower bowels to hunt for the pieces, as Cook and the kitchen staff had their hands full preparing the food. Unfortunately, the man and most of his attendants had been sent to the market to pick up the fresh meats and produce Cook had ordered in advance, leaving no one I'd trust to dig around House *Nuada's* antique breakables. Despite Cook's protests that my wandering around the dusty *isolach* (cellar) was highly "un-Lady-like," I didn't fancy waiting around for Tuck to return, so I set off to find the glassware I knew would make my table decor unforgettable.

Truthfully, I hadn't been to this lower level of the estate since my "voyeur escapade" in the dungeon several years back. I still didn't know my way around, needing to rely on Cook's detailed map magically sketched out on a linen tea towel. According to her diagram, after walking under the main stone archway, I was to head down the central corridor, take a sharp right at the first fork, and then a left at the first possibility. The room storing all the estate's vintage glassware and bowls was located down this corridor and had a wooden door marked with the shape of a wine glass.

I'd just made that final left turn when something odd caught the corner of my eye…a filmy shape about twenty feet away from where I was standing. I wasn't expecting anyone else down there, so it gave me a start while my heart thumped heavily in my chest. I called out in a loud voice, "Hey you down there…stop! You don't belong here. Who are you?"

The shape thickened and I could see the flash of a face. A familiar one. "*Oisin*? Is that you, Honey?"

The face registered an expression of pure panic and then the whole shape disappeared into thin air, leaving me, once again, alone in the hallway.

I am so stunned that, for a few seconds, I just stand there, letting my heart return to normal rhythm and my brain to register what I just witnessed. It was *Oisin* I saw. Of that I have no doubt. But how? And why was he so…well…ghost-like? All thoughts of tulip bowls and tea parties slip away like dust on the wind. I turn and head upstairs, set on finding the Tax Man and figuring this whole thing out.

TOOTHLESS 8

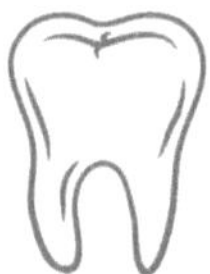

THE TROUBLE HAMMER FALLS

As USUAL, his Lordship is never where I expect him to be. Despite all the ongoing preparations for the Beltane celebration, my husband is in the stable checking on a mare due to foal in the next day or so. When it comes to horses these *Tuatha de Danann* types have a one-track mind. "How is she doing?" I ask, knowing perfectly well how the new mama-to-be must be feeling so near her due date; large as a barge, tired of carrying the extra load, and ready to welcome her little one into the world.

Declan doesn't look up, bent over as he is feeling the mare's round belly. "Won't be long now. She's vera' restless as if she ken' no sit still," he glances up at me smiling. "It reminds me of ya' right befar' wee Liam was born. Ya' insisted ya' had ta' re-arrange all the kitchen cabinets in the middle of the night." Then, the smile drops from his face as he notices my own troubled expression. He stands upright and grabs for my hand. "What is it, Lass? Ya' look like ya' have just seen a *spiorad cráite* (wandering spirit)."

He isn't wrong. The figure I saw in the sub-level of *Dun Siorai* did give the impression of being ghost-like. Still, I'm not ready to claim him as an Afterlife-bound spirit. For that to be the case, I'd have to accept *Oisin* is physically dead and my head and heart aren't ready to admit that. "I saw something odd. In the corridor below the estate where the older things are stored."

He furrows his brow in what I'm not sure is confusion, annoyance, or combination of both. "Ken' ya' be a bit mar' specific, Rosie Love? What da' ya' mean by 'odd?' Dangerous 'odd?' Or just weird 'odd?'"

I take a deep breath and try to explain what I saw. "I went down to the sub-level to look for some crystal bowls for the Beltane tea, and…"

The Tax Man doesn't let me finish. "I donna' understand why ya' went down there in the first place. 'Tis like a funhouse maze in the cellar. And dusty as well. Why did ya' no send someone from housekeeping?"

Now I'm just annoyed to have been interrupted for a lecture. "No one was available to go. If you haven't noticed, my Lord, there's a lot to be done in time for the sabbat," I reply, not hiding my sarcasm by using his title. "Honestly, that's not what matters. The fact remains that I did go down there and…well…I think I saw *Oisin*."

I'm pretty sure my husband never expected me to drop that bomb. His startled face says it all. "*Oisin?*" Here at *Dun Siorai?*" He tightened his hold on my hand and began to pull me towards the stable's exit. "Come, Lass. We need ta' find him befar' someone else does."

"Wait. I didn't tell you all of it. I don't think he was physically there. Like in the flesh," I explain, trying to make sense out of the senseless.

"Are ya' sayin' the lad was a *taibhse* (ghost)? That *Oisin* has left this world?" the tremor in his voice giving his emotions away.

"That's just it, Declan. I think he was very much alive... somewhere. Even though I could see right through his form, I felt a distinct connection to him. His aurora, if that's even possible." I ask the question we're both thinking. "Do souls that have left this plane give off an energy level that strong?" I query. "Because it was no small tug. This was the real thing. I could feel it in the soles of my feet."

Declan furrowed his brow, seemingly as lost as I was to explain what I had experienced. "Truth be, Love, I ken' no recall ever meetin' a wanderin' spirit, so I would have nothing ta' compare it to. Nor do I have the answers ta' how the lad could be in two places at one time. I have no doubt the Merlin ken' help answer that, but we ken' no bother him now. He and the House Druids are fastin' and purifyin' far' the Beltane rituals. It will have ta' wait until afterwards. Both he and the Black Knight have accepted the invitation to House *Nuada's* hunt and luncheon. Perhaps we ken' speak to both of them in private when they come ta' *Dun Siorai*." He paused as if another thought had come to his mind. "Da' ya' recall if the spirit boy was carryin' anything? A package or parcel perhaps?"

I try to recall, but the whole experience had happened so fast. Plus, I was completely thrown off my game at the idea of seeing *Oisin* here at *Dun Siorai*. "I'm sorry, Sweetie. The figure I saw was very misty. I'm not even sure I saw definitive arms or hands. Just a brief flicker of his face as he turned to look at me from several feet away." I get a flash of insight from my Eternal Mate's mind. "You don't think he stole something? Not on Beltane. He knows better than that."

Declan grimaces at my question and rubs a hand through his hair, a "tell" he has when he's especially anxious. "The lad has been with his damnable sire for over a year now. It is hard ta' say what bad habits he might have picked up under the tutorage of that evil soul." He continued pulling me toward the stable's exit. "Come with me, Lass. We need to at least try and see if we ken' be sure, one way or the other. If the boy has attempted ta' steal the House's luck for the comin' growin' season, then I'm afraid he's crossed a line he ken' no take back."

TOOTHLESS 9

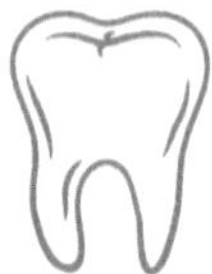

GOOD LUCK DIES...

THE TAX MAN and I spend the next hour and a half searching through all the storage rooms in that particular corridor to see if we can tell if something might have been stolen. In my heart, I know this is a waste of time we don't have. There is so much stuff jammed into these multiple, tiny rooms that it would be nearly impossible to tell if any one thing is gone. Making the search harder is the fact that we can't narrow it down to anything of particularl value; it could be something as inconsequential as a spoon, salt shaker, or even an old pot scraper, and still have the same effect. I've no doubt that my *Mo Shiorghra* is well aware that we are searching for the proverbial "needle in a haystack," but as of yet, he's not ready to admit failure.

To understand Declan's deep anxiety over a single stolen item, one needs to understand the Fae concept of *"ádh goidte"* (stolen luck), especially as it applies to *Beltane*. It's common knowledge that the residents of the Otherworld are highly superstitious souls. This most likely has something to do with the fact that they are all races and cultures centered entirely on magic, a reality folks in the Mundane world don't even accept as being real. On the other hand, Otherworld citizens firmly understand that, within the entire Universe, the seemingly impossible is very much in reach, and that luck, karma, fate, providence, destiny and recompense are all an active force. On sabbats, like today's *Beltane*, the power associated with these forces is much greater than usual.

The belief that "good luck" could be stolen from a person, clan, or House through the theft of a single item probably goes back several centuries with the practice of practitioners conjuring *piseógs*, malevolent charms used to cause misfortune, illness or failure. A personal item could be stolen from a household and channeled into a bad luck charm, though not without personal risk to the conjuror via *"Riail na Dtrí* (The Rule of Three), which states that any negative energy put out into the Universe could be returned to the sender three-fold.

Apparently, the threat of repercussions from the Universe wasn't enough to dissuade folks from using these charms and causing mayhem and chaos. Thus, when The Morrigan took up The Throne of *I Idir* as Queen, she made the use of *piseógs*, curses, hair magic, and other types of dark energy spells a capital offense. Still, old habits die hard, and the Fae were leery of giving up on the idea that the "good luck" the Universe doled out was finite, meaning one person could "steal" luck from another. This belief found its way into the traditional celebrations of *Beltane*, when hope for a productive growing season was especially high. Anxiety over lost "good luck" spilled over into the practice of not even lending out basic necessities of flour, sugar or eggs to one's neighbors, lest you unwittingly gave away your luck with it. There's even an old Fae cautionary fable told to children about a man who secretly lit his pipe from his neighbor's hearth on Beltane in order to increase his own crops while hoping to decrease the other man's farming success. Though the thief's crops were abundant that summer, his wife and two children, out collecting the harvest, were caught and eaten by marauding Fomorians, thus making true The Rule of Three.

It makes clear why my loving husband is covered in dust and already late in riding over to *Crann Bethadh* for the *Beltane* Ruling Council gathering he is expected to attend. The idea that his own half-brother, his own flesh and blood, would steal from the House on a sacred sabbat is devastating, but not knowing for sure, one way or the other, would just drive him crazy. At some point, however, my thoughts must leak out from behind my shield, because he dusts off his hands on the legs of his pants, and says, "'Tis no use, Love. Locatin' a single item in all of this mess would take more time and energy then we have to give right now. I suppose we should leave this search far' another day and concentrate on the upcoming festivities."

I pretend like that wasn't exactly what I've been thinking for the last thirty minutes. Instead, I calmly say, "I agree, Sweetie. For now, we'll just have to believe that *Oisin* was homesick for the sabbat day and only came for a quick visit. We can do a more organized search when we return to *Dun Siorai* for the summer. It's only another week or so."

We both turn to leave, but while on the way out, the toe of my right foot catches the corner of a wooden box that's sticking out a hair further than the others lined up next to it. Something pulls at my brain and I stop, not sure if it's my own intuition or a prod from someone else. "Hang on a sec, Declan. This box seems a bit out of place. I just caught my toe on it. I have a gut feeling about it. Let's quickly check this one before we leave."

Declan lifts the heavy box off the floor and places it on an old wooden table in the center of the room, pushing other items to the side to make room. He takes off the cover to reveal a collection of old pewter ale tankards, horn shaped with carvings of different animals on the front. "I remember these," he says. "My *athair* had them lined up on a shelf in his study. He said they belonged to ma' great grandfather and were a handfast gift from the man's *Mo Shiorghra*, ma' great grandmother, Lady *Moira* Lanigan *Nuada*. I always thought they were especially handsome. I wondered what ma' *mathair* did with them when she had his things packed up and stored when I took over that space." My mate rummaged through the browned paper they were wrapped in, pulling each one out, and lining them up on the table. "There should be a set of twelve," he explained. "Each one represents a *Tuatha de Danann* spirit animal."

I watch as the love of my life carefully unwraps each one, but in my heart, I already know what we'll find. Something dark settled in my chest the moment Declan opened that cursed box. As he sets down the last remaining one, it's clear there are only eleven tankards. One is missing. He names each of the carved animals that grace the front of the mugs. "Wolf, horse, owl, raven, badger, lynx, boar, bull, deer, hawk, and snake." He looks at me with eyes darkened with grief and I can hear the tremor in his voice. "I know vera' well which one is missing, *Mo Chroi* (My Heart.) 'Tis the fox tankard. The lad has taken the fox."

TOOTHLESS 10

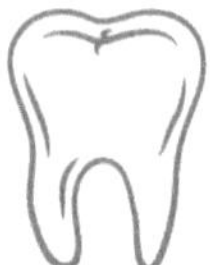

...AND LUNCH WITH THE GUYS

PRETENDING TO "CELEBRATE" when really bad shit is blowing up behind the scenes is thoroughly exhausting; all those fake smiles, tedious conversations, and the forced "musical-chairs-style" mingling sets my teeth on edge and fills me with unexplainable frustration. Despite the events of earlier this morning, Declan and I are both forced to spend the rest of the day playing the part of the gracious Lord and Lady of House *Nuada*, while neither of our minds are ever far from worry over *Oisin's* "snatch and grab" endeavor, or the meaning behind the specific choice of his loot. I go through the motions of the May Pole dance without much enthusiasm, which is truly a darn shame because it's one of my favorite traditions of the day. Cook has out done herself with the refreshments for the Ladies Tea, but all I can think about is how the search for those blasted tulip shaped bowls was the catalyst for me finding our young runaway in the lower caverns of the estate.

When Lord *Nuada* returns from the Beltane wild boar

hunt with his inner circle, I try to casually hang around outside of the solar parlor in hopes that my husband will eventually step out and I can ask him if he's had a chance to speak to the Black Knight or the Merlin regarding our little "situation." My subterfuge is totally unnecessary because in a very unusual break from protocol, I am invited inside to join the men.

For those of us who have spent most of our lives in the modern Mundane world, the cultural tenets of the Other-world would seem overly archaic and terribly sexist. I often explain to my sister, Claire, that though the traditional apparel of *I Idir* has heavy Renaissance Faire vibes, the societal norms are more in line with the "Ton" Regency period of Mundane England, especially among the *Tuatha de Danann* types. Into that regiment of Regency *"le bon ton"* (French for "good style"), one needs to mix a hefty dose of magical super-stition and strict adherence to *"Na Sean Bhealaí"* (The Old Ways) to understand everyday life among Ruling Council members and their "circles." Jane Austen would have had a field day here.

It's the reason why my getting invited to join the gentlemen in the solar parlor directly after their hunt is such a monumental break in protocol, more so because it is *Beltane.* The tradition of chasing down wild boars on horse-back using bow and arrow goes back at least one thou-sand Otherworldly years. Because the tradition is associated with the ancient god *Moccus*, a Celtic version of the Roman god Mercury, it may even go further back than that, but the tradition of the hunt of wild boars on the *Beltane* sabbat has been part of its celebration for a long time.

To the *Sidhe*, the *torc fiáin* (wild boar) has always symbol-ized courage, strength, fertility and ferociousness, traits admired by warriors since the beginning of written Fae history. These attributes were also the reason for the hunt taking place on *Beltane*, a day meant to honor the growth of new life at the hearth and within the fields, along with the ability of the *Ciann Ti* (Head of Household) to protect those *Beltane* gifts. Every year on the sabbat, all the House mages would fast for three days before selecting a half dozen of the strongest, most fierce wild boars amongst those that had been captured alive specifically for this hunt. The largest most prime specimen would then be selected to have a red cord tied around its tail. The six wild boars were released ten minutes before the hunters, giving the animals a slight advantage over their predators whose job it was to track every released boar, lest they lose a share of the new season's *ádh mór* (good luck). Traditionally, it was believed that the hunter who slew the boar with the red cord around its tail was promised an extra fruitful year, along with a silver trophy and bragging rights in the months to come. (Not to brag, but my awesome Tax Man has proudly worn the red cord around his wrist for the past two *Beltane* sabbats)

A hearty lunch is always served to the hunters and their closest comrades at each of the attending Houses, a strictly male affair as the riders came directly from the hunt to the meal without the benefit of a shower or a change of clothes, making it a rather "gamey," testosterone-filled gathering. Spiritually, it was strongly believed the men also came to lunch with "blood lust" in their veins and the aura of death upon them, which was thought to be a personal affront to any feminine energy. Thus, the post-hunt lunch was always a "no girls allowed affair," and my being invited into the solar parlor signaled something very serious was afoot.

My apprehension must show in my face because Ambrose Myrdynn, our current reigning Merlin, greeted me with a Beltane blessing while taking both of my hands in his. "May the fires of Beltane inspire in you the peace, prosperity and power of the new growing season, Lady *Nuada*. Blessed be!"

A slow warmth spread from our joined hands up my arms and into my chest and I let go of the breath I'm holding. Ambrose is so unlike the Merlin figures of Mundane myth, whose enigmatic, menacing mysticism held the center of Arthurian legend. Our 26th Otherworld Merlin is more in line with the ancient Druid beliefs of reverence for the natural world and an interconnectedness of all living things. He is the calmest man I ever met, even in the midst of great danger, and a perfect foil to the red-hot intensity of his only offspring, the Black Knight.

"I'm most honored to be invited in, Lord Merlin. A blessed *Beltane* to you as well," I replied, trying hard not to react to the overwhelming odor in the room that even several open windows couldn't dispel. The rumors I heard about this luncheon being…well…odiferous… were spot on. The air inside the space was a nose-alert symphony of male and animal body sweat, horse shit, and what I guessed was wild boar blood and entrails, mixed in with the steaming dishes of food brought in for lunch. How anyone could contemplate dining in here was a mystery to me.

Duncan is the next to greet me, adding the customary kiss to the cheek, designating him as close family. Most *Sidhe* refrain from touching one another if at all possible, lest they transfer knowledge of the strength of their magical energy, something considered rude as well as poor personal security. "*Beannchtaí na Bealtaine* (Beltane Blessings), Lady Cousin. May I offer ya' somethin' cool ta' drink? Some ale ar' peach wine perhaps?"

The thought leaves my stomach rolling, especially after I get a good whiff of something nasty and gooey on the sleeve of our cousin's normally fastidious tunic. "Thank you, Duncan. I believe I'll pass." I look across the room to where

my husband is standing next to the Black Knight. I don't
need telepathy to know he's very tense. It's written in every
plane of his face, and as much as I'd like to savor this unusual
breach of *Sidhe* protocol, the urgency of the moment, as well
as the smell, pushes me forward. "As much as I'm honored to
be invited into your celebration gentlemen, I've no doubt
there's a very good reason you've broken with centuries of
tradition. Perhaps we should just get down to why I've been
invited to your secret male soiree?"

TOOTHLESS 11

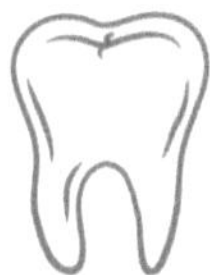

ROSIE RAISES THE ALARM

THE BLACK KNIGHT'S laugh breaks the tense silence in the room. "As always, Lady *Nuada* cuts right through the protocol bullshit. Bravo, Rosie. I respect team members who speak their mind." He takes a chair near where he is standing and points to one across from himself. I don't really care to put myself in a position that reminds me far too much of an interrogation, but ultimately decide that expressing my opinions will only go so far amongst this audience. I take the chair as requested, while Beck adds, "I was hoping, dear Lady, that you could give us a run-down of what you saw in the cellar of *Dun Siorai.*"

I am relieved that the Hand of Justice uses the term "saw," instead of "what you thought you might have seen." Nothing's worse than having the Powers That Be insinuate that perhaps you've lost your mind and are visualizing apparitions around every corner. For support, I look across the room at my husband, but his face is expressionless and he has his mental shield up at full strength, blocking me from getting any reading about what I'm supposed to say. Thus, I am left with the blunt truth. "I've no doubt my Lord has already filled you in on the events of earlier today, but I will repeat them if that is what you wish, Lord Knight."

"I'd be most grateful to hear your thoughts, Rosie. You may be able to shed additional details regarding your missing brother-in-law's presence at *Dun Siorai*."

I repeat my story for the assembled group; how I was down in the cellar on a mission to find some crystal bowls in the storage rooms; how I saw a misty image several feet in front of me; how I'm absolutely certain I saw *Oisin's* face staring back at me when I called his name; how Declan and I searched for anything that might be missing and how we discovered the fox themed ale mug was not among the others in the collection. I find it remarkable that I am as calm as I am, all things considered.

Everyone listens intently, and when I finish speaking, our Merlin takes over the questioning. "Lady *Nuada*, can you tell me if the form of young *Oisin* was composed of cloud-like substance, or was it made-up of tiny, fragmented pieces?"

"Fragmented pieces?" I ask, unsure of what the sorcerer means.

"Yes, dear Lady. Was his form created from tiny bits of what might have looked to you like colored glass, or was he more of a rolling mist?"

I close my eyes and try to bring the scene to my mind despite a dozen pairs of eyes on me. Pulling from my memory, I recall that I could distinctly see the wall behind *Oisin* through his shape. I answer with more confidence than I feel. "He was definitely more misty than solid, Lord Merlin. I could see right through him, the whole wall behind him, as if he were made of smoke, so I don't believe he was made up of those little pieces you mentioned."

"Thank you, Lady *Nuada*. Your remarks help narrow

down the type of magic the lad most likely used to breach the estate's security. Astral projection is very difficult to pinpoint when normal wards are being used. It makes sense that the boy was able to maneuver the cellars without being detected, though I must admit to being impressed with that level of magical skill in one so young and untrained."

"I doubt the kid remained 'untrained' very long under the tutorage of Callum Fitzpatrick," the Black Knight replied. "The man has had well over a year to brainwash the boy into his practice of magic."

Next to him, I see Declan cringe, still uncomfortable, even after nearly seven years, with the heavy mantle of guilt his father has forced upon the family name. I ignore the Knight's comments, true as they might be, and address his father instead. "I'm not all that familiar with the process of location magic, Lord Merlin. Perhaps you could enlighten me."

"'Tis not a magical skill easily accessed by most practitioners, thus the understanding of it is not universal amongst the Otherworldly folk. It requires absolute mental and spiritual focus to separate the *anam* (soul) from the physical body for the purpose of traveling to different realms of reality."

The wizard must see the incredibility in my expression. He smiles and explains. "I heartily sympathize with your disbelief, dear Lady. Astral projection is a concept that defies logic, even in the magical world. The ability to reside in two different planes of the Universe at one time is powerful mental sorcery, usually taking years to master. To those untrained in the practice, separating the soul from the physical body would cause the latter to wither and die in a very short time. It is why the only true way to end the life of a *Sidhe* is to remove its head, thus severing the body from the brain, the area we believe the true *anam* resides. Both body and soul must work in tandem for life to exist, making the traveling of one's consciousness away from its physical home both incredibly miraculous and equally dangerous at the same time. The practitioner must, for all intents and purposes, 'fool' the body into thinking the soul is still present, while sending out the *anam* to its different location. It's a special ability usually found only among Fae Druid candidates, however, with the lad's unique Elven genetic background, it appears he's been remarkably gifted."

"Thus, making him a huge security risk," the Black Knight interjects. He shifts in his chair to turn and speak directly to my husband. "Look Fitz, you know I've always been fond of the kid. Rooted for him from the first days he came to live with you. Nobody has worked harder to attempt to locate and retrieve him than this team. But you understand that I can't ignore that he has this powerful magical skill, a skill he used for breaking and entering, as well as possible burglary. Frankly, none of this makes *Oisin* look like the 'innocent hostage' we had hoped he was, and now that we are aware he has this bad ass magical ability, we need to find him ASAP. More so than ever, before his sire uses the kid as some secret weapon against the kingdom of *I Idir*."

"I think it far too early to judge the boy guilty of treason, Theodore," the sorcerer replied, the only one to ever call the infamous Black Knight by his given name. "I have no doubt his faithless *athair* has asserted a tremendous amount of influence over him, but I feel it is not beneficial to our cause to assume he no longer holds any loyalty to his bloodline here in *I Idir*. Young males with strong souls often struggle to find their rightful path," he argued, looking pointedly at his own son and making me think he wasn't just talking about our *Oisin*. There's always been a multitude of tales regarding the tumultuous relationship between the 26th and 27th Merlin, and I'd wager a lot of them were based in fact.

As one would expect, the younger heir to the Merlin line

ignored his father's inference. "Whatever 'path' you presume the kid is on, Lord Merlin, even you will agree it's prudent we find him as soon as possible. We have no idea how involved he is in the development of the biological weapon we believe the Mundane governments are working on. For everyone's safety, the boy included, we need to extract him from his father's clutches."

"But haven't we been doin' just that far' over a year now, ma' Lord?" Connor Dell asks. "Every time we get close ta' locatin' the lad, we seem ta' find that he's been moved once again. 'Tis like they know in advance when we are on ar' way, makin' me think that there is a traitor among us."

"I don't disagree, Dell," the Queen's Hand of Justice says. "I have my suspicions regarding the possibility of a mole, but at this point, it's only conjecture. However, there are ways of getting around fucking traitors. Be aware that going forward no one team member will have knowledge of all the parts and pieces of any given mission. It's my hope that the mole will thus reveal his or herself by their action within this constraint."

I think to myself that not reading everyone into a plan is the Queen and her Sword Arm's usual M.O., but I hold my opinions until I am alone with my husband as Beck continues his explanation. "In the meantime," he adds, "perhaps Lord Merlin can give us some insight on the kid's location via his astral projection abilities."

"That is something I can help with," the wizard replied. "Magical astral projection only works in moving the soul's presence from one plane of reality to another. The practitioner can move his soul from the Mundane World to some layer within the Otherworld, or vice versa. He or she cannot soul project to another location in the plane where the physical body is located; for example, they can't project from one hemisphere in the Mundane world to another. Therefore, it's a sure thing that when he appeared at *Dun Siorai* earlier this morning, *Oisin* was physically somewhere in the Mundane world while he was projecting in this one. In addition, building enough energy to draw the soul from its physical body would require a strong elemental amplifier to boost the focus, especially in one so young and untrained in mind control. Water is the most powerful element, and in this case, I don't mean just a lake or stream. I'm speaking of some larger body, like a sea or ocean, and logic would assert that he would choose somewhere near a major ley line. His location would also have to allow for privacy. The ritual components for out of body experiences are complicated and the boy would need somewhere he wouldn't be disturbed during the various stages of the spell. I'd focus on remote areas, possibly near caves or deserted structures that would offer shelter along with seclusion. I suggest we look at some detailed online maps of the Mundane world and pinpoint a few possibilities that can be explored."

"That sounds like a logical plan, Lord Merlin," the Black Knight said. "You, me, and Fitz can sit down in the next day or two and map out some possibilities. Once we have a list of places to search, I'll meet in private with each of you and supply the details of your next mission. Until then, I suggest we keep the knowledge we've gathered today to ourselves. Lady *Mac Badh* has been undercover now for two weeks. I am hoping we hear something from her very soon that might be able to aid us. Our immediate goal today is to get through this *Beltane* bullshit without anyone poking their noses into our business."

It's no secret that the Black Knight didn't hold to any of the spiritual aspects of the Otherworld sabbats. How he expected to be reigning Merlin someday is beyond me, as tradition demanded they must be a practicing Druid. I felt some uncomfortableness in the room regarding our fearless leader's lack of reverence for the Old Ways, but no one was brave enough, or stupid enough, for that matter, to contradict him. The men gathered in that room understood that though their Queen's Sword Arm was unconventional in his role, he was steadfast in his loyalty to The Morrigan and the people of *I Idir*, and had proven on many occasions his willingness to put his own life on the line while doing so.

Once the man in question rose and headed for the luncheon buffet, the level of tension in the room subsided, and everyone turned back to celebrating the sabbat. I'm both surprised and disappointed that the missing fox mug, as well as the implications of it being taken on *Beltane*, hasn't been discussed. I think about asking my husband about it, but he's already put on the mantle of gracious host, and I realize I am expected to politely excuse my feminine self. Thus, I do as tradition dictates, but I leave with a sense that something important has been left out of this little discussion and I can't help wondering why that is.

TOOTHLESS 12

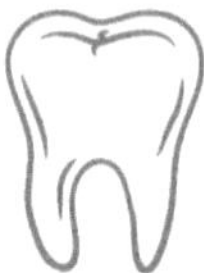

BUYING SOME CHARMS

THE HECTIC ITINERARY of *Beltane* doesn't allow me a moment of privacy to converse with the Tax Man over what had been discussed within the walls of the solar parlor after I left. Nor was I able to question him over why no one mentioned the missing fox mug or the threat of *droch ádh* (bad luck) that it presented. It isn't until much later in the day, while we are dressing for the evening's festivities, that I finally get my answers.

As I put the finishing touches onto the fresh floral wreath I will wear to the bonfires, Declan hands me a small linen, draw string bag. "What's this, Sweetie? A little romantic token for your *Beltane* true love?" I jokingly ask, as trinkets of affection are often exchanged during the various sabbats.

My *Mo Shiorghra's* mouth curls into a frown. "In truth, I wish it were such a thing, Rosie Lass. Ya' know I would pull the stars from the sky far ya' if I could."

I'm starting to think maybe I don't want this particular gift. "What aren't you telling me, Declan?"

"Just open it, Love, and I will explain," he answers.

I untie the strings and shake the contents out in my hand, then examine the odd pendant attached to a long leather cord. The centerpiece of the necklace is composed of a flat, silver disk on which the familiar Celtic Shield Knot is elegantly sketched. Characterized by its unique four corner design, the *Snaidhm Sciath Cheilteach* (Celtic Shield Knot) is an ancient symbol of protection used by the Fae for nearly a thousand years to ward off evil intentions and ill luck.

Four small holes have been drilled into the bottom of the disk and from each dangled a small bead on a very short silver chain. I recognized the beads as being made out of black tourmaline, citrine, smoky quartz, and a strange blue tinted stone I guessed to be labradorite. As it lay in my palm, the magical energy vibrated against my skin. "This is a *piseóga* (magical spell worked into a charm or amulet), isn't it? To protect against bad luck."

"Aye. I had one made for all of us," he states as he pulls his own out from under his linen tunic.

"For all of us? Even the kids?"

"Of course. 'Tis possible that the *droch ádh* (bad luck) could affect any member of ar' family. I've even included

Birgit and *Niamh*, Duncan and Mel, as well as ma' Lady *Mathair*, though I donna' relish havin' to give it ta' her. She will no be pleased that we have been cursed in this manner. Ole' Sean Murray, *Dun Siorai's Piseogaí* (Charm Setter), spent most of his sabbat hours creatin' these far' us. 'Twas a monumental task and I am vera' grateful for his speed in completin' the whole batch befar' tonight's bonfires."

By now you would have thought I would have learned that nothing about life in the Otherworld, or magic, for that matter, could be taken for granted. I guess part of me was naively hoping all this "bad luck" stuff was just silly superstition. Fat chance. "How long do you believe we're going to be stuck wearing these amulets?" I query.

His answer is a shrug. "Depends on what the Merlin discovers," he adds.

"So, the Merlin is aware of the missing fix mug?" I ask, frustrated at the slow-going of this interrogation.

"Aye. They all are," his Lordship concedes.

"Then why the hell didn't someone bring it up at the blasted 'secret meeting'?"

He runs a hand through the hair not caught up in the man bun at the back of his head, then looks off to the left, a tried-and-true Declan "tell" when he's deciding how much he actually wants to "share" with me. "This is your chance to come clean, Tax Man. Out with it," I order.

He takes the pendant from my hand and puts it over my head before speaking. "'Tis bad luck ta' speak out loud about *droch ádh*, Lass. I did no wish ta' take a chance of it settlin' upon the others."

"You do know how ridiculous that sounds, right? This idea that just mentioning bad luck causes it." I scold. "Bad luck isn't some contagious disease you can catch. It's just superstition. Your belief in it gives it power."

I get the dreaded husbandly sigh in response. The one

that screams "Poor Misguided Rosie." "Maybe 'tis how it works in the Mundane world, Lass, but not among the Fae. Luck is a finite commodity. All Fae treasure whatever luck the Universe has deemed should come their way and they are expected ta' guard against the theft of it. There will always be Fae in the Otherworld who will desire what is not theirs ta' take. In that way, 'tis vera much like the Mundane world."

As far as I am concerned, bad behavior and lack of ethics abound in both worlds, but I'm not in the mood to be drawn off topic. "You still haven't clarified how everyone in that room learned that the fox ale cup was stolen."

"When I confessed that I had a topic that was far too taboo ta' speak aloud, especially with this bein' the sabbat and all, the Merlin offered ta' conjure up *Amharc Scáth*," Declan explained.

If the parties involved are not speaking at the speed of a run-away train, my comprehension of the Old Language is much better now than it was when Declan and I first met, so I'm able to translate what supposedly went on in the solar parlor. "'Shadow Viewing?' Whoa! That's some heavy magic! No wonder the floor under my feet was literally vibrating when I first walked in there. I figured someone was using big juju. Hell, Tax Man, there's only a handful of practitioners in *I Idir* and Avalon that can handle that powerful type of ritual magic. It sure makes me glad Ambrose is one of us. I'd hate to have someone so magicaly gifted as an enemy."

Amharc Scáth, or "Shadow Viewing," is a top-level magical skill that allows a very focused practitioner to draw memories and thoughts from another's person's mind and string them together to form a bubble-shaped, filmy, video-type, for lack of a better description, physical manifestation. I, personally, have never witnessed a Shadow Viewing, but in my limited studies of Otherworldly magic I've seen it described, and it blows my mind to think something like that took place in our solar parlor.

Declan responded to my comment. "Aye, Love. Ambrose Mrydynn is a quiet, reserved man by his vera' nature, a true believer in the Old Ways, but the power of his magical energy runs deep. 'Tis little wonder the Raven Queen has forged such a long-lasting relationship with the Merlin line. The wizards are central to her holding the Throne of *I Idir* for as many generations as she has."

"I can't imagine how weird it must have been for you to see your memories and thoughts projected like that. So out in the open. I know how you are about keeping your personal feelings to yourself. It couldn't have been easy for you," I console.

"Never a truer statement, Rosie Love. I was beyond grateful the Merlin filtered out my emotions regardin' being betrayed by my own flesh and blood, though I have no doubt the others would have readily sympathized with my feelins'."

"So, was anything decided? Was the theft of that ale cup a deliberate attempt to…well…you know…do what you think it was meant to do?" I ask, careful not to make matters worse by speaking the words aloud.

The Tax Man nods in agreement. "Sadly, both Ambrose and Beck believe my sire is behind this latest attempt to wreak havoc for House *Nuada.* The fact that the fox cup was signaled out was meant as a message. It was the Merlin himself who suggested I have the *piseóga* made far' my near and dear, as a necessary precaution."

I lift the pendant from my chest to examine it, then let it drop. "That's it?" I ask, not bothering to hide my bitterness. "That's all we're gonna' do about your father's repeated attempts to destroy our life? When do we say enough is enough already, Declan? Surely between Herself, the Merlin, and the Black Knight there's enough magical juju to find him and do what needs to be done."

The look I get in return breaks my heart, changing my bitterness and frustration over the situation to guilt. If ever there were a man so wholly devoted heart and soul to his family and his House it's my mate and husband, Lord Declan Fitzpatrick *Nuada*. Having not only his father betray him, but the child he's called "brother" as well, must cut the deepest parts of him. Despite the Tax Man's feelings about sympathy, I throw my arms around him. "I'm sorry I lashed out, Sweetie. I'm just frustrated and afraid. I know everybody is doing whatever they can to end this terror. It's just so hard having it affect us so personally."

He returns my hug. "I know, *Grá Ma Shaol* (Love of My Life). 'Tis a lot far' one family ta' carry along their path. But I have faith The Morrigan will find the end ta' all of this. The Otherworld must stay closed ta' the Mundanes. There ken' be no compromise on that directive far' the sake of all we hold dear and the future of ar' home."

TOOTHLESS 13

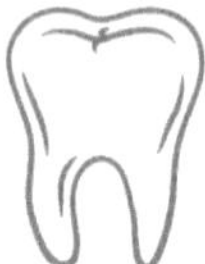

TROUBLE WITH THE LADS

I WOULD LOVE to say that the dark shadow of Callum Fitzpatrick didn't follow us into the final evening celebrations of Beltane, but of course that would be far too simple and a lie to boot. Before Declan could bestow the *piseóga* on the rest of the family, the slithering snake of *droch-ádh* had seemingly managed to wind its way through our household.

When we went to gather up our children and their nannies for the evening Beltane bonfires, Declan and I found the nursery in total childhood chaos. Dylan's eyes were red-rimmed as he hotly glared at his younger brother while *Birgit* held a large ice pack to the top of his head, the result of a whack by his younger brother's wooden sword. Liam was too busy howling to notice his brother's discontent as *Niamh* appeared to be working an especially deep splinter out of the tot's finger using a healer's touch magic, a *scathach* trait that ran in certain bloodlines. The only child not having an emotional meltdown appeared to be our youngest, Ronin, who, sitting in his booster chair, happily stuffing the peas from his dinner plate up his nose.

Birgit looked up at me, pink-cheeked and thin-lipped, her embarrassment over the state of the nursery obvious. "A million pardons Lord and Lady *Nuada*. As ya' ken' see, we are not quite ready far' tonight's festivities. This afternoon has been a nightmare with one mishap after another plaguing these vera' walls. 'Tis like *Fear Gorta* (ancient Celtic spirit of famine and ill luck) himself gained access ta' *Dun Siorai*."

As the *scathach* related all the things that had gone wrong since earlier that morning, she couldn't help but notice the glances Declan and I kept exchanging. "I no mean ta' over-step ma' boundaries, Lord and Lady *Nuada*, but it appears ta' me that our troubles here in the nursery are no surprise ta' ya' both."

I stay silent as my husband telepathically describes the incidents from earlier that day to the two nannies, never actually mentioning the words "bad luck." Though the expressions on the faces of *Birgit* and *Niamh* register their understanding and alarm over these turn of events, as consummate professionals, they don't react negatively to the burden this situation forces on themselves and their respon-sibilities. Instead, they both reinstate their pledge to guard our children from any attack, physical or magical, and appear exceptionally moved by his Lordship's decision to have a *piseóga* made for each of them along with our children.

"Ya' greatly honor my cousin and I with these gifts, Lord *Nuada*. Ta' be included in yar' warded *teaghlach* (family) circle is a *bronntanas* (gift) no *scathach* can freely expect,"

"I speak far' ma' Lady and ma'self when I say that we consider ya' both a sacred part of ar' family. 'Tis a bond forged in a spirit of love and devotion," Declan replies.

I see *Niamh* wipe a hand over her eyes, overcome with

emotion. For many Houses, a *scathach* is little more than hired help, a mercenary baby-sitter of sorts, with no more House standing than other key members of the estate's staff. Because of Declan's dysfunctional family environment, his relationship with *Magda*, his beloved *buime* (foster mother/nanny) *scathach*, carried a much closer emotional tie than those of other House heirs. Thus, it is no surprise that he wants the same for our children with *Magda's* own offspring.

While the nannies place the amulets inside their clothing, my Tax Man tries to explain the situation to Dylan and Liam in the same mode he used with the *scathachs*. Because Dylan is seven years old, and Liam four, they are astute enough to understand that something important is up, especially when their Da speaks to them mentally instead of physically. Even at such a young age, the boys are *Tuatha de Danann Sidhe*, possessing a Fae bloodline that goes back a thousand years. Their *athair's* (father's) words command their attention and both children nod their understanding regarding the wearing of the amulets at all times. As Ronin is too young at two years old to fully understand these newest developments, it will be *Niamh's* duty to make sure the toddler is in contact with the *piseóga* at all times, no small feat with an active tyke.

Dressing the children for tonight's bonfire ceremony is suddenly easily accomplished, due in no small way to the presence of the children's father in the nursery. Any of the usual complaining or bickering is put to the side in deference to their Da's Lordship personae on a high sabbat and the serious nature of what they'd been told earlier. Even Liam, who detests the feel of things around his neck, tries his very best not to fuss with the amulet lying beneath his chemise and tunic.

As I finish fishing the peas out of Ronin's nose and see to

the last of his House attire, I say to my beloved mate, "I believe we are as ready as we'll ever be, my Lord. This being *Beltane*, all is in the hands of the Universe." At the time, I had no idea just how prophetic my words would turn out to be.

TOOTHLESS 14

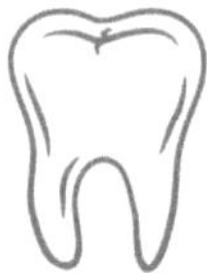

GOOD COWS GONE BAD

ONE OF THE oldest and most sacred aspect of the celebration of *Beltane* is what the Fae call in the Old Language, *Beannacht Dóiteáin* (Fire Blessing). The ritual begins with the lighting of two huge bonfires made of carefully dried oak branches that have been pruned from the Merlin's Sacred Grove on the outskirts of *I Idir,* and set several feet apart to allow a walkable pathway between them. Before igniting the pyres, our Merlin sprinkles both piles of wood with an aromatic blend of nettle, mistletoe, vervain, sage, mugwort, yarrow and meadowsweet, all natural elements used to purify and protect.

Ruling Class Houses as well as *Sidhe* Citizen Class Clans would each present one of their finest pair of male and female bovines or sheep decorated in wreaths and floral garlands, and led by the male and female heads of each family group through the pathway between the two bonfires. The smoke from the fires was meant to purify the animals before their journey to the summer pastures, thus assuring fertility within the household, the success of an abundant harvest, and a fruitful growing season free of mishap, adversity and hardship.

Since Declan's appointment as Lord of House *Nuada* years earlier, he and I have joyously participated in this ritual, leading *Dun Siorai's* finest pair of cattle down the path between the fires. Until our unusual discovery this morning, I had no reason to be concerned about this evening's participation. As I waited with the other Ruling Class couples, a small part of me was filled with angst about all the ways tonight could go very badly for we Fitzpatricks. I could tell through our unique telepathic bond that my mate had some misgivings as well, but he worked to set both of our minds at ease.

"All will be well, Ardaigh mo Chroí (Rose of my Heart*). I trust that the good will of Universe is stronger than ma' sire's curses."*

I desperately wanted to believe with all of my mate's faith that the Universe had an understanding of karma and that the evil deeds of Callum Fitzpatrick would not overshadow us as well. However, I had enough years behind me, along with a big dose of Mundane practicality, to acknowledge that the power of the Universe often did not share the same sense of justice as its inhabitants.

When it was our turn to walk the path between the two bonfires, I tugged at the reins with my left hand and *Áilleacht* (Beauty), a sweet, chocolate-brown heifer, calmly followed my movement. Next to me, with my right hand clasped in his, Declan did the same with *Láidir* ("Strength"), the three-year-old bull who was the pride of our breeding stock. Within seconds, I could tell something was amiss. The male bovine was hesitant in his gait, causing my husband to pull harder than usually necessary on his reins. I could hear his Lordship murmuring soft words of encouragement toward the animal, but the bull seemed unwilling to walk through the smoke of the bonfires, something he had done with no problem the two previous years. After we'd only taken a half dozen steps, the bull refused to go any further.

I could feel the Tax Man's angst over the situation, but outwardly he showed no sign of frustration or unease. He whistled loudly and a group of stable men came to aid in the pulling and pushing of the bull down the rest of the path. Because it was a high sabbat, and everyone was on their best protocol behavior, no one said a word to us regarding the spectacle we'd made, or the problems it indicated. But I could feel their eyes upon us and I knew, without doubt, that with their hands hidden in their laps, many in the crowd were wedging their thumb between their index and middle finger, an ancient talisman against the "evil eye."

As Lord and Lady *Nuada*, key members of *I Idir's* Ruling Council, the rest of the evening's events required our focused participation so I had little chance to discuss the alarming actions of the bull. It seemed as though most people were giving us a wide berth, waving greetings from afar, but not engaging in any close contact. Still, I let myself believe that perhaps I was letting my imagination run away with me and kept my opinions to myself. An hour into the post-bonfire celebration, our stable manager sought Declan out to make him aware that *Seamair* (Clover), the pregnant mare, had gone into labor and was struggling. An animal healer had been called, but the prognosis wasn't good for either mother or baby.

All seven of us returned to *Dun Siorai* where Declan immediately headed toward the horse barn with the rest of us moving to our family quarters. A heavy mantle of apprehension and concern hung over my little clan, so I did my best to try and keep the conversation and mood as light as possible. When Liam asked for milk and cookies before bed, I agreed, fully knowing he would mush more cookies in the milk than he would eat. I offered Dylan some quiet time in the solar parlor with the magic story book, free from the distractions of his younger brothers, a treat he graciously accepted, while the nannies and I fussed over Ronin, drank chamomile tea, and chatted about everything except the metaphorically loud elephant trumpeting in the room.

By the time my husband returned from the barn, the household was settled, with all three boys and their *scathachs* tucked in bed. Only I was still awake, unable to shut down my mind to the trauma of the day. From his aura, his body language and the grim expression, along with his blood-stained clothes, I could tell the news was not good. I forced myself to calmly ask, "So…how are they?"

"We lost them both, Love. Mare and foal. The *bairn* (baby), a male, was still born. The animal healer thought the babe's oxygen might have been compromised during early labor. Poor *Seamair* struggled so hard to bring her foal inta' the world, and when he was born dead, she completely gave up hope. Laid on her side and refused ta' fight. She no would work ta' discharge the afterbirth. The healer thought it a grave injustice ta' force her stay on this plane of the Universe if she no found it acceptable ta' do so. I agreed. Though she be a mare, she is entitled to the journey of her own spirit."

He flopped into an empty bedroom chair and loosened the tie holding his hair at the back of his head, hair that would undoubtedly be shorn as soon as we returned to Salem. "I am sick of heart, Lass, knowin' that 'tis ma' own sire at the core of all this grief. I am at a loss as ta' what I shad' do. The *Nuada* spirit prods at ma' pride ta' track the *draoi truagh* (wretched sorcerer) down no matter what the Raven Queen orders. The need ta' just be done with the man under the weight of ma' sword, once and far' all, is a temptation I'm havin' trouble not surrenderin' to. Yet within ma' mind, the wise fox spirit guidin' me warns that my reactin' in that manner is just what my evil sire expects me ta' do. If somehow, I lose my battle with him, you and the children wad' be at his mercy. That be a risk I no 'ken take."

"Oh, Declan, I'm so…so…" I let the words trail off. D.P. Fitzpatrick is not a fan of pity in any form.

He doesn't respond but notes the bed clothes I am wearing. "I am disappointed ta' see ya' ready far' a good night's sleep, Love, though I suppose it's logical at this time of the night. There was something I was hopin' ta' surprise ya' with tonight. While 'tis still Beltane."

For the life of me, I can't fathom what "Beltane surprise" would require me to be clothed, and truth be told, I've had enough "surprises" for one day." Still, I hate to disappoint my Tax Man when he has planned something special. "I can throw on some clothes if you'd like?" I suggest.

His countenance lightens. "It wad' please me vera' much, Love. I've been anticipatin' sharin' this surprise with ya' far' some time now."

I get up from the chair with plans to change into some fresh clothes. "Are we going somewhere in public? Do I need proper dress and hair? I ask, secretly hoping the answer is no.

His Lordship grins at me, and in that moment, seeing that smile replace the heavy shadow of grief, I know I would sky dive off a cliff or run with the bulls in Pamplona if it meant keeping that expression on his face. "This will be a 'private surprise,' Lass. Just you and me. Anything you want ta' put on is fine, and I love yar' hair just as it is. Though may I suggest ya' bring along a wrap of some sort. The spring evenings ken' be on the cool side."

* * *

The mention of a "private surprise" gets my libido going despite the strain of the day. The Tax Man's seduction scenarios never disappoint, even seven years into our relationship. I'm even happier when he draws a chalk circle around the both of us, signaling that we are traveling magically and are without the need of a horse or buggy. Leaving Duncan and Mac O'Kelly on family watch, I put my arms around my husband's waist and dutifully closed my eyes as I am told. There is a great deal of whooshing noise, but no pop, signaling that we haven't left the Otherworld. The smell and the weight of the air around me is a dead give-away, and I know without opening my eyes exactly where we are. We stand in the quiet, night air on *Tir na Fathach* ("Land of the Giants"), the property deeded to House *Nuada* by the Queen herself. "Oh, Sweetie! What a lovely surprise! We haven't been up here in months. It's the perfect place to heal our hearts."

Tir na Fathach is the place where the Tax Man and I had what I consider to be our first official "date." It's also the spot where we spent a joyous night after our handfast, and too many loving, memorable moments to count over the past seven years. The mountain side is a special place for both of us and one we keep entirely for our own. I lean in and kiss him. "Thanks for bringing me here, Tax Man. It's just what I needed," I say, inhaling the cool, pine scented air.

"I am glad you are pleased, *Solas mo Chroí* (Center of my Heart)," he says, returning my kiss. "But 'tis not the only surprise. Come. I'll show you." He takes me by the hand and leads me down a familiar path to what I'm guessing is our favorite spot within a large clearing of ancient oak trees. I expect to see some romantic, tented love nest in the usual Declan style, but what sits in front of my eyes takes my breath away. Set in that small clearing is a replica of my beloved house in Salem. Not the way it currently stands, all remodeled and spread out; but the way it was when Declan and I first met, early in our relationship when it was just the two of us so crazy lost in the magic of our destined love. I'm too overwhelmed to speak, and I can feel my lip trembling, a sure sign I'm going to have a whole mess of waterworks coming.

"Do ya' like it, Sweet Rosie Lass? Are ya' surprised?" he asked

"It's amazing, Darling! I…I can't even find the words. Is the inside a copy as well?" I question in a voice two octaves too high.

"'Tis not altogether finished yet, Love, but that is the plan. The builder promises it will be completely ready by the *Litha* (Summer Solstice) sabbat. There are a few things that may require yar' input, as there were some Mundane elements the par' builder was not sure he understood. I told him he would need to speak with House *Nuada's* Lady and she wad' set his straight," he adds with another spirit- raising grin.

I can do nothing more than throw myself at him, wrapping my arms around his neck. "You, D.P. Fitzpatrick, are the most wonderful husband any woman could ever have! I love your Beltane surprise!"

"I am so glad, Lass. I was worried that the events of the day would temper yar' enthusiasm. My heart is glad ya' ken look beyond this situation. I must confess though, ta' this not bein' entirely my own idea."

"Oh, really? Then who should I thank for this absolutely perfect love nest, Sweetie?"

"Truthfully, the credit would go ta' Fr. Kevin," he admitted.

"Fr. Kevin? He's an odd person to ask for romantic advice," I replied.

"The man does have a way of gettin' to the heart of things. He's a good soul, no doubt about that. He happened to stop by ma' office regardin' Ruling Class business while I was lookin' over some plans from the builder. I expressed ma' frustration because nothin' in front of me seemed to be what I was lookin' far. It was then he asked where I thought we were our very happiest, and when I mentioned yar' little cottage in Salem, he said I had my answer. It seems the Black Knight and his Lady have their own special "get away" place in the same vein. The *Banphrionsa* was most pleased with his efforts."

I wasn't sure how much I liked the idea of copying romantic advice from Mr. Shark Teeth, but I did like Fr. Kevin. Very much so. And he wasn't wrong. The cottage in front of me made my heart sing.

"Even though the house is not quite finished, I was hopin' my Lady Love would consent to a few hours alone here with her besotted mate. I have tried to make it temporarily comfortable for the two of us," he suggests.

"Hmmm. A few hours?" I question with a coy smile "However shall we spend those hours, Tax Man?"

The expression on his face is wistful. "'Tis still the wanin' hours of Beltane. Perhaps the goddess *Brigid* will especially bless our union on this sacred sabbat. I know yar' heart yearns for another *bairn*, a wee *inion* (daughter) who looks like har' *mathair*. Perhaps on this special night, in this special place, we ken' make that happen, Sweet Rosie Lass."

Perhaps he's right, I think to myself as I take his hand and head for the cottage. Perhaps.

TOOTHLESS 15

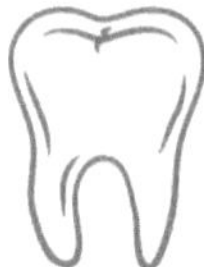

WORRY IN OUR HEARTS

His Lordship and I return to a quiet *Dun Siorai* in the purple light of dawn. We are met by a grinning Duncan, who asks, "Did ya' find ma' Lord's *Beltane* surprise satisfactory, Lady Cousin?"

"More than satisfactory, Duncan. Down-right amazing is more like it. I must say, I don't know how in the world you and Mel kept it a secret from me. You both have a reputation for accidentally spilling the beans," I tease.

"'Twas a tough enough challenge, Cousin Rosie. I know ma' own Lady was close ta' hinting to ya' about it on several occasions," he replies. "It was surely the fiery wrath of his Lordship that kept us from revealin' the surprise."

That statement elicits a round of laughs, Declan included. "Cranky Declan" is not pleasant to deal with, but using the term "wrath" to describe his anger is…well…ridiculous. If anything, Lord *Nuada* reacts to irritation with cool, calm, stinging sarcasm, which I sometimes find worse than fury because it reminds me so much of his Dragon Mama.

Changing the subject, my husband asks, "Nothing amiss here at *Dun Siorai*, Cousin?"

"No, ma' Lord. "Twas a very quiet night," Duncan states.

"Too quiet, if ya' ask me," grumbled Mac O'Kelly, the team's lone leprechaun. "Should we no have heard somethin' from the Lady *Mac Badh* by now? She's been gone for nearly two weeks. Surely, she has made some contact with the evil sorcerer."

Out of respect for my husband and their given House, the men in Declan's circle refuse to address Callum Fitzpatrick by any sort of title. Thus, he is always referred to as simply "the evil sorcerer."

"Ma' sister has been warned ta' only make contact if and when she ken' do so without being challenged, and only if she has information important enough ta' risk being found out," his Lordship explains. "We ourselves have been tracking the man far' years and as of yet have been unable to take him into custody. You ken' no expect Lady *Mac Badh* to handle it all in a matter of weeks."

The leprechaun shrugged, taking no insult from my husband's disagreement. "Yar' words are sound, ma' Lord. I speak only from frustration. I no ken' figure why the Universe and its gods and goddesses allow the man's wretched soul ta' still walk among us, spreadin' dark magic," he argued.

"I feel far' yar' anger, Mac, but 'tis always the way of the Universe. It moves as it deems ta' move. We are set on this path and walk it we must," Lord *Nuada* replies. An awkward silence follows, a testament to the fact that, undoubtedly, the other two *Sidhe* males feel the same way as Mac O'Kelly, but are holding to the "party line."

Once again, it is Duncan who moves the direction of the conversation. "If you have no further need of me, ma' Lord, then I will take my leave. My Lady is expecting me ta' join her far' dinner in the Mundane world, though it barely be breakfast here. I shad' like to wash up befar' meetin' her."

"Ya' both are free ta' be on yar' way. My Lady and I appreciate yar' diligent watch over our family. We will be returin' to Salem ourselves later this morning ta' finish up the last of Dylan's school year, and expect ta' return to *Dun Siorai* within the next 10 days or so," Declan stated.

"Then my wish is far' ya' all to have a…peaceful visit until ya' return ta' these walls," Duncan says as he leaves with a respectful bow. Yet another member of our inner circle who is carefully working at ignoring the huge elephant in the room waving his bad luck flag.

* * *

As planned, the seven of us pass through the Veil and return to our Salem home in the Mundane world. We arrive to what feels like a sauna, with hot air blowing through the air vents and the thermostat registering the temperature at 84 degrees. "Why is it so damn hot in here?" I ask no one in particular.

"I have no idea," says Cranky Declan. "The thermostat was set at 68 degrees when we left. I suppose I better go see what's going on," he grumbles as he turns and heads for the house's heating and cooling system.

While *Birgit* and *Niahm* round the kids up and usher them upstairs to settle in and change clothes, I walk through the lower level into the kitchen, my nose catching the odor of over-ripe fruit in the bowl on the island, literally baking in the steamy temperature. My indoor herb garden tucked into the kitchen's east window hasn't fared much better, the stems dry and droopy in the afternoon sun. As I contemplate if there's anything worth trying to over-water and save, I hear several clicks coming from the vent, followed by the welcome burst of cooler air.

Passing through the dining room on my way upstairs, I meet up with my husband, whose aura is still vibrating with magical energy. "Looks like you were able to fix the problem. Any idea what went wrong."

He frowns and shakes his head in the affirmative. "Aye. The main thermostat seems to have undergone some type of electrical short. I was able to zap the electronics back into correct order, but I suppose I should have someone come in and look at it. I hope ya' haven't found anything else amiss?"

"No," I reply. "The appliances all seem to be fine. What-ever it was that caused the thermostat to go crazy didn't seem to affect anything in the kitchen." I open my mouth to add something else and then close it. I hesitate asking for a "magical favor" as I know how my husband feels about using his gifts for what he considers "frivolous" purposes. On the other hand, I spent a lot of time and energy keeping that herb garden going all winter. I'd at least like to try and dry a batch for use next fall.

Because we always have that open line of communication, my request is noted without me having to ask. "I'll see if I can't perk up yar' little plants, Lass. Ya' know ma' gifts are yars' far' the askin'."

I give him a hug. "I know, Sweetie, and I appreciate that. I try not to use you as my personal "magical maintenance man."

"Ya' ken just go on usin' me any way ya' need," he says with a suggestive grin. He leans over to kiss me but is inter-rupted by a loud crash above our heads that causes the light fixture in the dining room to shake and sway. We both dive up to the second-floor nursery to find the heavy wooden armoire tipped over and lying on the floor, with Liam wailing in *Niamh's* arms and the rest of our clan looking on in horrified silence.

"Hell's Bells! What happened here?" I take my still sobbing middle child from his nanny's arms, and quickly check him for injuries, which, thankfully, appear to be non-existent. Knowing my Liam as I do, I ask, "Was he using the armoire as a jungle gym again?"

"Nay, ma' Lady. Liam was just putin' away his clothes in the bottom drawer like I'd asked him to, when suddenly, the *cófra* (cupboard) pulled away from the wall. 'Twas only *Niamh's* speed that kept our par' boy from serious injury."

I turn to Declan who looks physically ill. "How could this possibly happen?" I question with a shaky voice. "The armoire was bolted to the damn wall."

His Lordship is already on it, poking and prodding his fingers in the ragged edges of the plaster that once held said bolts. "The drywall in this area feels damp and mushy. There must be a pipe leak somewhere upstairs that has caused water damage to the plaster. Given how soft it is, 'tis no wonder the bolts gave way."

I don't even want to consider what might have been. That armoire must weigh at least two hundred solid pounds. To think of Liam in its way causes my stomach to roll. Seemingly to sense my physical angst, the four-year-old puts his arms out to his father, who takes him from my grasp. I try to thank *Niamh*, but she waves me off, neither of us wanting to even consider how badly this might have turned out. And in that moment, I understood, without doubt, that the two-ton, circus Jumbo of magical bad luck had followed us here to Salem.

TOOTHLESS 16

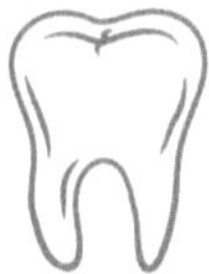

DA'S RUNAWAY CART

It's the same in either world; it's all about who you know. Within two hours of the armoire incident, Ambrose Myrdynn arrives at our home to do what he can to counter the dark mantle that seems to have settled itself upon our family. I sense that my normal cool, calm collected Tax Man is at a breaking point, his rage over what might have happened to Liam a living breathing entity, and I pray that I'm the only one privy to the curses of retribution against his father that play out in a loop in his head. In The Morrrigan's *I Idir*, patricide without the prelude of personal self-defense is a "big sacred no-no," a decision that could cost him everything he holds dear for a fleeting moment of revenge. I do my best to remind him of this while having my own dreams of watching the life drain out of the evil bastard.

What most people don't understand about ritual magic is that it is the caster alone who holds the spell together. Our Merlin can try and counter the effects of the spell, but he can do little to end it. A ritual spell is entirely owned by the practitioner who has sent it into the world. There are caveats to magical energy that even the mega-powerful entities like our Raven Queen must adhere to. Even if she were to find a way to successfully disrupt the parameters of the spell, the energy behind it wouldn't be lost or gained, only transformed, and magical energy without set boundaries was a very dangerous thing.

We all watched as the wizard burned enough sage to make the house smoky, ground some type of gray lava rock to sprinkle around the front and back doors, and anointed all of our palms with salve that smelled of pine needles and tallow. After that was completed, we politely withdrew to other spaces to give the Merlin some privacy in order to deeply meditate in the quiet of our living room.

Despite all the time I'd spent in *I Idir* the last several years, I hadn't seen a lot of conjured ritual magic. Most *Sidhe* used the quiet personal energy they were born with, though there are others, mostly those with *Tuatha de Danann* bloodlines, that have the ability to successfully amplify their power through ritual and spells. Growing up in a Mundane culture peppered with human-written fairy tales and fantasy stories, it always amazed me as an adult to learn that so much of the practice of magic had a strong biological and scientific foundation. And if the concerns of The Morrigan and her Black Knight were horrifyingly true, the rest of the Mundane world was now fully aware of that fact and using technology to bridge the gap.

Upon leaving our home, Ambrose explained the parameters of his casting. "Protective spells are hard to cast as an infinite, especially away from the Otherworld." he explained. "You will find that the ritual spells cast here in the Mundane world work much more efficiently when contained to a set space. Therefore, you will likely find your general well-being safer in the confines of this house than when you are out and about among the rest of the Mundane world. May I suggest that during this week until the time you return to *Dun Siorai* you limit your travels outside the house to a minimum?"

I open my mouth to explain that our whole purpose for returning to Salem was so we could finish things up for our summer hiatus, but Declan cuts me off. Touching his hand to his forehead in the *Sidhe* gesture for respect, his Lordship says, "I am most grateful for your efforts toward the protection of my family, Lord Merlin. We will abide by your advice whenever possible, though I am hoping *Mac Nuada* will be able to finish his school year at *Cerridwen.*"

"I fully understand, Lord *Nuada*. My granddaughter *Mairead* can talk of nothing less than the school field days coming up this week. Considering their unique relationship, I have no doubt the youngest *Banphrionsa* would be very disappointed if your son were unable to join her. I plan on popping over to the school and seeing if I can't lay down some extra words. I don't believe the administration will have a problem with that," the wizard replies with a knowing smile.

Dylan's intense connection to the daughter of the Black Knight and the *Banphrionsa* of *I Idir* is public knowledge. The two are inseparable, though I've always felt it was more of an ongoing competition than a friendship going back to a time when they were both toddlers. There's no denying the two children are extremely fond of one another and undoubtedly share the burdens their birth order places upon them. However, as his mother, I secretly hoped Dylan would get a chance to get out into the world, Mundane and Fae, to meet other people before settling on a future devoted to the reigning heir of *I Idir.*

My mental musings earn me a "look" from my husband as our 26th Merlin prepares to take his leave. The mood in the house is tense, Liam's near miss leaving our little clan apprehensive and somber. I tell myself it's only ten days. We can handle this. Still, the phrase "famous last words" bounces around my head like a chaotic rubber ball.

* * *

We work out a viable plan for our short Salem stay: *Birgit* and *Niamh,* along with the two youngest children are basically housebound while Declan drops-off and picks Dylan up from school with plans to work entirely from his home office. And me? Well, I'm the only "stubborn one who insists on cuttin' the feckin' safety net," as my Eternal Mate so colorfully puts it.

What the Tax Man doesn't seem to understand is that my profession doesn't offer the flexibility of caring for my young patients through the impersonal luxury of FaceTime and Zoom. Knowing that I would be away for the summer months, I had scheduled three oral surgeries and two orthodontic consultations weeks in advance, cases I felt couldn't be delayed for three and a half months. Thus, for six of the ten days, I trot off to my office in the Witch City Mall to take care of business.

I would like to say that it was no big deal and that I competently maneuvered around the *droch-ádh* (bad luck) that had befallen our family. Unfortunately, that was not the case. In the six days I left the safety of the house, I incurred a hit and run to my car in the mall parking lot, lost one of my favorite ruby earrings, stained my new Lauren blouse with silver diamine fluoride, had the entire records network go down for most of one day putting us way behind schedule, and sprained my wrist trying to catch a heavy stack of file folders as they fell off the top of my desk. As bad as all those incidents were, what's truly annoying is listening to my Tax Man's "I told you so" verbiage.

It's why I am so shocked when he himself "cuts the feckin' safety net" on our last day in Salem. What's even more crazy is that he takes on the risk over something utterly ridiculous. I watch as he dresses in expensive khakis and some designer polo shirt to spend the day playing golf. "Seriously, Declan. I can't believe you're going to endanger yourself over a silly golf game. You don't even like the sport."

"Aye, Love. 'Tis a vera' slow challenge, I will agree. I much prefer somethin' a bit livelier. But this invitation came from an associate I hope ta' make a client of and it's far' 18 holes on the course at The Country Club in Brookline. I'm not sure if ya' are aware, but this club is one of the top courses in Massachusetts. Very private and elite. I could no pass up such an opportunity."

I shrug in response. After all the badgering I received for attending to my professional duties, I feel his golf game outing is a tad hypocritical, but when his Lordship makes up his mind, there's no changing it. "You have to do what you have to do, Sweetie. Just…please…be careful. I'm proof that this bad juju follows us around."

He kisses me in response. "I promise, Rosie Love. I will take every precaution," he vows, pulling the amulet out from under his shirt.

I'm not convinced that *piseóga* is going to be much protection. It didn't seem to work very well on my end, but there's no use arguing with my husband when he has one foot out the door. Truthfully, I have enough on my plate today, packing for our summer at *Dun Siorai* and getting the house closed down for extended absence, to go head to head with my mate over a stupid golf game.

I'm grateful to have all three children safely under our roof today. Because he bested *Mairead* Beckett in two of the school's field day competitions, Dylan is in a pleasant enough mood to consent to playing with his younger brother, thus allowing me uninterrupted time to handle my necessary chores, already made more difficult by the sprained wrist. Later in the afternoon, as the six of us are enjoying picnic-style tea on the screened porch, Declan returns home. For a moment, we all just stare at him in shock until Liam blurts out, "Look at Da! He's a mess!"

My four-year-old isn't wrong. My normally fastidious Tax Man IS a complete mess. His pristine and perfect pressed khakis are wet and muddy, as is his pale, yellow polo shirt and top-of-the-line Pioneer golf shoes. Worse yet, he reeks of stagnant pond water. "Oh hell! What happened to you," I ask. "Are you okay?"

"Obviously I am far from 'okay,' ma' Lady," he grumbles. "Let me change out of these wretched clothes and then I will explain."

I don't say anything along the lines of "I told you so," but Liam is not as astute. "Da is a mess, Da is a mess," Liam repeats in a sing-song voice.

"Liam, Honey, don't tease Daddy. It's not a nice thing to do," I gently scold.

My little man just shrugs and smiles at me. "Okay, Mama. Da is no a mess," he corrects as he happily goes back to eating his toast and honey.

None of us say much of anything until his Lordship returns to the sun porch, freshly showered and wearing clean clothes. Liam slides off his chair and runs to his father. "Ya' look vera' nice now, Da," he politely states.

Declan laughs and then picks the boy up and settles in a chair with Liam on his lap. "I should expect yar' all wantin' ta' hear my tale of woe," he says.

"Only if you want to share it," I counter.

Liam pats his father's cheek. "I want ta' hear yar' tale, Da," he bluntly adds.

"Then, of course, you must hear it, *Mo Mhac Ionúin* (My

Beloved Son). It would seem yar' par' ole' Da did not follow his own rules regardin' stayin' home. I foolishly decided 'twas mar' important I should go off ta' Brookline ta'play golf and curry some new business. The golf club was vera' impressive…vera' large and richly appointed."

"I bet that ya' won first place, didn't ya', *Athair*?" Dylan remarked, freshly off his own triumph over the *Banphrionsa*.

"I'm afraid we did not get ta' finish our game, Dylan," Declan explains. "As I was sayin', 'twas a large course and the holes were spaced quite far apart. My associate decided ta' rent a cart far' the four of us, which would have been wholly pleasant if it weren't far' the overpowering scent of his after shave or cologne. It smelled as if he had bathed in pine resin and flower petals. I did no care far' the smell at all, but it seemed the wee *beacha siúinéir* (carpenter bees) liked it vera, vera' much. We must have bothered a nest of them goin' over a wooden bridge near the eighth hole because they came at us in a swarm, goin' hard at my smelly associate who was drivin' the cart. As he attempted to swat away the bees, he lost control of the cart and drove it inta' the pond at the eighth hole, submergin' all four of us in the mucky water. Truthfully, 'twas quite disgustin'.'"

Okay. I'll admit I was working hard to be a good motherly role model and not laugh out loud at my mate's misfortune. It was, however, an admittedly funny story, and Dylan and Liam couldn't hold in their giggles, followed by Ronin who I'm sure didn't understand the story, but nevertheless, didn't want to be left out. Pretty soon, we were all laughing, even Declan himself, and I let myself naively believe we Fitzpatricks could handle whatever *droch-ádh* shit was being thrown our way. I could have never imagined it would all go down the way it did.

TOOTHLESS 17

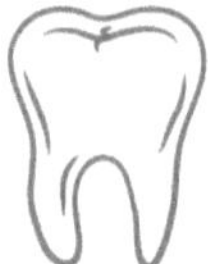

A VISIT FROM A BIRD

We had been settled in at *Dun Siorai* for nearly two weeks when the first mysterious raven-gram arrived, sadly along with definitive proof that the goddess had not generously blessed our *Beltane* union with another child. While I was shocked by the first event, the later wasn't much of a surprise. I'd been having crampy, lower back pain for a few days, clueing me in that I probably wasn't expecting baby number four. Perhaps it was the lingering disappointment over my lack of fertility that made me so emotional following the arrival of that damned bird and his wretched missive. Or maybe it was the fact that this whole situation simply sucked.

I was alone in the parlor when I heard the creepy tapping and scratching at the far east window. Over the years, I've made no secret of my personal disgust over those beady-eyed harbingers of bad news. Normally, when Declan is around, I let him retrieve raven-grams. This morning, however, he was up and out to the horse barn before dawn to monitor the spring shoeing. Our return to the Otherworld had so far been welcomely free of the over-bearing bad luck we experienced in Salem, but his Lordship wasn't taking any chances with the safety of any part or person who called *Dun Siorai* home.

The children and their *scathachs* were out in the vineyards watching the new budded vines be pruned and trellised, followed by a highly anticipated breakfast-style picnic in the west gardens and topped off with a rousing game of kick ball. His Lordship was adamant that his children, especially Dylan, should begin learning about the running of the estate as early as possible. Though I agreed with him on point, I promised myself I would make this last summer of freedom for Dylan as pleasantly child-like as possible, as next summer, at age eight, he would begin daily summer studies at the Academy.

These circumstances left me, and me alone, to answer the urging tapping. The first thing I noticed upon opening the window was that the blasted corvid wore no leg band of House colors, which usually signaled that the message the bird was carrying was of dubious origin. Every person in *I Idir* belonged to one House or another, whether it be by bloodline, handfasting, or employment, and House colors made it easy to recognize who belonged to what clan. Thus, a raven-gram without a colored House band was akin to receiving spam phone calls or junk mail.

The fact that it was an un-banded message made me less apprehensive. From my experience, House-sent messages were, more often than not, invitations to events you didn't want to attend or simply bad news rolled up in scroll form. With a sigh, I foolishly assumed this particular missive was little more than nonsense. I took the paper from the bird's mouth. The feathered creep continued to eye me, but didn't move. "Go on, now! Shoo!" I say as I waved my hands at it.

Crazy as it sounds, the raven uttered an annoyed "tisk tisk" and then flew off.

I pulled the string from the scroll and unrolled it, but the writing on the page made little sense. In fact, it wasn't really writing at all; only a series of numbers with a few random words scribbled at the bottom:

50.2374 20.8478

47.6558 8.8580

36.7462 5.1612

36. 7538 3.0588

Bab Lads - Bab Risk

Despite staring at it for several minutes, I couldn't, for the life of me, figure out what this message meant. Mathematically, it made no sense as a receipt or an equation, thus I assumed the numbers were a code for something else. I thought perhaps the numbers matched up to letters of the alphabet of either English or the Old Language, but that didn't seem to make sense at all, nor did the odd words at the bottom ring any bells. Still, my Fae intuition poked at me, giving me the vibe that I was missing something of importance.

Though I hated to pull my husband away from his responsibilities in the horse barn, I sent out a mental communication. *"Hey sweetie, are you there?"*

He answered immediately, his angst reaching me before the words did *"Aye, Love. Is something the matter? Are ya' all okay?"*

"Everything's fine here. It's just that a raven-gram came to us this morning. From an unmarked bird. It's well...very strange."

"Strange how," he asks.

"The message contains a list of numbers and a few nonsensical words. I tried figuring it out but nothing is coming to me. I really think you ought to take a look at it as soon as you can get away. In case it has anything to do with Black Knight business."

"Give me a few minutes here, Love, and I will join ya' shortly. I need ta' see ta' this last stallion befar' I ken' leave. Just so ya' are aware, I'm gonna' touch base with Beck, so don't be surprised if he shows up there before me. Ya' know how he likes ta' be on top of things."

"Okay, Sweetie. See ya' soon." I broke the mental connection then thought to myself that I really hoped the Black Knight didn't arrive before Declan. The man was a terrible tease who I believed thoroughly enjoyed making me feel uncomfortable. In the meantime, my Lady of House *Nuada* protocol kicked in so I ordered late morning tea service to be sent to our quarters, because goddesses forbid a guest to *Dun Siorai* not receive perfect *Sidhe* hospitality. The world could be burning to ashes and those *Tuatha de Danann* types would still expect appropriate refreshments.

As predicted, the Queen's Hand of Justice arrived ahead of my husband, but thankfully had brought the *Prionsa* of *I Idir*, aka Fr. Kevin O'Kenney, with him. Both men were dressed in casual Mundane apparel, which I suppose was to be expected as it was the late evening yesterday back in the Mundane world. "It's always a pleasure to see you again, Lady *Nuada*," the priest said with his usual friendly politeness. "I hope we haven't caused you extra trouble popping in this way."

"No trouble at all, Father. And please, call me Rosie." I lead them to the parlor and say, "May I offer you gentlemen late morning tea? I realize it's evening back in Massachusetts, so I had the staff add an herbal pot to the tray if you'd prefer something decaffeinated."

"Thank you, Rosie," the Black Knight replied without taking a seat, "but I'm mainly interested in the raven-gram you said you received."

His brother-in-law gave him a withering look, and added

"That's very thoughtful of you, Rosie. We'll both have a cup while we wait for Fitz to join us."

I could tell by the clenched jaw that our fearless Knight did not like being over-ruled by Fr. Kevin, but he couldn't very well scold the *Prionsa* of *I Idir* in my presence, so they both took a spot on the sofa and busied themselves with the tea tray. While we waited for Declan, the three of us engaged in friendly chit chat. "Will Maureen and the children be spending any time in *I Idir* this summer, Beck?" I ask, the informal use of first names already established.

"I believe at some point all of them will relocate here for several weeks in July," our "Spy Boss" said. "*Mairead* is signed up for some gymnastics day camp the rest of May, and my wife's family always plans a reunion vacation at our home on the Cape during the first few weeks of June. After that, Maureen and the kids will come to *I Idir* and stay at *Crann Bethadh* and I'll continue to commute back and forth. Like your son, this will be our daughter's last free summer, as next year she'll begin her courses at The Academy," he says as he takes a sip of the tea. "My wife and I want her to enjoy the *Bon La Vie* (French for "Good Life") while she still can."

"I feel sorry for both children," Fr. Kevin countered. "So much responsibility at such a young age. In my opinion, Maureen and I were lucky not to become aware of our heritage until later in life. We were able to enjoy a pretty normal Mundane childhood." He smiled and then added, "Though I am one hundred percent sure Herself would not agree. My Great Grandmother holds that our human upbringing was 'an abomination' to all things *Sidhe*."

I smile back politely, though part of me is waiting for some caustic reaction from The Morrigan over Fr. Kevin's casual mention of her. It always shocks me how unafraid and natural he is when he speaks of her, as if she were like any other normal human family member. Truthfully, the Raven Queen still scared the shit out of me.

It's during this interlude that my husband finally makes his appearance, still in clothes meant for the barn and not for a meeting with some of the kingdom's top movers and shakers. "Welcome ta' *Dun Siorai*, gentlemen. I appreciate ya' both comin' on such short notice. I hope ya' will excuse ma' appearance. 'Tis shoeing season, and I was in the horse barn all morning."

"No problem, Fitz. Now that you're here, I need to take a look at the raven-gram message you received," the Black Knight said in a tone that indicated he didn't particularly enjoy wasting time drinking tea and conversing on the topics of domestic life.

"Rosie, ken' ya' show us the scroll that ya' received this morning," Declan asks me.

I stand and retrieve the parchment from the mantle where I placed it earlier. "Here it is, gentlemen. It came at about 9:30 this morning from an unmarked bird. At first, I thought it might be just some kind of advertising, but when I read it, I found it to be very odd."

I remove the tea tray and spread the mysterious message out on the low table between us, using the sugar bowl to hold one side down from curling, and the creamer to hold down the other. "I believed it might be a code of some sort, but of what type I can't be sure. Don't bother trying to match up the numbers to letters in either alphabet. I tried that and it didn't provide any clues," I explain.

"That's because these numbers aren't a code, Rosie. The arrangement of them with the decimal point where it's placed suggests that these numbers are coordinates," Beck states.

"Coordinates?" I ask, not fully following his thinking.

"Yes. Longitude and latitude numbers. I strongly believe

these are specific locations. Shit! It's times like this I really miss the fingertip access of technology within the Mundane world," the Black Knight complained.

"I think there might be a map of the Mundane world in the library, Beck. I ken' find it if ya' think it will help," my husband offers.

"Unfortunately, figuring the points would take time none of us have to give. I'm going to pop back through the Veil, look these numbers up on my phone, then come back with clarification," the Knight replied. "It shouldn't take me very long. I'd like you all to stay here and wait, if that's possible. If what I'm thinking is correct, we'll need to make further plans based on my findings."

"Look Bro, didn't you just promise Maureen you weren't going to jump back and forth so often. We're all keenly aware that excessive Veil crossing can cause physical damage on a cellular level," Fr. Kevin interjected.

"Do you hear that, Tax Man," I mentally convey to Declan. *"You need to start keeping track of how much you go back and forth as well. Too much Veil tripping isn't good for you."*

My husband doesn't reply while Beck grins with his shark teeth and teases his brother-in-law. "Aww, isn't that sweet. You worry about me, Kev. Come here and give me a big hug."

The priest didn't move, instead giving the Black Knight a disgruntled look. "It's not funny, Ted. You've seen the risks first hand."

"I appreciate your concern, Kev. But I'm not *Sidhe*. I'm *Draoi a Rugadh* (Wizard Born). We come from invincible stock. I'll be fine. Be back before you know it." Then, without any additional conversation, the 27th Merlin drew a chalk circle on my hardwood floor and disappeared.

TOOTHLESS 18

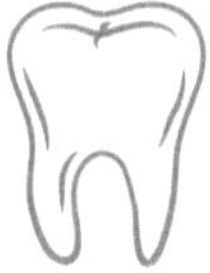

GIVEN THE OFFICIAL WORD

UNDER ANY OTHER CIRCUMSTANCES, the Black Knight up and disappearing like that, leaving us just sitting there waiting on him, would have been a tad awkward. But the Prince of *I Idir* is such a pleasant, likeable person we are caught up in his chatter. He soon had Declan and I laughing at funny stories about his very large, Irish family back in Boston, who sadly aren't in the least bit Fae and who can't share any of his adventures in *I Idir*. I can commiserate with him in earnest. The hardest part of my dual "citizenship" in both worlds is that I can't share one very important half of it with my older sister Claire and her family. There have been so many times over the past seven years that I have thought how wonderful it would be if Claire could have shared some of my Fae life here in *I Idir*. As a long-time hobby horticulturist, I absolutely know she would marvel at the formal gardens of *Dun Siorai* and take great delight in the variety of Mundane similar animals that make their home here. Alas, the best I can do is verbally describe it to her while showing her some of the simple sketches one of the house staff has drawn for me.

It's because of Fr. Kevin's social light-heartedness that we don't even notice how long Beck is gone until he pops right back into the parlor with no advance warning. "I was right," he announces. "The number sequences are longitude and latitude coordinates. They match up to specific small towns across the globe." The Hand of Justice speaks directly to my husband. "Fitz, do you think you can dig out that Mundane world map you talked about? I want to plot these places and see if there's any connection or additional clues in where they are on a map."

While Declan goes to find the map in the library, I have questions of my own. "Do you have any idea who might have sent this message? These coordinates? I would think knowing who sent them would be just as important as the information."

"I don't disagree, Rosie. I don't believe this message came from any of our regiment assets in the field. The locations these coordinates focus on are very small towns scattered across the globe in places that haven't been on our terrorist radar. Three of the towns are located in Europe, while the fourth is miles away in Algeria. Our vetted assets would have no reason to be in those obscure locations without orders from me, but I suppose I can't absolutely write off that possibility. More than likely, this message came from Lady *Mac Badh*. When she went into the field a few weeks back, I left it up to her ingenuity to get information to us without being found out. She'd be more familiar with using raven-grams."

Beck's logic was sound, but something about the whole idea didn't ring true for me. Meghan had never seemed to me to be of the personality to enjoy puzzles or cryptograms. I remember Declan telling me once that he'd gifted her a Mundane jig saw puzzle for Solstice when she was about seven years old. Although the completed puzzle would have shown a painting of wild horses, a theme she adored, the girl returned the gift to him a few days later stating "'Twas not ta' her likin' and much too time consumin' ta' bother with."

Declan came back with the map and we all gathered in the informal dining room area so the folded paper could be spread across the entire table. The map was not an up to date one, but very detailed. The print date on the corner stated a publication date of 2004, but the man in charge didn't think it would matter much for our purpose. Grabbing a felt-tipped pen and a post-it-note from his back pocket, the Black Knight plotted out the coordinates. "Okay…so the first set of numbers is for a small town in south-eastern Poland called Zalipie."

Our four pairs of eyes scour the map for Poland then try to hunt down the dot signifying Zilipie. Fr. Kevin is the first one to see it. "There," he says, pointing to a tiny circle on the map "In between Krakow and Czestochowa. I think I saw a documentary on the Travel Channel about this place. It's considered one of the prettiest villages in Poland because of its painted cottages."

"Excellent," Beck replied as he made the dot for Zilipie larger and darker with his pen. "Now, we're looking for Stein am Rhein in Switzerland. By the numbers, I'm guessing it's most likely in the Eastern part of the country."

"Right here," my husband says. "On the banks of the Rhine River."

The Knight again uses the felt-tipped pen to enlarge the dot marking *Stein am Rhein.* "Rosie, do you have something I can use as a straight edge ruler?"

I glanced around the dining room, looking where I remember seeing a coloring book Liam left there earlier in the day. "Will this work?" I ask, holding it up.

"That's fine," he replied taking it from my hand. Using the

spine edge of the book, he drew a line from the town in Poland to the one in Switzerland, crossing directly through Germany. "The third set of longitude and latitude points to Ronda, Spain. I know it's in the Málaga Province so that means southern Spain," he says as he inspects the map. "Yup. Right here," he concurred as he marked the paper and drew another line from the spot in Switzerland to the lower point of Spain. "That just leaves this last set of numbers which is actually almost directly south of Spain, across the Mediterranean. A place I happen to be very familiar with…Algiers, Algeria." Marking the map with the final dot, our Boss drew a straight line from Ronda to Algiers and then from Algiers back up to Poland. Looking at the dark line shape the four cities created, the man asked, "Does anything jump out about these four places to anyone? Observations?"

"The only location I know anything about is Zilipie," Fr. Kevin offered "It's a small, quaint little community. Not sure what they would have to do with terrorism, at least the sort we're concerned about."

"Agreed. That one threw me off a bit as well. On the other hand, you can't always judge a book by its cover. For all we know, Zilipie could be a hot bed of anti-Fae sentiment," his brother-in-law suggested.

"I donna' have first-hand knowledge of any of these locations, but accordin' to the map, only Algiers has a port. The other three are land-locked, forcin' the sendin' and receivin' of materials or men to be by train or truck. Makes the logistics far mar' difficult. I donna' see how these locations would be beneficial ta' any espionage, unless obscurity was yar' motive."

"I thought the same," Beck agreed. "Algiers is better suited for general logistics, and I can tell you from my experience, a lot of shady shit moves through there."

Pushing my luck among these seasoned "spies," I bring up

my question from earlier. "As I mentioned before, Lord Knight," softening my perseverance with his title, "I really think finding out who sent this raven-gram might help us zero in on the motive of sending us these coordinates."

"I don't disagree, Rosie. I will check-in with all my European assets to verify it wasn't one of them, though we usually use modern Mundane technology to make contact rather than raven-grams. Still, I can't discount that theory out of hand, so I'll double-down on checking myself. But, as I told you earlier, I believe this message is from Lady *Mac Badh*. It makes the most sense as it fits with what we asked her to do."

"Ya' think ma' sister sent the raven-gram, Beck?" my husband questions.

"It does make the most sense, don't you think? We told her to be creative in her transfer of information so as to not let her father catch on. It would be a good sign that she's doing okay. She's been gone for two weeks now and this is the first intel we've received. Truth be told, I was starting to worry."

"Aye. I was as well," Declan replies, but knowing him like I do, I can tell he's not totally convinced of the Black Knight's theory by the flexing of the fingers on his left hand. I take the high road and keep my thoughts to myself for the time being.

"If you ask for my opinion, I think we need to do some reconnaissance on all four places. Just to see what we can dig up," Fr. Kevin chimed in.

"I'm in agreement," his brother-in-law concurred. "You have time this week to join me?"

"If we avoid Mundane travel and jump to *I Idir* and then to wherever, I could probably give you most of this Wednesday. I wouldn't be able to do commercial travel, though. Takes too long," the priest stated.

"No problem. We can jump." Beck turns to my husband.

"Can you and Duncan take on an exploratory mission to Zilipsie, Poland? Maybe get two of your guys to do the Switzerland location, and I'll get *Mac Badh* and his man Turner to do Spain. Since I know the city of Algiers, Kev and I will take that one. I'm looking for a quick turn-around on this. In and out. Reconnaissance only with no engagement until we know what we're dealing with. Meet at *Crann Bethadh* or here at *Dun Siorai* next Thursday?"

"Aye. That I can do," my husband says, carefully ignoring my disgruntled expression. Then, he totally shocks me "As it is only a reconnaissance mission with no engagement, I wad' like ta' take ma' Lady as ma' second. It would be gad' practice far' her and if I ken' be honest with ya', I would prefer that Duncan stay here with ma' family while I am away. "Tis too much been goin' on as of late."

I secretly pray that the Black Knight won't disagree. It's been a long time since my husband and I have been on a mission together and I really, really want to do something to help find *Oisin*.

There's a tiny bit of smirk forming on the man's face, but he seems to accept my husband's request. "Good plan, Fitz. It will probably be easier to move through the town as a married couple. You'll call less attention to yourselves and it will be easier to poke around. And you're absolutely right; our Rosie needs to be more visible on the team. Time to run with the big dogs."

I'm not sure I'll like the dog metaphor, but I'd be lying if I'd said I wasn't tickled pink over the idea of going to Poland with my Tax Man.

"As for the odd words at the bottom of the paper, all I could come up with is an alphabet cipher code. Switching the letters out for numbers, it comes up **212-121419-412-1891911**," the Knight said. "Too many numbers for a phone number, but definitely could be an alarm or entrance code.

Maybe even a safe combination. I want all the teams to take a copy of this sequence with them in case it might be useful." The man gathered up the original scroll as both he and Fr. Kevin prepared to cross the Veil back to the Mundane world. Before leaving, he turned to Declan and myself. "Have fun, kids. But stay on your guard. I really have no idea what this is about so play it safe, keep to yourselves, and…absolutely no engagement."

Later that evening, alone in our bedroom, I bring up the misgivings I have over the identity of the raven-gram's sender. "I don't want to rock the boat right out of the gate, Sweetie, and I know I'm only a junior spy, but I just don't think your sister Meghan sent that message. It's too…too 'puzzle-y' for her. I always felt she was very literal in her speech and thinking. I get the feeling you think the same thing."

My mate puts down the paperback he's reading, some new best-selling techno-thriller he brought with him from Salem. "Aye, Love. It does no suit her personality or logic. Meghan never wanted ta' attend school in the Mundane world. She always had private tutors here at *Dun Siorai* along with her magic classes at the Academy. I would be shocked if she knew anything about Mundane geography or coordinates. Plus, mathematics and numbers were never har' strong point. Far' a time, she had her heart set on working with Robyn in the genetics field, but she just didna' have the aptitude or grit ta' tackle the math and science involved in that field of study. Her sendin' that coded raven-gram doesn't make sense."

"I'm just going to say it, Declan. I think *Oisin* sent that message. He's always been a whiz with Mundane technology and I could fully see him looking up those numbers on the internet. Plus, you know as much as I do that the kid loved puzzles of all kinds. He always had a Sudoku he was working on. I think he's trying to tell us where he's at. And shocker of shockers, I'll bet any money that the Black Knight thinks that as well. He's not fooling me one little bit. That man is always three steps ahead of everyone else, and there's no stinking way he thinks your sister could come up with that secret message."

"I agree with ya', Lass. The man never shows his full hand. It appears we are goin' ta' have ta' wait and see exactly what cards he's holdin' so close ta' the vest."

TOOTHLESS 19

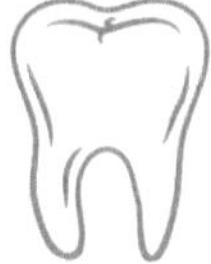

A EUROPEAN TRIP

Because of pressing responsibilities at *Dun Siorai*, Declan and I don't leave for Poland until two days later. I've been my husband's second on a handful of "missions" over the years, and truthfully, none of them have been what one might describe as "scintillating loads of fun." The few I've been invited to participate with fell into two basic categories; surveillance or information gathering, neither of which was very exciting. I have spent countless hours sitting in a car with my Tax Man watching the comings and goings of "people of interest" from a particular location, along with searching through dusty documents and such in libraries, government departments, and the occasional suffocatingly small storage unit. When I complain about "not getting my hands dirty," my always practical husband reminds me of my one and only "hands-on-field-mission" with him to Asgard in which I was wholly miserable.

This mission would be different. Better. I'd thoroughly convinced myself that in the last six and half years I'd come a long way in my role as a "spy." I'd taken and passed the basic self-defense training and now had a better understanding of how the Raven Queen's secret intelligence network actually worked. People generally found me easy to talk to, and when you're in the information gathering business, that's a huge asset. Plus, as much as I hated to admit it, the Black Knight had been right regarding my growing social status, thanks in no small part to the rumors that followed us out the woods on that awful *Oíche Fiáin* (Wilding Night) nearly two years ago. Despite my connection to the shamed Callum Fitz-patrick, I suddenly became more "intriguing" to the gossip-loving Ruling Class, and thus was invited to join more circles where I was taken into confidence, a boon my Spy Boss expected me to use exclusively for the Queen's benefit.

With my spy confidence level high, I asked my "Superior Officer" what he thought I should pack for our trip. His reply took my zeal down a level or two. "'Tis not necessary ta' take anything along, Lass. We will only be in Poland for a short time. Just long enough to discover what someone wants us ta' find in Zilipie. I have no plans ta' stay the night. I'm hopin' to be back at *Dun Siorai* before the children are put ta' bed. I would suggest, though, a pair of sturdy hikin' boots and comfortable Mundane clothing. It is likely we will spend several hours on our feet. I ken' provide us with anythin' else if the need arises."

"Oh. Okay," I reply without a whole lot of enthusiasm.

"'Tis no a vacation, Lass," my Superior Officer says with Lordship bluntness. "We have a job ta' do at the command of the Queen. She and Beck will expect us ta' focus on the single task at hand." Seeing my glum expression, the husband in him quickly adds, "'Tis an added bonus that I get ta' spend the day with my gorgeous Eternal Mate. There is no one I'd rather have at ma' side than you, Love. And if you find that ya' enjoy the sights and sounds of Poland, then in the near future you and I shall plan a romantic trip there. Just the two of us."

It's on the tip of my tongue to say that Poland isn't on my list of romantic get-away locations, but I don't want to start the day off in a negative way, so I hold onto my sarcasm. After much debate, it is decided that I don't have anything appropriate to wear for marching through the woods, so I rely on Declan to conjure something up for me to wear. At least this time around, I don't have to appear as a dowdy, old peasant woman, and the tourist hiking clothes and boots he creates for me are casually chic, comfortable and attractive, which I take as a sign that maybe the day won't be as unappealing as my mate has made it sound.

Once Duncan arrives, looking less than thrilled that I'm going with Declan instead of him, we cross the Veil into Poland. Because Himself is unfamiliar with the area and doesn't have Google Earth to pinpoint a specific secluded spot near Zilipie, we land in a wooded area two and a half miles from the edge of the village. Although the road is mostly flat, two and a half miles is still a long walk, and my legs are a lot shorter than my husband's, so I have to basically trot to keep up with him. The rural town itself is very small but absolutely charming. All the buildings, sign posts, and barns are lavishly decorated with hand-painted floral artwork in every color of the rainbow, the creativity and dedication to visual appeal reminding me in many ways of *Groenn Dalr* in Asgard.

"Oh Declan, this place is amazing. Look how quaint and pretty all the little houses are! Did you know it would be like this?" I ask as I stop and study an intricate bouquet of pink and red peonies painted on a wooden mailbox.

"Only by word of mouth, Lass. I have a client who has family in Tarnów, Poland, who once chatted with me about a nearby 'painted village.' I recognized the name when Beck mentioned it the other day. Since he was sending me here, I thought ya' might enjoy seein' it with me. It did no seem like a place that would be especially dangerous and there has been no evidence of any recent terrorist activity here."

"That's very sweet of you, Tax Man," I reply with an edge of annoyance. "But I was hoping you were taking me along because you thought I could be a good partner. That you believed I could help you get the information we need. I have been trained, you know. I can take care of myself."

"There's no need ta' get all ruffled up, Rosie Lass. I love havin' ya' with me. Ya' see things other people blindly miss. Yar' one of the smartest people I know, and it is obvious the rest of the team feels the same way, Beck included. But we both know if the time came where ya' needed to defend yar'-self, you would hesitate in the decision ta' hurt someone, especially ta' the point of takin' their life. That way of thinkin' ken' get ya' killed and I will no ever risk that. Not in this lifetime or any other."

"I'm sorry you think I'm such a coward, ma' Lord," I grumble as I pull my hand from his, suddenly not as charmed by my surroundings as I was a minute ago.

"*Mo Ghrá* (My Love), ya' are a wee brave Lass, but ya' have a vera' soft heart. Ya' don' even want ta' kill the spiders in the barn. I wad' never put ya' in a situation where ya' might be called ta' make that decision. It's far too risky. And if that makes ya' angry with yar' par' *Mo Shiorghra*, then I will just have ta' bear yar' discontent. 'Tis much easier than ever takin' a chance with the center of ma' Universe."

It's hard to stay angry when the love of your life is professing his truest feelings. I slip my hand back in his as we walk along the road through Zilipie. Truly, there isn't all that much to see here except the beauty of the artwork. We stop in at the richly decorated Catholic Church of St. Joseph, and then the museum dedicated to the talents of Felicja Curylowa, the village's most famous artist. There is little in the way of commercial buildings, and nothing that looks remotely sinister. "Are you sure the Black Knight has the right location?" I question. "Honestly, I don't see or feel anything out of the Mundane ordinary. And yes, I know it's currently daylight hours, but even during the day I can still pick-up magical vibrations. I got nothing. Nada. Could this possibly have been a silly prank of some kind, someone sending us on a wild goose chase.?"

"I am a bit frustrated as well, Rosie. However, ya' are not entirely correct about the lack of magical elements. They are being heavily veiled, but they are here. If 'twas not daylight, ya' would feel it as well. A brush of something dark and ritual-like."

His words send a tingle of fear up my spine, but the last thing I want to do is have him sense my angst and rush me back home. "If that's the case, then we need to keep looking. Like you said, Her Majesty is counting on us."

Tired of walking, I stop in front of a small heavily painted building with the word *Kawiarnia* (cafe) lettered on the glass window next to an image of a steaming bowl of soup. "I don't know about you, Tax Man, but my feet are killing me. I think this might be a diner of sorts. What do you say to a cup of coffee and a bite to eat? I had Polish food once in Boston and it was very tasty."

My mate is quiet and still for a moment, as if magically checking something out. Then he smiles. "'Tis a perfect plan, Love. I would no want ta' miss the opportunity ta' try those polish dumplings ma' client is most impressed with."

As to match the outside of the building, the dining area is tiny and covered in the same flower motif as the rest of the town. The place is lunch-hour crowded, several people conversing in Polish as they enjoy their meal. A man at the counter waves us in the direction of an empty two-person table near the back of the restaurant. Once seated, he comes to our table and drops off a laminated menu along with two glasses of water, then stands there without saying a word.

The menu is in Polish, which is not a problem for Declan. I sometimes forget he is multilingual which is one of the leading reasons he's as good as he is at this spy work. He and the waiter go back and forth in conversation without any input from me until my husband is seemingly satisfied. "So, what are having?" I ask when the waiter leaves.

With a grin he says, "'Tis a surprise. But don' worry, Rosie. I have ordered plenty of options. I think ya' will find something you like."

As we wait for our food, I let myself take in the beauty of the painted details, thinking how something like this would look lovely in our backyard gazebo in Salem and wondering if my crafty self was up to the challenge. As I glance away from the painted designs, I catch the eye of a man sitting across the room at a table intently staring at me. His dark eyes are unblinking, almost snake-like, and I instantly look away as a weird feeling settles in my forehead and makes the hair on my arms stand straight up.

Instantly, my Eternal Mate is on it. *"What is it, Rosie? I just felt your fear rise up. What's wrong?"* he asks me in the solitude of my mind.

"That man over there...near the window...I caught him staring at me. It felt icky and the hair on my arm stood straight up." I explain.

"The man wearing the brown sweater? Medium build with dark hair, combed back?"

"That's the one. How did you know?"

Declan leans back in his chair, blocking the man from my view. *"I sensed him when we came in. He's definitely seems Otherworldly. Not Sidhe. Something else. He's wardin' full-on, so it's hard ta' get a close read on him."*

"Shouldn't we be warding as well?" I question, trying to rein in my fear.

"No worries. I extensively warded the both of us the moment we arrived in Poland, My Love. It would be risky ta' wander around here unprotected, especially since we had no clear idea of what we might find. Until we came ta' this cafe, I felt nothing magically focused. But now I feel it. 'Tis not unusual ta' run across Other-worldly folk out and about the Mundane world, but there's something off about him. Something dark."

The waiter returns with our first course; steaming bowls of *borscht*, creamy beet soup, a woven basket of dark, coarse, rye bread, and a small crock of creamy butter. It smells delicious, but I'm too anxious about the strange man to take a bite. *"Go ahead, Lass, enjoy yar' lunch. If I ken' read him, then he ken' read me as well. Surely, he is aware of my stronger magical skill, and it's doubtful he'd attempt ta' engage with me. He's definitely worth keepin' an eye on, but I do not believe he is a threat."*

Somewhat pacified, I pick up my spoon and tuck into my soup, which tastes as wonderful as it smells and is chocked full of cubes of boiled potato. The soup is followed by a hearty stew called *bigos* made with pieces of veal, sausage, and shredded cabbage, a plate stacked with *plaki ziemniaczane*, crispy potato pancakes alongside a generous helping of sour cream, and a huge serving of the fluffy dumplings Declan's client mentioned. The *pierogi*, as they're called in the Polish language, include some stuffed with ground meat, some with fresh sauteed mushrooms and cabbage, and even a few with a sweetened cottage cheese mixture. Everything is delicious and when I finally put my fork down, I'm very full. "That was amazing," I proclaim. "I'm stuffed. Couldn't eat another bite," I confess.

"I hope that is not true, Rosie Lass. I have ordered some dessert. They have these biscuit-like cookies stuffed with fruit filling called *kolacyki*. Surely you have saved a little room?" he teases.

"Well, maybe a little," I grin. "Order me some coffee, would you, Sweetie? I'm going to go find the ladies' room."

I follow the signs down a narrow hallway to the restroom, not giving the strange man at the table another thought. In hindsight, it's a serious rookie mistake, and one the Lord Warrior, who helped train me, would have a tantrum over. I realize the error of my ways when I step out of the restroom and come face to face with Mr. Snake Eyes in the brown sweater, holding ground in front of me and completely blocking my exit.

TOOTHLESS 20

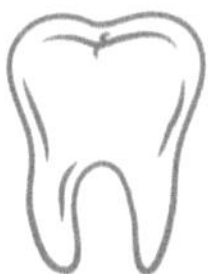

ROSIE GIVES HIM THE SLIP

FOR A MERE SECOND, I am stunned into immobility as the man grabs my right wrist, wrapping his fingers tightly around it as he uses his other hand to try and push me back into the restroom. "*Przestán walczyc, ty wrózko* (Stop fighting, you Fae bitch), he sneers at me. I don't understand what he's saying but it rings hostile, and when he speaks, flecks of spittle fly from his mouth and hit my face, totally grossing me out and causing a violent reaction from me as well.

My training suddenly kicks in and I use my free hand to grab hold of one of his fingers and bend it as far back as I can while simultaneously bringing my left knee up and ramming it as hard as I can into his balls. He lets go of my wrist and I change my stance, ready to gouge at his eyes with my fingernails, but it appears not to be necessary. Mr. Snake Eyes slides to his knees with a groan, covering his family jewels with both hands.

I push past him and almost run back to the table where I plop into my chair across from Declan, who is sitting calmly sipping his coffee and eating his dessert. "Did you somehow not pick up on what just went down back there?" I huff with breathless indignity.

"I am fully aware of what happened, Lass. Nicely done, by the way. No doubt the feckin' bastard will be pissin' blood far' a few days."

"I can't believe you sat there eating frickin' cookies while I was fighting for my damn life," I snarl.

I get that notorious one eye brow lift. In a carefully measured tone, he says, "Ya' have repeatedly complained ta' me that ya' are not being treated as a full member of the team and that ya' donna' wish far' me ta' coddle ya'. This was a gad' opportunity ta' let ya' have at it and build on yar' training. I saw him follow you ta' the back hall and I would have intervened if I felt ya' were in any serious danger. But, truthfully, 'twas a pleasure ta' see ya' handle yar'self so admirably. However, we need ta' work on the issue of ya' not notin' the man was just a few steps behind ya, or that three second hesitation ya' experienced befar' goin' into fight mode. Those errors ken' be improved with mar' practice. I am more than willin' ta' work with ya' on that, Love, if ya' promise not ta' knock ma' balls inta' ma' throat," he replies with a half-attempted grin. "I ken' guarantee 'twad no be beneficial far' ar' love life."

I'm not sure whether I should be embarrassed, insulted or pleased. To be honest, I'm kind of proud of myself that I caused Mr. Snake Eyes to go down so quickly. "I think he called me something nasty," I replied. "It was in Polish so I didn't understand."

"Aye. He called ya' a Fae bitch," he says with more calm than I would have expected.

On one hand, I love that my Tax Man believes I can handle myself. On the other, it's a little disconcerting to see him so...well...bland about it. Normally, his Lordship is very touchy about people showing me any kind of disrespect. It's been that way since day one. "Aren't you just a little bit upset that he called me that?" I ask.

"I am furious, Love. I'd love nothing more than ta' beat the little fecker' ta' a bloody pulp. But doin' so would not be vera' advantageous ta' our mission. Besides, Lass, 'revenge is a dish best served cold,' as Master Poe so intelligently claimed."

"You think Mr. Snake Eyes is the reason we're here in Zilipie?"

"I believe he's tied to it," my super spy hubby reveals. "As we speak, yar' snake is slitherin' out the back door in plenty of pain. We will finish up here and discover where he's off to."

I stand up from the table ready to leave, but the Tax Man motions me to sit back down. "We're going to lose him if we don't get moving," I say.

"Sit and enjoy yar' coffee and dessert, *Rós mo Chroí*(Rose of my Heart). I've got it covered." He slides the plate of Polish *kolacyki* toward me. "Try the apricot ones," he says. "They are most delicious."

* * *

Declan is not wrong. The apricot *kolacyki* are yummy. But then, so are the raspberry and poppy seed filled treats. I can't say I didn't love every bite, but part of me is chomping at the bit to discover how the Snake Man is connected to the mysterious raven-gram. When we leave the cafe, my Eternal Mate heads eastward down the road in purposeful fashion. "You look like you know where we're going," I comment.

"Aye. I put a tracker spell on him as he went by me toward the restrooms. I'm following his path," Declan explains.

"I thought you said he was full-on warded?"

"He was. But his mental focus was on trappin' you, so he let his wards slip. His magical energy is of a dark nature, but 'tis not vera' powerful. Nor does he understand how to use it properly. It takes a great deal of skill and training to call up a ward and keep it focused while goin' about other business," he says.

I think about the fact that my hubby is carrying the wards for both of us while at the same time being one hundred percent on his game. It's sometimes hard to wrap my head around how damn magically talented he is as most of the time he works at downplaying his gifts in deference to my lack of them. My heart is filled with love and gratitude for this special person the Universe has blessed me with. I give his hand a squeeze which makes him stop walking and look at me quizzically. He takes the hand of mine he's holding and brings it up to his lips. "I love ya' too, Sweet Rosie Lass. But you are mistaken in yar' thinking. 'Tis I who has been overly blessed. No man has ever been as graced with a loving mate as perfect far' him as you are far' me. I will spend ma' whole life and beyond makin' sure you believe it as well."

We spend a few minutes in full embrace while locking lips as we stand on a dusty road in a tiny, obscure Polish village with painted houses, far off in the Mundane world, and my soul wants to giggle at the absurdity of my life. A life I wouldn't trade for all the wealth in either dimension.

My Eternal Mate is the first to pull away. "I am askin' far' a rain check on this moment, Love. Far' later. Right now, we must finish this trackin' of that vile creature from the cafe."

As we get further and further away from the center of Zilipie, we come across fewer and fewer houses and out buildings, while seeing less and less people. The area is mostly rural, a patchwork of farms and small cottages, still painted, but not as well kept as the ones we viewed closer to the cafe. An occasional cow or a few sheep are our only audience. Just when my feet are about to start complaining, Declan points to a run-down square box of a building devoid of the floral motifs of its neighbors. The wooden sign above the door reads *Klinika Nowego Życia.* "It says 'New Life Clinic'", my husband translates.

We note the old model Toyota parked behind the building, but other than that, we see no signs of other people. "How good is yar' acting ability, Lass?" Declan asks.

"Passable," I replied. "Why?"

"I need ya' to pretend that ya've sprained yar' ankle. I'm hoping ta' gain access inside."

"I can do that I say," as I begin limping on my "sprained" foot.

When we reach the clinic's entrance, the door is locked and there is no sign of activity. A handwritten note is taped to the inside of the door's window that reads *"Tylko powczes niejszym umówieniu* (By appointment only). We try ringing the bell, then knocking repeatedly but no one comes. My husband walks around the side of the building to where there are two small windows with the shades pulled all the way down, but otherwise, there are no additional entrances or exits.

"Are we going to try and break in," I ask.

"No. Not today. This is a 'no engagement' mission. I had hoped to get inside and look around, but it seems that it's not ta'..." His words trail off as a man's face suddenly appears in the doors window.

"Zamkniete idz sobie (We're closed. Go away)!" the man shouts through the glass. It's then I notice that he has the same dark, unblinking eyes as the man in the café.

Declan tries to explain to him in Polish that I have sprained my ankle and am in need of medical attention, but the man continues to shake his head in the negative, when suddenly annoyed, he pulls out a small caliber pistol and waves it in our direction.

Hands up in mock surrender, we back away from the door and begin walking and limping in the same direction we'd just come. When we reach a bend in the road that's out of view from the clinic, we take up a hiding spot behind a rusted, deserted tractor. "If I'm right, Lass, our friends will be in a hurry to leave and report our presence here in Zilipie."

Sure enough, a few minutes later, we watch as the old Toyota we saw in back of the clinic drives past our hiding spot. The car contains two men; the man in the brown sweater and the bald guy who threatened us at the clinic.

"Are we going to go after them," I ask, rather hoping my Tax Man will answer in the negative. I'm far too full from lunch to chase after bad guys, and even in my originally comfortable hiking boots, my feet have had enough for one day.

"Nay, Love. We have the information we came for. Something treacherous is definitely going on at that clinic. Those men gave off Otherworldy energy signals, but from what I ken' tell, they are not folk from our other dimension."

"They're not? Then where are they from?" I ask, knowing full well I'm not going to like the answer.

"I believe they are most likely genetically altered humans, Rosie. Humans with just enough magical energy ta' be a threat ta' the Otherworld."

TOOTHLESS 21

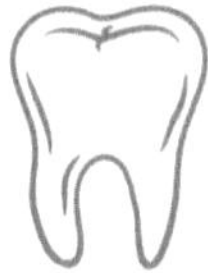

BAD LUCK ATTACKS

WE RETURN to *Dun Siorai* and are welcomed back by our little man clan as if we'd been gone for multiple weeks and not the seven hours we were actually away. There is, of course, the expectation of "souvenirs," as their father has made a tradition of it when he has to leave either of our homes for "business." He presents each of his sons with a handmade toy from Poland; a miniature tool bench with delightful tiny tools for Dylan who has inherited his mother's penchant for anything small, a hand-carved wooden train with moving wheels and a pull string for the always-moving Liam, and a set of animal decorated building blocks for Ronin who has just discovered the joy of stacking things and then knocking them down. From where and how these toys appeared in our Otherworldly home, I have no idea. We certainly didn't make any purchases in Zilipie. It's just part of the magic that makes Declan Phineas Fitzpatrick who he is.

Dinner is a family affair so the true nature of our trip to Poland isn't discussed. It's not till the kids have been tucked into bed and I have collected on my "rain check" from earlier in the day that we discuss the strange events that took place in the painted village. Despite the miles of walking in Poland and the athleticism of our lovemaking, neither one of us can settle our minds down enough to fall asleep. I rise from our bed and throw on a robe. "I believe I'm in the mood for a nightcap. Care to join me in a glass of port, my Lord?"

"A vera' good suggestion, *Mo Chroi* (My Love). Let's have the Fonseca, '77, shall we?" Himself recommends.

I raise my eyebrows at the suggestion. It's a very expensive choice for a nightcap. "I didn't know we were celebrating."

"What is not ta' celebrate, Lass? We are home safe and sound, our wee *bairns* sleep peacefully in their beds, and I have just spent a most enjoyable hour with the woman who owns ma' soul. 'Tis much to be thankful for," my mate replies.

"Can't argue with that, Tax Man," I say as I open the Fonesaca and pour it into the two glasses I've snagged from the cabinet in our suite.

My husband slips on a pair of boxers and joins me, and after doing all the sniffing one does with good wine, he lifts his glass. "A toast to ma' favorite 'second' and by far the prettiest one on our team. *Slainte* (Health)!"

I answer his toast and take a sip, letting the sweet, rich wine play on my tongue and tastebuds "This is very good," I say.

"Aye. That it is. A parfect' way to end the day," he agrees.

"You know what would be great with this?" I add, holding the glass in front of me to eye the wine's lovely amber color. "One of those raspberry *kolacyki* we had at that cafe."

In a blink of an eye, a plate magically appears on the small table between us with a half dozen of said pastries on it. "Thank you, Sweetie. This is amazing." We sit in content silence, enjoying the port, the sweets, and each other's company. It seems wrong to ruin the mood with conversations on tough subjects, but my concern over today's events forces me to ask, "My Lord, if what you say about those horrid men in Zilipie is true, that they are mostly human, what does this mean for protecting our borders?"

My spy guy puts his glass on the table. "It means that we in *I Idir* are not nearly prepared enough far' what is ta' come, Love. Originally, we believed the governments of the Mundane world were only using limited military personnel in their experiments to cross the border, but if what we saw in Poland is any indication, and they are offering these gross biological alterations ta' human civilians in out-of-the-way locations, then our problem is much larger than we all anticipated. Those men today were not soldiers. Their hands were callused and weathered. They are probably farmers, local people drawn into something they ken' no possibly understand. And what is most worrisome is that I could tell from their level of magical energy 'tis unlikely they would be able ta' cross the Veil and still survive vera' long.

Whatever has been done ta' those men in Poland is not the same level of magical genetic engineering as what we've witnessed on trespassers at the Veil border. I am not sure what purpose altering humans at such a low level would serve. Yes, they would give off an aura of being Otherworldly, but they would be unable to cast even the smallest of spells or manifest anything inta' reality. It makes no sense at all ta' me. I am looking forward to hearing what the others have discovered at our meeting tomorrow. Perhaps one of the other teams ken' shed some light on this quandary."

* * *

Due to scheduling and security purposes, our secret team meeting is held at *Cuach an Fhithich* (Raven's Hollow). At least that's what we're told. To my mind, I believe it's just *Cillian Mac Badh's* way of making himself seem higher up in rank than he actually is. I think this as our carriage rolls along toward the most opulent estate in *I Idir*, after, of course, the Royal Seat, *Crann Bethadh*.

"Rein those thoughts in, *Mo Rós Beag Dealgach* (My Thorny Little Rose)," my Eternal Mate says. "I donna' disagree with yar'opinion, but 'tis bad form ta' insult a Lord Heir in his own home, and sometimes yar' feelings' overwhelm yar' shield. I agree that the man's character at times has been questionable, but there is no denyin' he is good at what he does and is an important asset for the Network. If the Black Knight trusts him, then I suppose we shad' as well."

"The Black Knight likes *Mac Badh* because they both have the same questionable moral guidelines," I counter.

I get the raised eyebrow and the "husband sigh," which after nearly seven years together, I understand to mean that the Tax Man is not terribly happy with the way this conversation is going. Still, I'm entitled to my opinions.

"You may personally feel whatever way you wish regarding the man, Rosalinda," my husband says, using my entire first name, a sign that is often a preclude to "Cranky Declan." "Your reasons for feeling the way you do are, I am sure, absolutely valid. The Black Knight can be difficult, brutal and single-minded, and he does seem to take pleasure in teasing you. But he is the Queen's Second, *I Idir's* Hand of Justice and the only reason the Kingdom has not yet fallen to the Mundane world. The man has turned his back on the country of his birth to protect a race of people he's only recently become aware of. For that reason alone, ya' owe the man his due respect," He pontificates. "And if I may add, I think he teases ya' because he considers ya' a close member of his inner circle. Do ya' not see how he good-naturedly needles Fr. Kevin? His kin is the *Prionsa* of *I Idir* and yet Beck's jests are often quite…biting."

I have never appreciated being scolded, especially when it comes from my *Mo Shiorghra*. Besides being vastly annoying, it hurts my feelings. And frankly, the relationship between the Black Knight and his brother-in-law has nothing at all to do with me. However, as we are on our way to discuss things of monumental importance, I hold my peace, and answer with a curt, "As my Lord wishes," which earns me yet another dramatic sigh.

We pull up to the gates of *Cuach an Fhithich* (Raven's Hollow) just as the driveway lamps are being lit with fairy light. In the purple glow of spring twilight, the estate appears ahead of us in the manner of a Mundane fairy tale castle. Whereas the architecture of *Dun Siorai* has always reminded me of a 17th Century French Chateau, symmetrically oblong-shaped and classical, the seat of House *Badh* is reminiscent of the various Mundane castles one can see along the Rhine River in Germany, complete with rounded turrets, teeth-like crenellations at the top of the towers, and even a coat of arms pennant flying from its highest point. It is an impressive building reminding you before you even enter that this is a House blessed with ancient history, magical power and abundance of wealth.

As our carriage pulls up to the main entrance and before we disembark, my Eternal Mate turns to me. "Being at odds with ya, *Mo Stór* (My Darling), hurts more than a thousand knife wounds. Ken' we call a truce until we return home. I will need ma' focus ta' be on the important discussion of the evening. I promise that ya' we will face this disagreement together at *Dun Siorai* where it belongs."

As well as I know my Tax Man, he knows me. Undoubtedly, as history has proven, by the time we get home later tonight much of my annoyance over being scolded will have evaporated. And what he says about the stark realities of our meeting isn't wrong. These are difficult times for the Otherworld. Now is not the time for petty couple nonsense. Not when the safety of *I Idir* is at stake. "I agree to your call for a truce, my Lord. There are more important topics ahead of us."

He takes my hand and kisses it as we disembark the carriage. We are met at the estate's main entrance by uniformed footmen, one of whom directs the carriage toward the guest livery stable, and another who admits us to the house and leads us to the "Gentleman's Parlor," an impressive high ceiling room that reeks of...well...patriarchy. We apparently are the last guests to arrive, and I am not all together surprised to see my husband's mother in attendance. She is, after all, a semi-permanent guest of House *Badh* while her youngest daughter is away doing undercover work in service to the Crown.

"Good evening, Lady *Mathair*. How fares the wee *Féchín?*" I politely ask.

"The *bairn* (baby) grows stronger and more active each day, but 'tis obvious he misses his sweet *mathair*. He seems to look for her at every turn. As you yourself are aware, Lady *Nuada*, 'tis difficult for a child not to be under the tender care of its loving mother," says my mother-in-law.

"Aye. I agree. It's very difficult for both the mother and the child to be separated from one another for long periods of time. I shall petition the goddesses to return Lady *Mac Badh* safe and sound to her child as quickly as possible," I reply.

In response to my statement, Dragon Mama raises that genetically endowed single eyebrow. "It almost seems like you actually believe that sentiment, Lady *Nuada*."

"Of course, I feel that way. I am no monster, Lady

Mathair. Although I don't in any way condone your daughter's murderous actions toward me, I certainly do not wish that an innocent babe be robbed of his *mathair's* loving care."

Lady *Siobhan* examines me as if I were under a microscope, then replies, "You do seem ta' be honest in your feelings, Rosalinda. It is a trait that will certainly lead to your downfall. But I will gratefully accept your petitions to the goddesses in my youngest *inion's* (daughter's) name." She fingers the *piseóga* my husband had made for the entire family when the fox mug was stolen on *Beltane.* "I am worried that this ill wind will blow towards my Meghan. She is in enough danger as it stands."

At Dragon Mama's words, the amulet around my own neck seems to vibrate ever so slightly. I push down my own angst so as to not increase Lady *Siobhan's.* "Meghan is no longer considered a Fitzpatrick *Nuada*, Lady *Mathair.* Since her handfasting to Lord *Mac Badh*, she is, by sacred law, now part of House *Badh.* Any *mallachtaí* (curses) laid upon us would have no power on her. Even our own Merlin has stated thus."

"So, I have been told. Yet I fear something terrible is afoot. I myself have witnessed three different omens in this last week alone. I have heard the whistling of a cricket from my very own hearth every night before bed. Then, a few nights ago, during that awful storm, the large hawthorn tree in the south gardens, the one under my windows, was hit by lightning and completely split in two. Now, worst of all, just today one of my chamber maids took down the gilt mirror in my sitting parlor to give it a good polish. The heavy thing slipped out of her hands and fell to the floor where it shattered into a million tiny pieces. The House Mages were quite in a magical uproar over the incident."

As someone who grew up almost entirely Mundane, believing these common annoying events were a prelude to genuine misfortune seemed silly. But the Fae were univer-sally, profoundly superstitious, and since our own little inci-dent with the stolen fox mug, along with the havoc that occurred after it, I was more inclined to take stock in Lady *Siobhan's* omen. Despite all logical otherwise, a tingling shroud of fear lingered over me at my mother-in-law's prophetic words.

TOOTHLESS 22

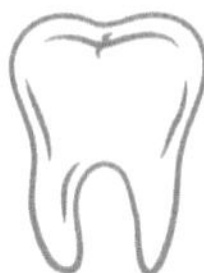

SORTING THE FACTS

Across the room, I could see my mate observe me as I chatted with his mother. He gave me a questioning look before I heard him in my head. *"Is there a problem with my mathair?"*

I didn't like lowering my shields low enough to mentally converse with him amongst a group of magical power horses, but I didn't want to add another concern to my Tax Man's already full plate. *"Nothing we can discuss here,"* I say. *"I'll fill you in later."*

I took a glass of white wine offered by the wait staff and found a seat next to my husband. Lord *Mac Badh* was making the rounds as host, a job that would have been his mate's had she been there, but I could tell there was little interest in the trappings of hospitality despite the generous array set out for the group. Everyone gathered seemed focused on the business at hand, especially the Black Knight, who was literally tapping his foot in impatience.

The group consisted of the four of us who had originally

deciphered the mysterious raven gram, plus a few high-ranking members of the Black Knight's A-Team, including Declan's mother and Ambrose Myrdynn, our Merlin. It surprised me that The Morrigan was not in attendance, but I've learned it's never worthwhile to try and guess the Raven Queen's intentions because she was always three steps ahead of whatever you were thinking.

Once he held everyone's attention, Beck welcomed the members and gave a brief recap for those new to the mission regarding how the raven-gram had come into our possession and the method we used to decode the strange message. Then he and Fr. Kevin gave a report on what they encountered in Algiers.

Curiously, our Spy Boss begins by speaking in the Old Language *"Is ionann draíocht a aimsiú in Algiersagus stria saor a lorg i measc na gcéibheanna* ("Finding magic in Algiers is like looking for a cheap whore among the wharves").

The males all snicker, except for Fr. Kevin, who comments, "Really Bro, that's a rather 'colorful' comparison there, especially considering that there are ladies present."

"The *Prionsa* is correct, Lord Knight. There's never a need to be vulgar," Lady *Siobhan* chimed in, always on the look-out for the proper tenets of protocol.

"I did not mean to offend, Lady Donnelly. I do apologize if I have somehow offended your delicate sensibilities," the Black Knight replied, obviously not sounding the least bit apologetic. He attempts to corral me into his little web. "What say you, Lady *Nuada*. Do you share your Lady *Mathair's* opinion of my figurative speech?"

I'm not stepping into that little trap. I hold up my hands in mock surrender. "As my wise woman once told me, Lord Knight, *'Ná scall do bheola ar leite fear eile* (Never scald your lips on another man's porridge).'"

My quip gets everyone laughing, especially the gentlemen

and even Dragon Mama cracks a little smile. The quote is meant to advise against getting involved in someone else's affairs, but I suddenly realize too late that it could be considered a double-entendres of a much smuttier nature, causing heat to rise into my cheeks.

The Queen's Hand of Justice raises his glass to me, "Well played, Lady *Nuada.* Your natural wit is a blessing to this group in such dire times." Then he makes it ten times worse by winking at me.

The others join in the toast offered for me, and I want to slide right under my chair in embarrassment, but next to me my Tax Man is smiling. *"Ya' certainly do have a knack far' makin' the heaviest of situations lighter, Love. I am a lucky man ta' have ya' by my side."*

By this point, I want the group's attention off of me by any means possible, and thankfully, the Black Knight comes to the rescue. "Seriously, boys and girls, Algiers is a hot mess of magical activity. For several centuries, the Djinn Tribunal has attempted to keep their folk in line, but as you are all aware, when it comes to rogue magic in that part of the Mundane world, the djinn run a criminal enterprise that puts the Russian mafia to shame. I have personal experience dealing with that element and, frankly, I don't believe they would align themselves with humans bent on breaching the Veil or destroying the Fae. They keep entirely to themselves, isolated in the Oman city of *Bahla* as they are, and their disdain for the Mundane populate is well known.

Removing the djinn from our search narrowed the magical pool a bit, but because of the crossing ley lines and the water element there are numerous sorcery transplants, a conglomerate of dimension-crossing expats who feed literally and metaphorically on the unsuspecting human population. If it weren't for Kev's obsession with a Turkish snack called *bourek* (Turkish style eggroll) we might have left Algiers without the information we needed."

"Seriously, people, if you ever get to Algiers, or even a Turkish restaurant in Boston, you have to try them. So good," the priest interjects with a chef's kiss before getting an annoyed look from his sister's husband.

"As I was saying," our Boss continued, "We were doing reconnaissance of the open-air market when Kev kept pestering me to make a stop at one of the *bourek* carts. It's just by chance that this one was owned by a *Bichura*, a shape-shifting house spirit who picked up on our auras despite our attempts at self-warding. As I have said, Algier's unique geographical location gives it a huge magical energy boost. Turns out, the *bourek* guy has a second cousin who works as stableman for House *Lir* and is married to a local *Puca* woman. The cousin and his mate are very loyal to our Queen for allowing unions between Fae Folk and other Worldly races, a freedom not allowed in some of the other conserva-tive kingdoms, thus he was very chatty. Pointed us in the direction of the Port of Algiers. Claimed he had heard rumors that a group of sorcery outsiders had opened a dock-side clinic of some sorts that mainly catered to the local population and claimed to be a 'holistic rejuvenation' center with organic vitamins and natural tonics. No one in the *Bichura* circle seemed to have a definitive word about what went on there, but he'd heard it said that many people became seriously ill after seeking medical advice from the clinic's staff.

Declan and I look at each other, the Black Knight's description of a strange clinic remarkably like our own expe-rience. We hold our comments while Fr. Kevin takes over the report. "We found the clinic the *bourek* vendor described about six blocks from the port's dock. It was a poorly maintained, ramshackle building. Nothing you would expect to see as a medical facility. The place appeared to be closed and no one answered our persistent knocking while a handwritten sign in both Arabic and French stated patients would be seen by appointment only. While Ted and I were discussing the best way to get inside for a look-see, we saw five men come out the back of the building carrying heavy canvas bags which they loaded into a van. When they drove off, we followed them to the port's docks where they offloaded the bags onto a small fishing boat. The weather was bad with heavy storms forecasted so it seemed fool hardy for the small boat to go out, but when it did anyways, we decided against following it. Observing from a small coffee shop near the boat's slip, we saw it return about an hour later without its cargo, so we have to assume that whatever was on board got dumped into the Mediterranean Sea, most likely in the Algerian Basin based on how long the round trip took."

"Do you have any guesses as ta' what was in those canvas bags," Connor Dell asked.

The priest grimaced while Beck answered for him. "I dislike making guesses, even educated ones without any direct proof, but based on the size and shape, plus the way it took at least two men to lift the bags into the van and onto the boat, it seems plausible that the cargo was likely human remains. Corpses they meant to dump at sea. Whether they were some of the clinic's unfortunate patients or something entirely different is hard to say with certainty at this point. But I can say, without doubt, that some extremely shady shit is going down at that so-called 'clinic,'" our Boss stated.

"If I may interject, ma' Lord, ma' Lady and I had a similar experience," my husband says. ""Twas a strange place far' a clinic. The town of Zilipe is vera' small and located in a rural area nearly twenty miles away from the larger city of *Tarnów*. The place had only four commercial buildins'; a tiny cafe, a run-down gas station, a farm and feed store, and a museum focused on Zilipie's artistic history. Its only claim ta' fame seemed ta' be the decorative paintin' of the cottages, barns and mailboxes and no doubt the local economy relies heavily on the tourist trade.

We checked out the cafe because I picked up on some fluctuating magical energy and 'twas there that Rosie had a physical run-in with a nasty *bastaird* givin' off a modicum amount of Otherworldly vibe despite bein' mar' human than anything else," Declan explains.

"I can assume you are no worse for wear after that incident, Lady *Nuada*?" the Black Knight asked.

"I am fine, my Lord. The Lord Warrior's excellent training kicked right in," I replied.

"Ma' Lady is bein' far too humble. That *faobhar* (prick) won't be showin' his balls to the lassies anytime soon."

My husband's comment gets the group guffawing again and now I understood that the use of raunchy humor was a way to ease the growing tension in the room. These were dangerous and trying times for the Fae people, and a little occasional levity went a long way in hanging on to one's mental health and perspective.

"I'm sure the Lord Warrior will be pleased to hear that you benefitted from his instruction, Rosie. He's an excellent instructor." Turning back to address my mate, Beck asked, "Were the two of you able to get inside this Polish clinic and take a look around."

"Unfortunately, we were unable to gain admittance. They had a similar sign on the door of this clinic stating visits were by appointment only. We tried an injury ruse as a distraction, but another man came ta' the door brandishin' a small pistol and I thought it best to retreat. We noted a car leavin' the place shortly after, but as we were on foot and they were in a vehicle, we were unable ta' follow them. As yar' initial orders were not ta' engage, I felt it best ta' just report what was discovered befar' takin' any action."

"That was absolutely the right call, Fitz. Cleaning up the aftermath of engagement is both difficult and costly. I'd rather hold off on any confrontation until we can get more bang for our buck. It's not worth it to take down flunkies. It's disturbing, however, to find two of these supposed 'clinics' in different global locations," Beck replied.

"Make that three, my Lord," Cillian *Mac Badh* added. "We came across somethin' of the vera' same nature in Spain. As Turner and I were wanderin' the narrow alleyways, we came across Mundane folk with just a sprinklin' of magical energy. I doubt any of them even posed a substantial threat ta' the Veil Border. They could no conjure up a simple flea with the little trace of magic they had. Strangely, though, we did observe that many of those same 'hybrid' Mundanes were notably sufferin' with some type of human *tinneas* (illness). Their eyes were red and runny as if they had the *Súil Lofa* (Rotten Eye), and they seemed ta' be chokin' on their own breath. We kept clear of contact. I no wanted ta' bring a ragin' case of 'Rotten Eye' back with us and possibly expose ma' wee boy."

"Probably a wise decision on your part, *Mac Badh*. With a few exceptions, human diseases and viruses pose no threat to the Fae, but all things considered, we shouldn't take any chances. I'll talk to Robyn and get his input on whether or not he believes there could be any connection between these clinics and the symptoms you witnessed. Until then, we should all take necessary precautions," the Black Knight warned.

A shiver ran down my back at the thought that "Mr. Snake Eyes" had been as close to me as he was, going as far as to hiss in my face and touch my wrist. At the time, I didn't notice that he was suffering from anything as obvious as what *Mac Badh* was describing. Still, with human viruses, a person could be exhibiting no symptoms of illness but still be quite contagious. It was a sobering possibility.

Beck continued his interrogation. "You mentioned that there was a clinic in Rhonda. Did you gain any access to the building?"

"No, ma' Lord. There did no seem ta' be a lot of activity goin' on, but the place had armed security outside. No doubt Turner and I cad' have easily disarmed them," the young Lord bragged, "but we dinna' know how many more might be inside and yar' orders were not ta' engage, so we just observed the handful of Mundane folk that went in and out. There appeared ta' be a steady parade of them."

"Good work, gentlemen. The more information we gather, the easier it will be to make plans for action," his Boss said. Beck addressed the last mission team composed of Connor Dell and Mac O'Kelly. "Are we four for four regarding clinics, gentlemen?"

It was Mac who took the lead. Despite his small stature as a leprechaun, the man was as tough as anyone in that group and remarkably fierce in battle. "Nay, Lord Knight. Not what I would call a 'clinic' in the manner the others have described. The location in Switzerland was definitely some type of lab or medical facility of sorts, all modern built with a large parkin' area and secured with razor fencin', along with guards totin' top of the line automatic weapons. The place was easy enough ta' find bein' so conspicuous among the old-fashioned, half-timbered structures of the town, but gettin' inside would be no easy feat. Besides the usual Mundane security, the place was heavy-duty warded with dark ritual magic. Had we tried ta' gain access, we would have been immediately noticed," he explained.

"What makes you think it was a lab or medical facility if you didn't gain entry?" Fr. Kevin questioned.

"There were folk comin' and goin' and they all were wearin' white coats like I've seen Doc Robyn wear on many occasions. Some even had face masks and…" Mac stops and gestures toward his head, "*clúdaigh ceann* (head coverings). It did no seem like they was dressed far' makin' toys or sweets or anythin' simple like that. Not with that level of security."

"Well, that fucking doesn't sound good," the Black Knight commented, totally abandoning any pretense of polite proto-col. "Whoever sent that raven-gram had good reason to do so."

"It had ta' be ma' courageous Lady. Who else would want ta' tip us off in such a way," *Mac Badh* replied with the conviction of a man in love with his *Mo Shiorghra*. "She was told ta' be discreet."

"I agree that ma' youngest sister does seem like the logical guess ta' have sent it," my husband said, "as it was her mission ta' do so. But I am questionin' har' use of longitude and lati-tude ta' send us these clues. Those are Mundane concepts of geography not used in the Otherworld. I'm not sure how she would be familiar enough with them to think of using such a thing. Meghan was home schooled by Otherworldly tutors who I ken' no see adhering ta' the same curriculum used in Mundane schools. That leaves me curious about the real origins of that raven-gram."

Everyone remained silent pondering Declan's words. I was sure he wasn't wrong in his reasoning. I always felt something wasn't matching up regarding the idea that Meghan was the raven-gram's sender, though by the annoyed frown on Cillian *Mac Badh's* face, it is obvious he's not happy with my husband calling up doubt about his Lady's heroic role in this mission.

"I don't suppose anyone has figured out what the words at the bottom mean? If these are actually words at all and not some complicated cipher," the Boss asks.

Something is clawing at the fringes of my memory. Something to do with *Oisin*. "Do you happen to have the original raven-gram with you?" I asked the Black Knight. He reached for a table behind him and handed me the still curled parchment. That's when I noticed it. The odd slant to the letters "b" and "d." When the boy was first learning to read and write, he often confused the two letters, so much so that I made up a little nonsensical ditty to help him remember which way the bottom loop of both of those letters faced. "'B' faces away, while 'd' saves the day," I said out loud.

"I'm sorry, Lady *Nuada*, but I have no idea what you're talking about," Beck says.

I stand up and hold the raven-gram uncurled in front of me. "What if the person who sent this switched the letters 'b' and the 'd' for security purposes? Then, the message would read 'Bad Labs- Bad Risk,' which, considering what has been revealed here today about those longitude and latitude locations, makes a whole lot more sense, doesn't it?"

It takes a few seconds, but eventually the group sees the same thing I do. "That does fit, Rosie," Fr. Kevin said to me. "Good thinking."

"I agree. Even though it's ridiculously simple, it does seem to make more sense than an alphabet-number cipher. "Excellent work, Lady *Nuada*. May I ask how this solution came to you?" the Black Knight asked.

I take a deep breath because I know what I'm about to say will be controversial to some people in this room. "When my husband's half-brother was small and first learning to read and write in Mundane English, he was forever turning the two letters around. Over the years, it became a running joke between us. This message was sent to me at *Dun Siorai* because the sender knew I'd eventually figure out what they wanted to say. Lady *Mac Badh* didn't send this raven-gram… *Oisin* Fitzpatrick did."

TOOTHLESS 23

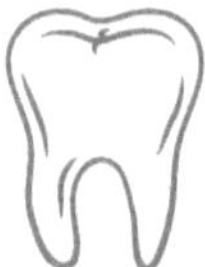

A MISSION FORMING

MY REVELATION about the raven-gram's origins did not have the shock factor I thought it would. It appeared that several group members had already considered that possibility, including my husband and the Black Knight himself. As expected, there were a few dissenters, mainly Lord *Mac Badh* and my husband's mother, a resistance, I believed, grew out of growing anxiety for their mate and daughter rather than any sound logic. Lady *Mac Badh* had entered the Mundane world three weeks ago on a mission to try and make contact with her father as an asset inside his terrorist organization, and as of yet, there had been no contact from her. The raven-gram had given both mate and mother hope that their loved one was alive and well, and thus, they were extremely reluctant to let go of that belief.

Their denial, though politely heard, did nothing to dissuade the Black Knight who deemed the information sound enough to move to the next level of operation. Gaining access to the suspect lab and pseudo clinics would be a highly specialized mission requiring the teams to breach all the locations at the same time to avoid one location notifying the other. Although they were geographically miles apart, three of the targets were in the same time zone, while the fourth, Algiers, was only one hour ahead. This made coordinating the breaches much easier than if one or two had been located in a different hemisphere.

Whether or not the goal of information gathering would go further on to include the complete destruction of said targets would require the Queen's input. Retaliation from Mundane world governments after her destruction of the North Korean lab and holdings involved in Declan's kidnapping was substantial, and only stopped after The Morrigan brought down their entire technology system. Since then, most of the Mundane governments had ignored their Fae counterparts, except for a few rogue terrorist cells, the largest of them being led by Callum Fitzpatrick and his secret cabal of wealthy investors.

I listened politely even though it was doubtful I'd be invited to participate. It would be naive to believe that even within the 'information gathering' parameters, the mission would be violence free. All the facilities seemed to be guarded by persons with conventional Mundane weapons, and though my training had included some basic handling of a pistol, it was a far stretch from being able to repel from a helicopter onto a rooftop with an automatic weapon strapped to my back. Plus, there was still that little caveat my Tax Man had recently brought up regarding whether, if push came to shove, I could actually take someone's life. That was a question I had yet been able to answer.

Dragon Mama, on the other hand, was all in, and from what my husband had confided in me, was a force to be reckoned with, known to have "a kill rate that was impressive even far' a seasoned asset." It was hard to conceive of the protocol-loving, social-climbing, fashion-heavy, former Lady of House *Nuada* being this blood-thirsty, ninja-like assassin, which once again proved to me how terribly "messed-up" my husband's family really was.

I was a reluctant observer, an outsider among insiders, while the people who moved in my circle, some of whom I called my own family, discussed the ending of lives and the destruction of property as if they were merely talking about a corporate merger. Even Fr. Kevin, who appeared generally uncomfortable with the details discussed, stayed in his chair until the very end.

We left that meeting, which lasted late into the night, with the Black Knight's soft plan of action for a second mission to the longitude and latitude locations. Until he spoke to the Queen and her inner circle, no final decisions could be made regarding logistics and manpower. I knew my Eternal Mate would be undoubtedly front and center in a leadership role and the thought frightened me. I'd never truly gotten over nearly losing him during that ill-fated mission to rescue the conniving Marcy Kilcrabtree, and even though logical me understood that since that terrifying event, my beloved *Mo Shiorghra* was ten times more powerful, both magically and physically, than he'd been seven years ago, I could already feel my heart beating rapidly in my chest over the idea he was once again going to put himself in danger.

I also was aware that although he would be sympathetic towards my feelings, Declan would never put his responsibilities to *I Idir* aside, especially with his own sire at the heart of the treachery. It was my role as his devoted Eternal Mate to fully support him, but as it turned out, the Universe had different plans for all of us.

TOOTHLESS 24

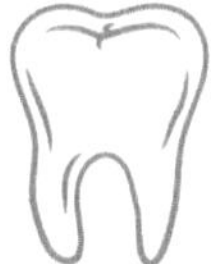

THE BANSHEE'S WARNING

LIKE BUSINESS PLANS and big deal projects in the Mundane world, covert Fae spy operations took a lengthy matter of time to put together. There were decisions to be made, bribes to be paid, and more assorted weapons of violence and trouble-making paraphernalia to gather up than the average mind could safely imagine. In the meantime, summer life at *Dun Siorai* continued as it always had, the competent running of an estate as large as ours requiring daily attention to a myriad of chores and spending.

Mixed into my role as Lady of House *Nuada* was that of Summer Camp Mama Counselor to three very active little boys. Though many of the activities in my children's daily routine could have been easily handled by their *scathachs*, I relished these stay-at-home vacation days when I was free of the pressing responsibilities of my full-time Mundane career and tooth fairy duties. Thus, my days were often filled with wooded day hikes, meadow-style picnics, bug and leaf collecting, messy craft projects, and copious games of kick ball, badminton, and American style soccer. In my quest to give Dylan a memorable summer, the youngest *Banphrionsa* often joined us, despite my growing unease at the ridiculously close bond the two children shared.

The effects of our Beltane bad luck curse seemed less intense here in the Otherworld than it had been in Salem. Whether it had something to do with the Merlin's wards being stronger here, or if the worst of the spell had finally passed into obscurity was unknown, though in my opinion, I leaned toward believing it was Ambrose Myrdynn's skill that kept us free of a constant barrage of ill fortune. It soothed my mind to have more faith in the power of our kind Druid sorcerer than that of my husband's dark-souled father.

Declan still commuted back and forth between both worlds, though not at the rate he once did. Our forced exile to the Otherworld after his rescue from the North Koreans was a hard lesson about having contingent business plans in case things went sideways. Like me, the Tax Man had added qualified staff to his firm so that if he is unavailable, things got done as needed. In addition, he's taken on some *Sidhe* clients in *I Idir* and Avalon who wanted to invest in Mundane holdings, allowing him to conduct some business in the Otherworld, albeit without the use of technology.

And yes, he's still doing the whole fox thing. So far, the red fox is still the only animal form my shifter husband can take on. I can't say I am crying tears of disappointment. One four-legged furry transformation in my marriage is enough, thank you very much. But I've come to accept it as part of what makes my Eternal Mate who he is, loving the fox in him as much as his multiple other magical abilities, his penchant for trashy crime novels, and that one damned eye brow. He almost always returns from his daily fox runs relaxed and upbeat, a brief respite from the burdens and responsibilities that weigh on his shoulders. I love him too much to be anything but supportive.

Thus, for two weeks we Fitzpatricks exist in relative peace, enjoying the glory of nature in each summertime outing without the pressure of the grinding school year schedule. Perhaps that is the reason we didn't take the early warnings of impending disaster as seriously as we should have. Or maybe, we just were flat out tired of all the drama that seemed to track our very existence.

It began with whispered rumors circulating amongst the staff, which frankly, is the life blood of any Ruling House estate. Like most of the nonsense that passes as fact in *I Idir*, Declan I didn't bother to take much stock in the wild gossip that *mná-síghe* (keening fairy women/banshees) were spotted gathering in the backwoods property of *Cuach an Fhithich* (Raven's Hollow). This part of the Otherworld is home to many birds that have human-like calls which hauntingly tend to echo in the quiet stillness of nighttime and it's more than likely that's what folks were hearing rather than the legendary *mná-síghe*.

In the diverse genetic nature of Otherworldly Fae, the *mná-síghe*, or "banshees" as they are modernly called in Mundane literature, aren't a separate ethnic group in the way of the *Pucas*, the Mer Folk, or even tooth fairies. They are, instead, high skilled *Sidhe* who have a magical inherited marker that calls them to perform the duty they do. The single purpose of the *mná-síghe* is to herald the impending death of another member of the *Sidhe* community by appearing together at night in small groups to wail or keen their sorrow. Because their presence is not a particularly welcome one among their neighbors, banshee women (and yes, they are always female) keep this part of their identity a secret and only other banshees know who is also a member of this out cast club.

Sidhe Fae, even those with mixed Mundane blood, don't die easily. Though they are not immortal, they age a lot slower than human beings and aren't susceptible to most Mundane diseases. Though they can magically heal themselves of injuries, a wound caused by a weapon made of brass disrupted the flow of magical energy needed to repair the affected part of the body, possibly causing an end to their life if not immediately and aggressively treated. There is also the problem of the "wasting disease," a blood cell mutation similar to human leukemia, but despite Dr. Brannigan's tireless research, there was still not enough information to help eradicate this affliction. And when it came to top-tier *Sidhe* with ancient pedigrees like the *Tuatha de Danann*, their head needed to be directly removed from their shoulders, thus spiritually separating the soul from the body, to absolutely guarantee they were not eventually going to heal themselves and come right back at you.

All of this is common knowledge, and during the nearly seven years I've been handfasted to Declan, I've been witness to only one true case of banshee heralding, and it was done for an ancient looking man, a widow, who was said to have lived 392 years and who was begging the Universe to set him on a new path in the Afterlife.

It wasn't until several days later that I heard the eerie sounds for myself. His Lordship and I were returning from an evening social event at the estate of House *Lir.* It was a balmy spring night so we'd left the carriage windows open. As we wound our way back to *Dun Siorai*, there came across the wind a high-pitched wail that made all the hair on my uncovered arms stand straight up. "Did you hear that?" I asked my husband.

"Aye," he replied. "It be nothin' but an old *ulchabhán* (owl). With a full moon, 'tis the perfect night far' birds of prey."

I tried not to notice that my Tax Man was crossing his left ringer finger over his left middle finger, the Otherworld gesture against curses. "There's been rumors, you know. About the *mná-síghe* out and about," I commented.

"I am aware. I had ta' scold the stable boy far' goin' on about it," he says. "'This *cac* (shit) starts out of some person's imagination and gits' carried around the kingdom at light-nin' speed. 'Tis only boredom among the young folk that is at the root cause. *Beltane* has passed and *Litha* is still a month away. They are only lookin' far' somethin' ta' gossip over. Trust me, Lass. There's nothin' ta' worry about."

* * *

Memories are a funny thing. The way the mind remembers the most inane of things at the most life-changing moments. What oddly comes to mind whenever I think about that awful day was the colony of red ants in the sugar bowl. Not an entirely unusual incident at an outdoor picnic. In truth, it was a rather common occurrence when you thought clearly about it. Logically. Still, logic never seems to play a role in my recollection of that terrible day.

The children, the nannies and I had just finished up a rousing competition of *liatharóid bata* ("stick ball"), a game similar to Mundane croquet. All in all, it had been a successful outing. Liam had managed to get through the entire match without accidentally walloping any of us in the head or shins with the heavy wooden mallet, Ronin was able to leave the balls on the ground where they belonged, and Dylan was thrilled to have outplayed *Mairead* Beckett, who was once again spending the day with us. So pleasant was the mood that it seemed we Fitzpatricks had finally rounded the corner in our fight against the *Beltane* bad luck curse.

Cook had made a wonderful lunch geared especially to the children with tiny finger sandwiches shaped like round balls and oblong mallets, while also including a dessert that featured fresh berries meant to be eaten over sponge cake with a topping of sugar and cream. I placed the sugar bowl within the reach of the children, but when Dylan lifted the hinged lid, an entire parade of large Otherworld red ants, the nasty biting kind, crawled out of it in a bug-centered parade causing all of us to jump up from the table and scatter. As I herded up the children, I caught out of the corner of my eye, *Birgit* and *Niahm* making that annoying finger gesture against bad luck.

This whole bad luck-good luck nonsense had worn my patience thin so I undoubtedly overreacted, sounding harsher than the situation called for. "What in hell's blazes are you ladies doing that for?" I questioned.

"Doing what, my Lady?" *Birgit* asked, her pink cheeks a testament to her embarrassment at being publicly scolded. Her position and our friendship deserved better.

"Making that gesture," I replied. "That one against the *'súil olc* (evil eye).' They're just ants, for Pete's sake, and we are outdoors! There's nothing catastrophic about freakin' ants!"

The two *scathachs* looked at each other, then *Niahm* stepped up and whispered in my ear quietly so the children, all big-eyed and startled, wouldn't be privy to her message. "Ants in the sugar bowl be an ill omen, ma' Lady. A vera' bad one. Trouble is on the way."

"That's simply ridicul…" I don't finish my reply, as across the lawn, I view the Lord Warrior, *Cú Chulainn*, the Queen's consort and personal body guard, moving toward us at a clipped and deliberate pace. The man is never far from The Morrigan's side so the fact that he is here and not at *Crann*

Bethadh is a dead giveaway that something is very wrong. And the fact that Duncan is trailing two steps behind him has alarm bells going off in my head.

When he reaches us, he gives a courtly bow before stating his purpose. "I am vera' sorry, Lady *Nuada*, ta' interrupt this fine summer outin', but I've come to escort you and the wee *Banphrionsa* back to *Crann Bethadh*. Her *mathair* is in need of her daughter, and you are ta' meet yar' Lord there as well."

I start to open my mouth to ask for clarification, but the giant of a man holds up a hand up ta' stop me. "I realize ya' are burstin' with questions, ma' Lady, but it be best ta' let yar' noble Lord explain it all ta' ya'. Duncan will escort yar' family back ta' yar quarters and stay there until you and his Lordship return."

I glance down at the gown I'm currently wearing, stained with grass at the hem and without the proper number of stays in my corset. I had dressed this morning for a sporting romp and picnic on the east lawn, not a visit to the Royal Seat of *I Idir*. "I'll need to put on more appropriate apparel, my Lord. It won't take me very long."

"I'm afraid expediency won't allow for the luxury, Lady *Nuada*. Rest assured, in this instance no one will mind this breach of royal protocol." He puts his arm through mine, and with his other, takes the *Banphrionsa* by the hand before striding back in the same direction as he came. I turn back to look at my children just in time to see Ronin cry out, "Mama no go" in a wail that tears at the very center of my heart. I do my best to hold it together, but I can feel the fear of the moment climbing into my throat.

In my head, I hear a voice, but it's not that of my husband. *"I know you are fearful, dear Lady. But yar' bairns will be fine. There are no better scathachs in I Idir, and young Master Duncan is mightily fierce. All will be secure at Dun Siorai."*

"And my husband?" I ask, *"is he..."* I can't even bring myself to think the words.

"Yar' Eternal Mate is without injury, though in need of the loving influence of his Lady wife. You will be with him shortly," the big man says.

"Is there nothing more you can tell me?" I ask, not caring if I sound desperate. But the Lord Warrior remained stubbornly silent.

TOOTHLESS 25

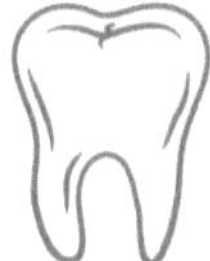

BIDDING ADIEU

THE *BANPHRIONSA* and I are led to a carriage bearing the Raven crest, one that apparently no one else can see. In fact, none of the staff seems to react to us as we walk right by them, signaling to me that we, along with the carriage, have been heavily veiled for the purpose of secrecy. This does nothing to ease my growing anxiety over what the hell this is all about. The legendary hero helps the princess into the carriage first, then assists me. Once we are settled, he takes a spot atop next to the driver, though I'm not sure if it is for security reasons or an excuse not to have to answer any more of my questions.

The maternal instinct in me kicks in and I focus my concern on the child sitting across from me. Disappearing from *Dun Siorai* with no explanation can't be easy for her either. Oddly enough, though she is quiet and somber, she appears calm, and if I could read aura (which I cannot, the princess being Raven born), I would guess it to be the palest shade of blue, a sign of inner peace and strength. "Are you doing okay, Princess? You can come sit next to me if you'd like," I coax.

"Thank you, Lady *Nuada*, but I am fine. I have been trained for situations like this. My Da has instructed me that if *Uncail Cullan* should come for me unexpectedly, I am to go with him without a fuss. He will make sure I get safely back to my parents. Do not worry, Lady *Nuada*. *Uncail Cullan* is very fierce and brave. He will protect us." She sighs and puts her chin on her hands. "'Tis a great shame, however, that I will not get a chance for a rematch of *liatharóid bata*. I realize now what I was doing wrong with my mallet, and I had hoped to correct it in our next game. Dylan will never let me forget I lost to him. Plus, I never had my dessert."

I always have a hard time wrapping my head around the thoughts and actions of the Beckett's eldest child. Since toddlerhood, *Mairead* has been older in words and actions than her chronological age suggests. As she's added real years, it is easy to tell that, that like her royal great grandmother several generations removed, she has a backbone of steel and a will to match. Plus, there is surely that whole wizard DNA range inherited from her father and grandfather. It is easy to see why The Morrigan has already named her as heir to the Throne of *I Idir*, though something tells me Herself has no plans to abdicate it any time soon.

It feels as if we arrive at *Crann Bethadh* far sooner than we should have, indicating magic was undoubtedly involved. We disembark in front of the same obscure side entrance I was led to when Declan had his fox trap injury on that horrible *Samhain* evening, an entrance that didn't seem to exist on future visits. There are troll guards waiting for us and we are whisked inside where the *Banphrionsa* is met by her *scathach*, the Lady Fury, and led away to the family's suite and to her waiting mother.

I, on the other hand, am directed down a series of twisting corridors to the same medical door my husband disappeared into nearly two years ago. I have no time to notice the room itself as a low keening sound has my full attention. The pitch and frequency of it stabs through my head like a swift arrow, and my heart is beating so wildly I can feel it in my temples. Before I can make sense of any of it, Declan walks through another door with a face pale and grim; his aura is a shimmering mix of rage and grief and he looks like an avenging angel unfolded from the pages of the Christian Bible.

"Oh, Declan," I murmur, too overwhelmed to form extra words.

My husband envelops me in his arms and a powerful wave of his poker-hot emotions flow over my body causing me to wobble a bit on my feet. "Rosie, Love, I am glad you are here with me. Yar' presence makes it all seem bearable."

I break away and place both my palms on the sides of his cheeks. "What's going on, Sweetie? Why all the secrecy?" As the words leave my mouth the mournful keening starts up again, and I get a case of the goosebumps so bad I shiver. "What is that noise, Declan? Banshees?" I question.

"Nay, Lass. 'Tis ma' Lady *Mathair.* She is singing the *Caoineadh Mathair ar son na Marbh* (Mother's Lamentations of the Dead), Love," with a voice hardly more than a whisper.

My translation of the Old Language is a few seconds behind his words. I blink a few times and ask, "Who, Declan? Who is dead?" In my head, I already know the answer. I just can't make my mouth say it.

"My Lady Sister has left this life, Rosie. She is walkin' the path ta' the Afterlife. 'Twas her death the *mná-síghe* were foreshadowing."

"But how, my Lord? She's *Tuatha de Danann.* Like you. She doesn't just die."

"Come, Lass. If ya' think ya' are up to such a sight, I will show you," he offers as he holds out his hand for me to take.

I am a physician. An oral surgeon. During my studies I saw plenty of dead bodies. Even dissected some. Still, I wasn't ready to see my husband's youngest sister without her head. But Rosie Parker Fitzpatrick is no coward. I take Declan's hand and follow him through the door he just exited.

I was ready for just about anything. A body missing its head. The shriveling effects of brass exposure. A gunshot wound to the brain stem. But not this.

The room is separated by a large plate glass window several inches thick. Behind the glass wall a figure walks around in a Mundane-issued, government hazmat suit, complete with attached respirator. "Is that Robyn," I ask in a hoarse whisper.

"Aye. He is takin' every precaution," Declan replies.

My eyes move to the autopsy-style table where my husband's sister lies covered by a sheet with only her head exposed. Her skin color is a strange bluish-gray, stretched across the planes of her skull like tissue paper over a Halloween skeleton. Her once intense green eyes are closed and sunk in, her lips are dry and deeply cracked exposing gums of the same awful color. "What happened to her," I ask, the words like cotton in my mouth. At that very moment, Lady *Siobhan* once again begins that soul-piercing wailing and it takes everything I have in the way of courage to keep from turning around and running from that room.

My Eternal Mate is quiet for a moment and then explains. "Doc believes it is a virus of some sort. Created to infect only those with a Fae bloodline and intended ta' be used as a biological weapon against us. It somehow causes massive dehydration of the body until the organs, including the brain, completely shut down. Robyn is no sure yet exactly how the virus works. He is plannin' on workin' around the clock ta' find answers, but currently we are at a loss ta' understand it."

Parts of my mate's explanation don't make sense. "But it's always been understood that human-type viruses don't affect Fae-born folk. Something in the evolution of your genetic make-up," I protest.

"We are immune to a majority of them, Love. But not all. The Doc thinks that whoever is behind this has created a mutated version of the norovirus as the delivery system. He found vomit on Meghan's clothes and the inside of her nose and mouth. But currently, 'tis only a guess."

"Oh, blessed goddesses, Declan. This is deadly! If it's mutated norovirus, it's likely contagious as hell."

"Aye. We believe it is. The two lads at the Veil Border who found her are in isolation in another room fightin' far' their lives. According ta' Robyn, between the vera' high fever and the vomitin' he can't keep them hydrated. Everythin' he puts in, comes right out. He is tryin' everything he knows but so far, the prognosis is poor."

I watch as Dr. Brannigan takes another blood and tissue sample from Meghan's corpse, then slips through an unmarked door on his side of the glass enclosed room. The poor man has an impossible job ahead of him, but if anyone can find answers, it's Robyn Brannagan.

Suddenly, it dawns on me that Meghan's *Mo Shiorghra*, Lord *Mac Badh* is not present. "Where is Cillian? Does he know? Why isn't he here?"

The Tax Man takes both of my hands in his with an expression so filled with emotion it makes me queasy. "He knows, Love. He was here. We let him have his privacy to grieve, though he could not even be in the same room with her, nor could he touch her one last time. 'Tis a heavy burden ta' bear, but it should be known that Lord Cillian *Mac Badh* honored his House in the manner expected of him. After his hour of grief, he went home to *Cuach an Fhithich* (Raven's Hollow) ta' make the necessary arrangements befar' he begins his *Bás Beo* (Living Death)."

I pull my hands from his while tears roll down my cheeks over the injustice of it all. I was not Cillian *Mac Badh's* biggest fan, but he didn't deserve this. No one did. "No, Declan. You can't let him do that! It's wrong. He's a young man with his whole life ahead of him." I start to pace the small room, while my mother-in-law ignores us both, lost in her grief and the privacy of her incantations. "He has a son to think of! Who will take care of that boy! It's a ridiculous concept...this 'Living Death' thing. A monstrous travesty to add grief upon grief. You have to do something!"

My Eternal Mate, the man I couldn't bear to live without, looked at me sadly. "I ken' no change sacred law, *Mo Stór*. This is all clearly explained ta' we House heirs befar' we undertake The Ritual and add to it the Eternal Bond. The gift of havin' the Universe select yar' perfect mate forever and always has its price. All magic does. *Mac Badh* will no shame his House. He will do what is expected of him and live the life the Universe has destined far' him. We are *Tuatha de Danann*. It is our ancient pledge, and none with honor will deny it."

"And the child? He's forced to suffer a life without either of his parents through no fault of his own? How is that righteous or honorable, Lord *Nuada*?" My voice cracks as I ask the question.

"Lord and Lady *Badh* will raise him with all the love they have ta' give. Undoubtedly, the *bairn* already wears the title of *Mac Badh* as we speak. One day, *Féchín Mac Badh* will undertake the Ritual, find his *Mo Shiorghra* and further the line of House *Badh*. As I have said on many occasions. 'Tis our way, Rosie, Love. Not our duty to understand, but only to accept."

"Your way, Tax Man. Not mine. If you think I'm going to ever let Dylan throw his life away on the writings of some lunatic sorcerers who lived a thousand years ago, you are in for a rude awakening." Then, I turn and leave that awful room.

TOOTHLESS 26

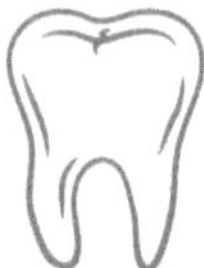

WHEN FEELINGS ARE TRUE

THE MOMENT I walk through that door to the common room I'm filled with shameful regret. Not for the truth behind my words. No. From the moment Declan and I knew we were expecting a son, I have been one hundred percent committed to not putting Dylan through the backward commitment ritual forced upon his father by some ancient and ridiculously outdated concept. Rather, I am deeply embarrassed that I thought this was a good time to bring up this long-term family drama in the midst of someone else's intense grief. My emotions must register on my face, or my shield is down and I'm leaking my pitiful emotions all over the place, because one of the two troll guards securing the space asks me if I'm in need of assistance.

"No. I'm fine," I stammer. "Just a bit…overwhelmed."

He nods his shaggy-haired head in understanding. "Aye. 'Tis surely evil among us," he growls as he forms the gesture against bad omens.

It's awkward standing here alone with the troll guards,

and I know I need to march back into that room and apologize for my behavior, even if I'm not sure what to say. I take a few tentative steps through the door when my Tax Man turns to me and opens his arms. I fall into them sobbing, clinging to the sleeves of his chemise as if my life depended on it. "I'm sorry, Declan. I meant to be supportive and I wasn't at all," I blubber.

"I understand, *Rós Milis* (Sweet Rose). 'Tis so vera' overwhelming and so far from what we know of life in *I Idir* that sortin' out yar' feelings is difficult. The words I threw at Beck will surely have me eatin' crow in the future." He looks at me and then glances at his mother, my cue that he expects me to apologize to Lady *Siobhan*, who has ended her lamentations and is sitting like stone, tearless, while she stares straight ahead at the body of her youngest through the plate glass window. He isn't wrong and I know it, but I also don't expect it to be an easy experience.

Dropping a very low and proper curtsy, I stand before her, hoping she can feel that I truly mean what I say. This is Dragon Mama I am dealing with, and in her mind, any sniveling, emotional apology would be considered self-serving and weak. "I ask your forgiveness, Lady *Mathair*, for my inexcusable behavior. I have embarrassed myself as your son's *Mo Shiorghra* and as Lady of House *Nuada*. This was neither the time nor the place to have angry words with my Eternal Mate. Not while your youngest daughter makes her sudden and unwarranted transition to the Afterlife. Please accept my deepest apologies and my heartfelt condolences over the loss of Lady *Mac Badh*."

The silence hangs between us for what seems like an eternity. I recall how I had once found her weeping over a photograph of Declan when he was lost to us in North Korea, and how it had shocked me. Sometimes it is hard to imagine *Siobhan* Donnely Fitzpatrick harboring maternal instincts, but I have come to see a different side of her in her relationship with our children, and it hits me square in the heart that she is a mother who has lost her child. A few tears slid down my cheeks despite my best efforts at holding my emotions steady, and I know, sure as the sun rises in the East, my mother-in-law will consider it a sign of inner weakness.

She doesn't look at me when she says, "Come now, Lady Rosalinda. Tears for my Meghan? You have made no secret of your feelings for my youngest daughter. Your show of false grief is unnecessary."

To my benefit, I have had years of Dragon Mama's caustic, cutting words, so I am prepared when she throws them at me. Perhaps I am even deserving of them in this particular case. I speak with all the honesty I can muster, hoping a vestige of the truth comes through. "You are correct, Lady *Mathair*. I found it difficult to have any positive feelings toward someone who has tried on three separate occasions to end my life. Your daughter and I did not have a relationship conducive to sisterly affection. But I swear to you on the bonds of my handfast, that I never once wished her dead. As to my tears, I confess that they are not for Meghan. She no longer needs them in the After Life, nor would she ever desire them from me. My tears are for you, Lady *Siobhan*. No *mathair* should ever have to witness the death of her own child. The Universe does not prepare for the shock of horrible emptiness I can only imagine it brings, and I, as a mother myself, am very, very sorry for the loss of your beloved daughter."

Her mouth tightens and I prepare myself for an especially harsh tongue-lashing. But as it usually goes with my false assumptions, I am wrong. In an emotionless voice she says, "You are correct regarding one thing, Rosalinda. No mother should ever outlive her children. It is an abomination to the feminine divine. My Meghan's heinous murder calls for sacred retribution and as I live and breathe, so shall she have it. Return to *Dun Siorai*, Lady *Nuada* and see to the care of my grandsons. You are a loving *mathair* and your place is with your children. 'Tis best to leave the warrior's game of revenge to those better suited to it."

TOOTHLESS 27

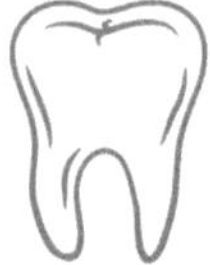

MEL GETS HER DREAM

THE AFTERMATH of Meghan's death was a whirlwind of secrecy, conspiracy, and grief. Like most citizens in the Mundane world, Otherworldly folk are not always privy to the under workings of their governments. *I Idir* is not unique in this concept. Without doubt, our kingdom's neighbors in Avalon, Asgard and the Jade Kingdom are just as clueless when it comes to the ways their reigning monarchs keep themselves in power and their citizens "safe." In *I Idir*, everyone is aware that the Black Knight is the Queen's Hand of Justice and the reigning expert regarding its civil and sacred law. What they didn't realize was that the famous bearer of *Caladbolg* was also the head of one of the Other-world's largest and most efficient intelligence network.

The covertness of this network was the reason that folks outside of the Black Knight's inner circle didn't pay much attention when Lady Meghan *Mac Badh* took a sabbatical to the Mundane world to "explore and audit the financial hold-ings of her husband's House." Meghan had been exiled to

Avalon for several years as punishment for her attempted murder of me, and the general public was never told any more than that in her generous mercy, the Raven Queen had commuted her sentence so she could return home and marry her fated mate. The fact that she was now Lady *Mac Badh*, mate to one heir and *mathair* to the next in line within an influential Ruling Council House, as well as related by hand-fasting to The Morrigan, led to common folks not asking too many questions, though rumors about her vicious temperament were abundant.

Therefore, when it was publicly announced that Lady *Mac Badh* had taken ill while in the Mundane world with a fast-moving case of the "wasting disease," and had quickly succumbed to the dreaded affliction, leaving behind a grieving husband and soon to be orphaned son, folks reacted with genuine sorrow and sympathy rather than any kind of suspicion. If, by chance, anyone was aware that the shroud buried in House *Badh's reilig* (sacred ground/cemetery) was actually nothing but old rags formed to look like a body, the real corpse being cremated, along with the two unfortunate lads who found her, in order to prevent the possible spread of disease, they were neither stupid enough nor brave enough to talk about it.

Cillian *Mac Badh*, his father, Lord *Badh*, Declan, Lady *Siobhan*, Dr. Brannigan, the Lord Merlin, the Black Knight, and myself were the only witnesses to the flames that claimed Meghan's physical body. It was a soul-numbing, deeply sad affair, but in truth, I was more shocked and confused at Cillian's appearance than the cremation of my sister-in-law. His once gloriously auburn hair, always neatly and fashionably braided, was now a startling gray color and left unbound except for a few tiny braids at the side of his head. Though Meghan's *Mo Shiorghra* was dressed in the traditional Fae mourning color of black, his form-fitting leather apparel was closer to battle gear than funeral wear, and his countenance strangely emotionless. I had asked Declan about Cillian's odd appearance after the cremation. My own Eternal Mate claimed to be as shocked by the man's appearance as I was, but something in his manner led me to believe he wasn't telling me the absolute truth, and as hard as I pushed at him, he never opened his thoughts to me on the subject.

No one except Robyn and Beck saw to the cremation of the two soldiers who were unlucky enough to be on duty that fateful day, their families told they had died heroically while on mission and their ashes returned with honors to the grieving families. A generous "sympathy consolation" of gold from Herself assured silent loyalty to The Throne from their next of kin.

Reaction to Meghan's "murder" was swift. A highly trained team was sent to all four locations, my husband and Duncan part of it. The Rhonda, Spain and Zilipie, Poland locations, were found to be deserted, emptied of anything that could be of use in unmasking the biogenetics of the disease and the people behind it. A decision was made to leave those buildings standing so as to not alert the other parties involved by burning them to the ground.

The Algiers location was still doing brisk business when the team arrived, but it was filled with civilians during daylight business hours, forcing the team to move in during the cover of night. As expected, the clinic had ample security, causing a substantial amount of Mundane bloodshed, though truthfully, I don't believe anyone involved gave it a second thought. A large collection of biological samples and paper-work were transferred to *I Idir* to await further examination by a team I was honored to be part of.

The raid on the lab in Switzerland was deemed the most successful, garnishing the Black Knight's team plenty of biological evidence along with the capture of two living scientists who were being held in a secure location inside the Mundane world. The Queen's Hand of Justice was confident that this mission would yield the answers we needed: what was the ultimate purpose of all this biological research, and who was behind it. Stuck at home in *I Idir*, I hoped he was right.

Thankfully, I didn't have to wait for the return of his Lordship on my own. Duncan, who had gone with Declan, insisted that his own mate and daughter spend the two weeks he was away at *Dun Siorai* for security reasons. Thus, what could have been an excruciating period of anxiety was made less awful by the presence of my best friend and her darling fourteen-month-old baby girl.

This miracle came to Duncan and Mel almost four months after *Oison* went missing. Months earlier, they had reached out to a young woman in Scotland named Leah who was of Fae bloodline and expecting a child conceived during a short-term affair while on vacation. The child's father had disappeared with no forwarding information, leaving the woman with an impossible decision. She herself, had no interest in her *Sidhe* heritage, it being a "gift" from a father who had long been out of her life, and though her totally human mother was pressuring her to keep the baby and raise her in Edinburgh, the Scottish lass had no desire for taking on the mantle of motherhood.

Adding to her dilemma was the fact that her baby, like she and her absent father before her, were by blood, kin to House *McCool*, a clan of considerable prestige within *I Idir's* Ruling Council. Lord *McCool* was insistent that the child needed to be raised among his own people and had offered to take the child on as his ward, but Leah wanted a more "normal," family-centered life for her baby. A week before her due date, Leah contacted Mel to ask her if she and

Duncan were still interested in adopting her baby, the only stipulation being that she wanted the child to be named *"Deirdre,"* a name meaning "sorrowful or broken-hearted."

Watching the adorable baby with bright carrot-colored curls and a sun-shiny disposition toddle around my parlor, I couldn't think of a more unsuitable name for this particular child. From the day she was placed in her parents' loving arms, *Deirdre McCool* Fitzpatrick was a blessing, mildly tempered and easy-going, and I couldn't be happier for our two dearest friends and their miracle baby.

"I see *Deirdre* is a little more sure-footed this visit," I say, as I watch the baby girl toddle off behind *Seamus*, who had taken on the role of doggy parlor nanny.

"Yes," Mel replied with a *mathair's* wistful smile. "One day she just up and went from cautious tip-toeing to confident running. She's growing so fast. I wish there was a spell to slow her down a bit. I want to hang on to babyhood for as long as I can."

"I hear ya'. Time seems to move in the blink of an eye where children are concerned. I can't believe Ronin is two already. He'd much rather chase after his two older brothers than sit in my lap for cuddles anymore," I comment with a sigh. For a moment, there's a slight and poignant pause in the conversation, a reminder that another baby is probably not going to happen for either of us.

I change the subject. "How's the new receptionist doing? She must be on top of things if you let her take over while you're gone."

Deirdre came back to her mother, arms up, and Mel pulled the baby into her lap. After kissing her daughter's curly head, she answered. "Linda's a go-getter, that's for sure. She's reworked the scheduling process so that there's an extra ten minutes built in for each patient. I originally thought it would just be a waste with doctors standing around with dead time, but it actually turns out that the office runs far more efficiently when we're not running behind all the time. Live and learn, I guess. With you on break and it being summer, things are a little slower than usual. If I had to be away from the office this was a good time for it to happen."

We talk a bit more about my dental practice, the remodeling she and Duncan are doing on their townhouse, and whether they should hire a full-time, live-in nanny for *Deirdre* instead of the commercial day-care associated with *Cerridwen* Prep she currently attends. Then, it's my BFF's turn to switch conversational tracks. "Rosie, what's really going on with this mission?" she asks.

Mel is not a member of the Black Knight's intelligence circle. That's by her choice. It was offered to her shortly after her handfast to Duncan, but at the time, she had insisted she didn't want to be a "spy" in any way, shape or manner. She's also well aware that because of that decision, I can't tell her a single thing about what is truly going on, so I hedge my answer. "Duncan goes on a lot of missions, Mel. Why so curious about this one?"

"Look, I know you can't give me the entire low-down, but can you at least tell me how dangerous this one is? The fact that Duncan packed Deirdre and I off to *Dun Siorai* tells me that this is something highly important with the possibility of serious backlash. We're off most people's radar because Duncan works really hard at keeping his undercover work a secret. The fact that he was worried enough to send me on a two week 'vacation' away from Salem has me worried," she related.

I think carefully about how I want to handle this. Mel is my best friend despite me messing up big time, not once, but twice, during our long relationship. I don't want to have to lie to her, but I am also sworn to secrecy. Lots of people depend on me keeping that promise. I tread carefully. "This is a particularly difficult but highly important mission, Mel. We both know I'm not allowed to dispense information, so please, let's just leave it at that. Both our husbands are very good at what they do. I expect they will be safely home soon and you can pump Duncan for more information."

Mel presses her lips together and frowns, indicating she's not fully satisfied by my answer. "You know very well that Duncan will not give me one iota of useful information, Rosalinda Fitzpatrick. At least tell me one thing. Does this have anything to do with your sister-in-law's sudden death? I mean…c'mon, Rosie…that was shocking! 'Wasting Disease?' In such a short time period? Seems pretty implausible to me. Please. Just tell me if this is something I really need to be long-term worried about. I have to think about what's best for *Deirdre*. If being in Salem is unsafe, then perhaps Duncan and I should take our daughter and move here to *I Idir* on a more permanent basis. Are we safer here? Give me some kind of clue, Rosie. What should we do?"

There's nothing more that I want then to give my dearest friend the answers she seeks. But the honest truth is, taking in how little I know…and don't know…about Meghan's death, I'm not sure any of us are safe in either dimension.

TOOTHLESS 28

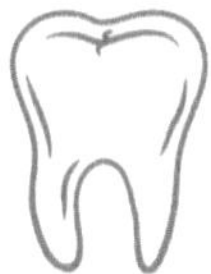

IT'S WORSE THAN IT SEEMS

THE NEWS DECLAN brought home with him was grim, but it took several days before he was willing to share it. His Lordship returned to *Dun Siorai* fourteen days after he'd left, climbing into our bed somewhere in the wee hours of the morning. Our bond let me know the exact moment he'd arrived back in the Otherworld, though it took a handful of hours before he actually made his way to our family quarters. "Are you okay, Sweetie," I asked as I felt the weight of him on the other side of the bed.

"I am now," he murmured as he tucked himself around me. Any thoughts I had for a "welcome home party" evaporated as I heard the almost instant wheezing of his snoring. This wasn't altogether a surprise. It usually took him a few days after an especially intense mission to decompress and relax, and from his quiet demeanor I guessed that when he finally did share what they'd discovered at those awful locations, I would be more than a little distraught.

Declan's revelation finally came three days after he'd been home attending to everything that had piled up while he'd been gone. *Mairead* Beckett had invited Dylan to the archery fields at *Crann Bethadh* for beginner's lessons in bow and arrow skills, while Liam and Ronin were off at the horse barn for their weekly riding lesson (Yes. Even my two-year-old rides. It's the way things go here). Given that we were alone, it was a good time to discuss things I surely did not want the children to hear.

We met in the solar parlor with a late morning tea tray. "I am not keepin' ya' from yar' business, am I, Love?" he asked in a tone that sounded rather hopeful that he might be off the hook.

"Not at all, Declan. Actually, I'm anxious to hear the details from your mission," I replied

"How was yar' visit with Mel and the *bairn*? She must be growin' like a weed, eh? Dunc says she's been walkin' for a few weeks now," he comments, looking to change the subject.

"We had a lovely visit, Sweetie. *Deirdre* is such an adorable baby. So good-natured, but I'm pretty sure you didn't ask me to join you here to discuss my time with Mel. Tell me about the mission. I can handle it."

He smiles with that "Tax Man's-on-the-move" look that I've seen hundreds of times over the course of the years we've been together. "Come sit in my lap, Lass, and we will discuss it, " he says sweetly.

"That's not going to work this time, Tax Man. You know as well as I do if I go over there we're never going to discuss anything of importance. I think I'll stay right here until AFTER we talk," I reply in my most convincing tone.

I receive a very dramatic sigh in return and some little "Old Language" ditty about a man whose wife is tired of his sexual advances. "Let's not play that game, Declan," I argue. "You know I would never in a million years tire of loving you. But this is too important to ignore. I can tell that whatever intelligence information you and the others have gathered has you majorly spooked. You've been off kilter since you've returned and your 'fox runs' have tripled in length the past two days. I know something is terribly wrong."

"I am sorry about shiftin' so much, Love. It seems the only time I'm free of this dread is when I'm out runnin' the trails in ma' fox form. 'Tis not fair to you, and I regret ma' need for isolation. It does no way reflect on ma' feelings' far' you and the children."

"I understand, Sweetie. And if you find you need a little 'escape' more than once a day, I'm behind you all the way. But as a full member of your team, I need to know what's going on. Robyn and I are supposed to meet tomorrow so that the two of us can go over the medical files you confiscated in Algiers and Stein am Rein. Please don't make me hear about it for the first time from him. I'd like some time to process it all."

"You are right, Love. 'Tis best ya' hear it from me, though it is so nightmarish I worry it will upset ya' greatly."

"Seriously, Declan…we've been in some serious situations together. I'm no shrinking violet," I offer.

"Aye. But durin' those times it was just you and I at risk. It appears now that we are all at the mercy of madmen determined ta' hurt us all…includin' the children."

His words are like an icy spear to the heart. Our children? "Just tell me already, Declan. Your hedging is not helping."

"I suppose 'tis best if I go ahead and speak honestly. The work you'll be doin' with Robyn will undoubtedly be frightenin' and vera' distasteful based on what I've learned on this mission. It seems our enemies have moved beyond just tryin' to make it easier far' humans to cross the Veil and spend time in the Otherworld. They've upped their game ta' wantin' to kill us off as well."

"With that norovirus mutation that Robyn thinks killed your sister, Meghan?" I ask, all the while trying to keep the rising panic from my voice.

"Aye. I think one of the things Robyn hopes you'll help him do is figure out how they mutated the virus enough to cause such a reaction in *Sidhe* folk," he explains.

"I'm no expert in virology, but I'll do what I can. I may have to go back to Salem and do some research," I reply. "I'll need the internet and research libraries."

"We assumed you would, but not without armed security. And only for short stints in different locations. I am sure our homes and places of business are being monitored, so we donna' want ta' set up any recurrin' patterns for them ta' track," my husband explains. "Truthfully, Rosie, Lass, I would prefer ya' stay put here at *Dun Siorai* with the children where I can keep ya' all safer. But I understand that you have yar' own responsibilities and you will do what you feel ya' need to do."

"Damn right, Tax Man. I love you to the moon and back, but I've always been my own person and that's not about to change now that *I Idir* needs me." As I say the words, I think to myself how ironic this must sound to someone who, when he first met me, complained that I held an unhealthy prejudice against all things Fae, myself included. Still, people mature. They change. And I would like to think my acceptance of my bloodline heritage, tooth fairy as it is, is a sign of my personal growth and understanding of my place in the Universe.

My Eternal Mate must be thinking the same thing. "Ya' are a vera' special woman, Rosie Parker Fitzpatrick, and I am a vera' blessed man ta' call ya' my One and Only," he says, staring back at me with those impossible eyes the color of spring leaves.

The bond is there. It's always there. I leave the chair I've been parked in and settle myself in his lap. "I agree, Tax Man. You are definitely 'vera' blessed' by the Universe, but I do believe you're about to get 'vera' lucky' as well," I announce, right before I throw my arms around his neck and kiss him vera', vera' nicely.

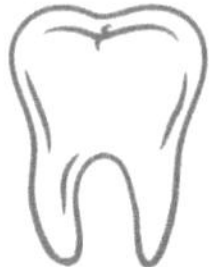

ROSIE RETURNS TO THE LAB

My first meet-up with Dr. Brannigan takes place in his home office and adjoining lab. It was a place I'd yet to be invited to and Declan teased that I should be especially honored to garnish an entry to Robyn's "Inner Sanctum." Robyn Brannigan, Prince of Avalon, Physician to the Royal Family of *I Idir*, and scientist extraordinaire, was an extremely private person. He kept his personal business to himself and, for the most part, shunned the social extravaganzas of both of the kingdoms he called home.

Even when he finally took a mate, an event highly anticipated by his Queenly Great Grandmother, as well as his all-knowing Raven Godmother from *I Idir*, he handfasted himself to The Morrigan's ward by sealing their vows in a manner that suited the two of them best; a very secret, decidedly private ceremony in the Doc's home with the 26th Merlin performing the Fae ritual and Fr. Kevin performing the Mundane Christian version at the bride's request, with the Black Knight and the elder *Banphrionsa* of *I Idir* as witnesses, and zero additional guests.

I let Declan guide me there through the Veil even though I've long moved beyond my earlier-life troubles with jumping back and forth between dimensions. For one, I was very nervous about how much I actually could help someone of Robyn's immense knowledge and needed to rest in my husband's unrelenting confidence in me, and secondly, I knew my Tax Man was dying to get a sneak peek at the doctor's home, a place he'd ever been invited to either.

Robyn and Roxanne Brannigan's stately home was located in the McIntire District, a location in Salem that housed some of the most beautiful examples of pre-1900 domestic structures in the United States. The couple's "honeymoon cottage" was actually a beautiful, historically protected, Federal Era style mansion boasting multiple bedrooms and countless baths. Both Declan and I took guesses on whether the home would be filled with antique pieces from the house's time period, or the stark, modern look reminiscent of the Doc's professional offices, and thus were surprised that it reminded us more of the Otherworld style found in many of the Ruling House estates with its heavy carved wooden pieces, overstuffed chairs, and rich, textured fabrics. This surprised me greatly, as I've always viewed Doc Brannigan as a Mundane-comfortable guy, more content amongst the advantages of modern technology offered by the human world. Which just goes to show you that you often don't really know people as well as you think you do.

Our friend met us in the spacious foyer, the floor of which was mosaic tiled with an image of an immense apple blossom, the national flower of Avalon, in varying shades of pink and white. Robyn noticed our attention to the details of the floor. "A 'gift' from my Great Grandmother after my nuptials," he says as he smiles. "A not so gentle reminder of my obligations to Avalon," he says with a wry smile. "She was not particularly happy with our decision to elope in private."

Doc Brannigan's Great Grandmother is the Lady of the Lake. Yes. That one from Arthurian legend, most of which the Mundane world has gotten wrong. Like our own Morrigan, the Lady of the Lake is considered a goddess within the Otherworld pantheon, she being descended from the Celtic goddess of the Underworld, *Bébinn,* and her river-goddess sister *Boann. Nimue,* as she is sometimes called in ancient literature, is known to be a sorceress of great magical skill and a renowned healer, which I guess makes Robyn an apple that didn't fall too far from the family tree. She also happens to be one of the Raven Queen's oldest and dearest friends, with *Nimue* asking Herself to be her only grandson's godmother, which explained why Robyn spent so much time in *I Idir* while growing up and his inexplicable loyalty to our Queen.

It seems to be the way with these hoity-toity *Tuatha de Danann* types, their long pedigrees reaching back hundreds of generations and tied to the mythological legends so gleefully devoured by Mundane readers. There are several legendary people in my own husband's *Nuada* line, the greatest being *Nuada Airgetlám,* the first king of the *Tuatha de Danann* and the guy with the silver hand. I try not to dwell on these kinds of things too often, as I'm pretty sure my tooth fairy-Mundane heritage doesn't fit gracefully among their golden histories. My parents, Edmund Parker, the Mundane bookkeeper and *Áine Fiacail* (Tooth) weren't the stuff of Otherworld legends.

These thoughts earn me a dirty look from my mate. It annoys the Tax Man to no end when I disparage my heritage, claiming that I am disrespecting all the Universe has done to make me who I am and bring me to where I now find myself.

I suppose in this particular instance, I just hope that somewhere the Universe has thought to wisely include some magical scientific insight into my DNA so that I might not be a total waste of Robyn's time today.

The Doc leads us up a curving set of stairs to the second floor and past a multitude of open doors. Most of them are bedrooms and baths that I nonchalantly try to get a good look at as we go by, our host sadly not offering a guided house tour. I wonder which one of the bedrooms is Robyn's and Roxanne's because…well…I'm fascinated by how other couples design their intimate spaces. This earns me another cranky Declan look and a mental admonishment from my Eternal Mate. *"Stop bein' a busy body, Rosie. 'What yar' thinkin' is rude…and a little weird."*

"C'mon…don't tell me you've never thought about it." I counter.

"Never." he says, the self-righteousness leaking directly from his head.

"I call bullshit. You've made comments to me that say otherwise." I replied.

"Perhaps I have. When we are alone. In private. Not when we are in another man's personal domain."

"Hmmm," is all I have left to say. I hate it when the Tax Man gets preachy with me.

We eventually reach the end of the hall where Robyn's office and lab are located behind a set of carved double doors, but the Doc doesn't seem inclined to invite my husband inside, a point I take pleasure over because, as I have said on multiple occasions, I don't much like being scolded by my One and Only.

"I would be happy to escort Lady *Nuada* back to *Dun Siorai* after we finish our work here, Fitz. Save you the trip," the doctor offered.

I could tell Declan was a bit put out over not being

invited into Robyn's private work space, but he is forever the consummate gentleman, so his response was seemingly cordial and polite. "That's vera' gracious of ya', Robyn. But ma' Lady and I have plans ta' briefly stop at Fitzpatrick's Folly ta' pick a few things up befar' we return, so I shall happily fetch her ma'self."

I neither knew of any such plans about stopping at home, nor did I particularly care for the notion of being "fetched" from anywhere. Still, I knew better than to contradict his Lordship in a public setting, so I bit my tongue, filing away my discontent for a later conversation. Then, with a bland kiss to the cheek, my One and Only disappeared from sight.

* * *

Robyn opened both wooden doors at the same time and ushered me inside, pausing a moment to let me get my bearings. The room was high-ceilinged and impossibly large for its Federal-era, architectural roots. One side of the open area boasted a modern science lab, all stark white counters and gleaming stainless steel. Behind the glass wall that kept it contained, state-of-the art medical technology hummed while the counters were home to a range of beakers, tubing, glass vials and microscopes. I had no doubt Brannigan's home lab was as well-equipped, if not better, than the one housed in Massachusetts General Hospital or the Dana Farber Cancer Institute in Boston.

The other side of the space was devoted to the pursuit of literary knowledge with floor to ceiling book cases filled with old and new tomes on endless topics within the fields of science, medicine, history, and magic. A few very old books, their covers worn with age and heavy use, were carefully housed in glass cabinets for protection, looking totally incredulous next to a bank of high-speed desk top computers, a few brand-new laptops, two odd-looking tablets, and both a traditional and a digital printer. Little thought was given to a reader's comfort. In regards to furnishings, the room contained a well-worn leather chair with an old fashioned hassock in front of a vintage Chesterfield sofa covered in an unusual shade of burnt sienna leather, and a few office-like, highbacked rolling chairs parked next to the table with the tech devices.

It was impressively stocked for the pursuit of scientific study, and comfortable enough if one was forced to spend long periods of time doing important research. But it was not what I was expecting. The way Declan had described Robyn's "Inner Sanctum," I had thought to find myself transported to some grand, mystical tower hideaway of a great wizard or mad scientist, the likes of Dr. Frankenstein or Faust. Despite being appointed with the best technology money could buy, the doc's secret hideaway seemed...well... ordinary.

I suppose I wasn't shielding either my thoughts or my facial expressions very well. Robyn grinned at my response. "Disappointed, eh?" he asked.

"Oh no," I say much too enthusiastically. "It's very impressive." Which wasn't exactly a lie. The fact that the man had a hospital grade research lab in his house was quite monumental. It would seem, however, that at times I still fall into the ridiculous notions Mundane people have about their Fae counterparts.

"Be honest now, Dr. Parker," he teased. "Based on all the rumors regarding this space, you were obviously expecting something a little more...flamboyant, perhaps?"

There didn't seem to be any reason to lie. I couldn't adequately concentrate on the work at hand and still keep a reasonably secure shield. As *Sidhe* royalty, Robyn's magic was undoubtedly in the *Tuatha de Danann* range. It seemed silly and a waste of energy to try to hide my thoughts from him. "Really, Robyn. I do think it's amazing. Honest! It's just that the way everyone carries on about it and the fact you allow so few people in here led me to believe…," I trail off, not finding the right words. "Oh hell! I don't know what I expected. And frankly, it doesn't matter. I'm just all together grateful that you felt I was a worthwhile colleague to join you in this pursuit. No one wants to find the answers about this evil, insidious virus more than me."

"It is I who am grateful, Rosie. For your input. You are the only member of Beck's inner circle who has any science and medical training. I know I don't have to start with the basics when we dive into our research. You know the structure and life cycles of viruses and how they replicate inside a host cell. That's way more than the average person knows. Plus, in the same way I've heard your mate say on more than one occasion, you always have this really unique way of seeing things other people miss. I couldn't think of a better partner in helping me find the key to how this virus was mutated and what we can do to counter it."

I'm appreciative, and a little overwhelmed, by Doctor Brannigan's confidence in me, but in good 'ole "Rosie fashion," I can't leave well enough alone. Something is still bothering me. "Doc, why all the secrecy about your," I wave my hand around the room, "work space? Why not invite your friends inside," I ask. Then quickly add, "If it's not too personal of a question to ask.

Robyn laughs with an easy-goingness that I don't usually see with him. He is the most professionally-mannered physician I've ever known, but right now, he looks like an overgrown student with mischief on his mind; his ever-present tie undone, the top button of his dress shirt unbuttoned, and a lock of his blonde hair is hanging in his eyes. "My goal to keep people out is a really practical, rather boring one," he explains. "Many of the books in this library are one-of-a kind magical records that go back a thousand years. It's the most complete collection of magical study in either dimension, and that includes the *Druid Akedemia* on the outskirts of *I Idir*. As a whole, this library contains knowledge that's probably best left unshared with most of my fellow Otherworldly residents. Plus, they're also very, very old, and very, very fragile. You might have noticed the air in here is filtered and the temperature controlled to prevent break-down and decay.

As to the lab, well it's obvious one needs to be extremely careful when working with biological samples. The less people in, the less chance of anything untold being brought in or carried out, especially with my *Sidhe* counterparts. They don't realize the magical energy residue they carry on their persons, but it wreaks havoc with the Mundane technology."

"Then, am I your only visitor?" I ask, hoping that's not the case. Robyn's "Inner Sanctum" is a pretty big mantle to carry as a secret.

"No," he replies. "Ambrose has been here many times, as has Her Majesty, though she less frequently. They've both come looking for knowledge on certain topics which I've never thought my place to ask about. And, of course, my wife has been here, mostly keeping me company when I'm working on something. Roxanne is not at all interested in magical or scientific research, but she is lovingly supportive of my work in both dimensions. As for the others, I've always politely turned down their requests for entry. Even Beck, who was surprisingly a good sport over my veto. Honestly, they've all been very amiable about the whole thing. Still, I will admit, rather sheepishly, that I find their rumor-mongering about my office highly amusing, so I've decided to continue to play along. Keep the mystique going, as they say." He says with a wink and a charming half grin, "You will keep my little secret intact, won't you Rosie?"

"Of course, I will, Robyn. I swear to it. And trust me, keeping secrets from my Tax Man is no easy feat, but I'm just the woman for the job," I reply.

"Aye. There's no stronger truth than that. Fitz can be very tenacious when it comes to solving a mystery, so I am grateful that you are up for such a daunting task, Dr. Parker," the doctor teased. "Now, shall the two of us get on with our study and see what we can discover about this wretched mess of information the team has brought back from their mission?"

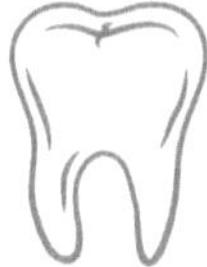

THE NEWS REMAINS BAD

I LOSE track of any sense of time working side by side with Robyn. There were stacks of reports and patient records to go through along with a slew of biological samples that required my foray back into the lab professionally decked out in protective gear. It had been over twenty years since I'd last been inside a lab for research work of any kind; probably not since my biology classes during my pre-med course of undergraduate study. Technology had moved rapidly forward in leaps and bounds since my college days, and it took me a fair amount of time to learn to correctly use the new equipment, some of which I guessed cost more than my current automobile. However, the basic concepts of the scientific method hadn't changed much since *Ibn al-Haytham*, an Arab Muslim scientist, first described a systematic approach to experimentation in his writings from the 11th Century, and after the first few hours, Robyn and I were researching together like a well-oiled machine.

At some point, a lunch tray appeared on the Davenport in

the office half of the space, but as we were busy in the lab, the tea and sandwiches simply sat untouched. Information from the patient records showed that every patient received a dose of 20mg of SX-36 stem cell therapy delivered intranasally. The cells were specifically targeted for the patient's frontal cortex where it was believed the Fae's genetic ability for producing magical energy was stored. This was not new information. The Mundane science behind producing "soldiers" who could cross the Veil dimensional divide and be able to physically exist in the Otherworld for any length of time had been an ongoing study for at least eight or nine years.

From recent observation of the few poor souls captured at the Veil Border, or of the bodies of those who perished on their own, the terrorist groups behind this exploration had not made enough progress to launch any kind of feasible offensive. What was odd about the patients mentioned in the recovered records from the Algiers and Switzerland locations, was the low dosage administered to the test subjects. 20mg was not nearly enough to make any kind of difference in their abilities. Though they gave off magical energy that could be picked up by a more sensitive Fae person, the humans with the low dosage would be unable to perform any magic whatsoever, and certainly wouldn't be able to physically survive any type of jump from the Mundane world to the Otherworld.

It wasn't until we discovered that some of these same people were also administered an injection containing a live mutated form of the *Caliciviridae* virus, one which causes inflammation of the stomach and the intestines, specifically the GII.4 type, better known as norovirus, that we could move forward in finding answers. It was logical for us to jump to the hypothesis that the human patients were probably being used to determine how this new mutated GII.4

virus reacted within the stem-cell-magically-enhanced Mundanes. Still, it seemed to be far too involved of an operation, one covering several locations and a wide range of test subjects, for the simple purpose of determining the virus's effect on the Fae population. It had been common knowledge for nearly sixty years that the *Caliciviridae* virus, i.e., the "stomach flu," was one of the few human diseases the Fae were susceptible to, and that among the Otherworldy population, GII.4 made them feel worse for a longer amount of days than their human counterparts.

With a bad case of eye strain and both of our stomachs gurgling with hunger, Robyn and I removed our protective lab gear and positioned ourselves in the office for an attempt at lunch. The conversation lagged, both of us lost in our own calculations and thoughts. All this talk of gastro viral pathogens brought back memories of when, early in our relationship, I had unknowingly infected Declan with the stomach flu, and how I had mocked him for his grown-man complaining of the symptoms, not realizing at the time he was *Sidhe* Fae and likely far more ill than I had been.

That's when another impossibly horrific thought came to me. I put my sandwich back down on the plate. "Robyn, what if the reason they're infecting low-dose stem cell patients with extra strength GII.4 is not so much to see how they are affected symptom wise, but rather to let the human host's immune system build up natural immunity against the mutated virus. Couldn't they then use these results to build a live-attenuated vaccine which they could then administer to their fully stem cell altered humans? I know it doesn't appear they've made that breakthrough yet, of getting humans to the point where they can sustain life in the Otherworld, but we both know from everything we've seen in today's documents that if they're not stopped soon, it's only a matter of time before they will eventually succeed. The people involved are ruthless enough not to care how many humans or Fae they harm." I don't add that if my wretched father-in-law is one of them, the man doesn't have a single shred of moral decency. If anyone knows what Callum Fitzpatrick is capable of, it's Robyn who cared for Declan after his North Korean imprisonment and torture.

Robyn Brannigan's stricken expression is proof that my hypothesis is a valid one. "If that's true, Rosie," he says as he puts his tea cup back onto the saucer, "and your supposition makes absolute perfect scientific sense, then they intend to vaccinate their own people against this deadly virus before sending them into the Otherworld to spread it to ours. Universe have mercy on us! We need to create a vaccine of our own before it's too late."

* * *

By the time Declan returned to see me safely back to *Dun Siorai*, I'd been working with Robyn for nearly ten hours of Mundane time. I was both physically and mentally exhausted, and my mood was somewhere between grim and despondent. Feeling as I did, the last thing I desired was a pit stop at our home in Salem; however, Liam had decided he could no longer live in *I Idir* without his "Master Turtty," a tattered, none-too-clean, stuffed turtle he'd used as a "lovie" during his toddler days and hadn't paid attention to for at least fifteen months, while Dylan had requested his left-behind Mundane sneakers so he could "run faster than *Mairead*."

On any other occasion, I would have been more than happy to use the unplanned visit to "Fitzpatrick's Folly" to take a short respite of privacy with my beloved Tax Man. Since we've added the "Eternal Bond" to our handfast, our intimate moments are no longer private, as we give off a wave of magical vibes when we're horizontally engaged that other *Sidhe* are sensitive around. Over the years, I've worked hard to try and not let it bother me. The Fae are a lot more open and casual about sex than their Mundane counterparts, and the "joining" of their Lord and Lady is considered a good omen for the entire House. Normally, I treasure those few opportunities that allow us to be alone together, but today is not one of those times.

As a tooth fairy after sundown, I can transport magically from one location to another in the Mundane world. My husband, on the other hand, cannot. It's the one advantage I have over him in the paranormal range of abilities. Thus, we are forced to either take a ride share or walk the ten blocks from Robyn's home to ours. Because it is a pleasant evening and the Hawthorn and Crabapple trees are in full bloom, we decide to walk despite my general fatigue. "Do ya' want ta' talk about it, Rosie Lass?" my mate asks.

"I wish that you wouldn't pump me for details about Robyn's 'Inner Sanctum,' Declan. I gave my word I wouldn't divulge any details," I reply, sounding more snappish in tone than I fully intended.

"I wasn't speakin' of the man's home, Love." he counters.

I then realize he's referring to the details of our research findings. I understood that I would be called upon to help Robyn explain every awful piece of information we had spent the day gathering to the team, but in the here and now, I just can't make myself rehash the frightening scenario. "I'm sorry, Tax Man. I just can't go over everything tonight. I promise I will tell you everything tomorrow morning. Until then, I just need to de-stress a bit with a long, hot shower and perhaps a cup of Cook's night time tea."

"Then that's exactly what ya' shall have, fair Lady. I swear we will not tarry long at the Folly. I would skip it all together ta'night if I thought Liam and Dylan would understand. Alas, our wee *bairns*, as of yet, take no notice regarding the trap-pins' of adult life."

"No worries, Sweetie," I answered with a tired sigh. "We'll probably all sleep better tonight if we bring Liam his Mr. Turtty."

As we approached our much-remodeled home, Declan veiled our presence with a slight wave of his left hand. Our neighbors all believed that the Fitzpatricks were away on their yearly summer sojourn to Ireland, and it made no sense to give them any reason to think otherwise. We enter through the back door, the wards my husband has set up recognizing our magical signatures and allowing us entry. I am thankful that all the lights inside and out are set on spell-induced timers, as I hate coming home to a dark house, especially with all the awful things I know are going on.

While Declan runs upstairs to locate Dylan's shoes and Mr. Turtty, I scrounge the near empty fridge and pantry for something to snack on, and thus, I am smearing peanut butter on stale oatmeal cookies when my Eternal Mate returns, items in hand. "That looks disgustin'," he says. "Why in the green valleys are ya' eatin' such a vile combo when I ken' easily conjure ya' up somethin' better?"

"I was just looking for something quick to tide me over until we get back to *Dun Siorai*, Sweetie. I don't need a three-course meal," I explain.

"No wonder ya' are feelin' so run-down lately, Lass. Sometimes ya' donna' make healthy food choices," he scolds, husbandly oblivious to my current mood. I hesitate over revealing a decision I made this afternoon, knowing he'll fuss and worry until we have some solid answers. Still, because of the bond, it's a lot of work to keep secrets from one another. "Well, I guess we'll find out if that's true, Tax Man. I had Robyn draw some blood when I was with him today. He's going to run a few tests, just to see what's what."

His aura immediately goes to a sickly yellow color, signaling his sudden stress and anxiety. "What else aren't ya' tellin' me, *Mo Ghrá* (My Love)?"

"Please stop, Sweetie. I'm not holding anything back from you. I don't expect my bloodwork to show anything serious. Truly. But it's always better to be safe than sorry, right?" I lie. Truthfully, because of my family history with "Wasting Disease," I have some concerns over my white blood cell count, but I bury my feelings deep and don't let on. "You'll see. It will be just as you said. I need to eat better, get more rest, and reduce my stress levels," I say with what I hope sounds like confidence.

I can see that my Tax Man is setting up for a long discussion I don't want to have right now when we are interrupted by a squeaky, metal sound coming from the parlor. We both instantly freeze, straining our ears to hear. When it remains quiet, my mate says to my mind. *"I need ta' check that sound out, Lass. I want ya' to stay here in the kitchen until I tell ya' otherwise. If I say 'go' I want ya' to be ready to immediately jump ta' Dun Siorai. Ask Duncan and the scathachs ta' secure the family quarters. I will return myself as soon as I ken'."*

I don't bother to argue. We have an established protocol for emergencies of this kind and it's the one Eternal Mate mandate I never question his Lordship on. I watched as my husband, gun in hand, dirk at waist, pushed the swinging door that separates the large kitchen from the dining room, parlor and upstairs staircase. I hear him shuffling around the rooms, then I hear the front door open and close. When Declan returns to the kitchen, he has an envelope in one hand and a pensive expression pasted on his face. He hands the envelope to me. "This was on the floor in front of the front door's mail slot. The sound we heard was the flap squeakin'. I knew I should have never allowed anything other than a solid wood door," he says. "It is addressed to you, Rosie."

I take the plain white envelope from his hand. There is the slight tingle of magical energy, and my name, Rosie Fitzpatrick, is printed in careful block letters. I look up at my husband waiting for the "all-clear" sign, then run my fingernail under the sealed flap. Inside is one folded sheet, again written in the same block letters.

> *Rosie*
>
> *Your sister is in danger. He is always watching and calls her his "Beloved Aine." He says he will take her to I Idir, and make her his Queen.*
>
> *Time is short. You must act in haste. Do not delay.*

My hands are trembling by the time I get to the last sentence. The Tax Man had been reading over my shoulder and when I turn to face him, I see his eyes closed, already sending telepathic messages to several people. When he opens them, I see the resolute fire of rage mirrored in those green eyes.

"He will get nowhere near her, *Rós Mo Chroí* (Rose of My Heart). I swear on ma' vera' life I will not let him touch her. Beck and the others are on their way. We will keep Claire and her family safe. Then we will take the evil bastard down once and for all," he says in a voice cold and distant.

I'm shaking so bad now I have to make a conscious effort not to let my teeth chatter. "You realize there is only one way that envelope got pushed through the mail slot, don't you? The wards wouldn't allow anyone near that door without immediately setting off a warning. Anyone, that is, but specific family members. You never excluded *Oisin* from the original ward spell, did you?" I asked.

"Nay, Love. I had always hoped he'd just return home someday. I dinna' want ta' make it difficult far' him ta' walk through that front door and back to his family."

"Then…bless all the goddesses, Declan! This proves that *Oisin* is still alive…and he's working for our side."

TOOTHLESS 31

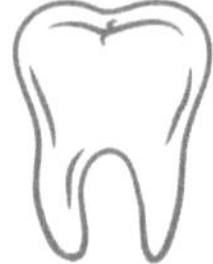

A DANGEROUS PLAN

THERE WAS a lot of back-and-forth discussion over where the most secure place is for us all to meet, but Beck ultimately makes the call to meet at Claire and Scott's home in Swampscott. His reasoning is based on keeping my sister and her family out of the hands of Callum Fitzpatrick. I am grateful for the Black Knight's determination to keep my older sister and her family secure, but the fact that he is so grim about it clues me in that he himself has deep concerns over what could happen.

Because he and Fr. Kevin both already reside in Swampscott, they are the first to arrive, but wait at the curb until Declan and I make the thirteen-minute drive from Salem to my sister's home. Don't ask me how my *Sidhe* husband managed to veil the removal of his car from our garage without our neighbors being any the wiser. I mean…shit… it's an entire car, for Pete's sake.

It's nearly 9:00 PM ET in the Mundane world, and Claire and Scott are obviously shocked to find the four of us unexpectedly at their door. Their unease grows when Beck tells Claire's husband to step out and pretend to be checking his porch light which appears to have gone out only seconds before. The four of us are heavily veiled, though by whose spell I can't say for certain. The light bulb charade is to placate anyone who might be watching the house, leading them to believe that Scott is just attending to home maintenance rather than greeting someone at their front door, someone who obviously can't be seen.

My elder sister, Claire, has been privy to my Fae life with Declan since day one, and because Ted Beckett is also Essex County's Sheriff, she and Scott know perfectly well who the man is, what he does within both worlds, and completely understand that his being here so late in the evening means something is likely terribly wrong. "Rosie, Honey, what's this all about?" Claire asks. My big sister is doing her best to appear cool, calm and collected, but the higher pitch to her voice and the way her hands are curling and uncurling at her side tells me she is absolutely terrified.

Beck takes immediate control of the situation, suggesting everyone sit down so he can explain things, then asks after her twin boys. "They're probably in bed, reading or playing on their tablets," Claire replies. "I'd prefer if they weren't involved in this if that's possible. They aren't one hundred percent clear about their aunt and uncle's Fae heritage. We were hoping to wait until they were older and better able to understand the need for complete secrecy."

Our Black Knight's expression is sympathetic but firm. "We will try and keep information on a need-to-know basis for your boys, Mr. and Mrs. Kellogg, but they may eventually have to be told the truth. Fr. Kevin here can help you with that. He's very good at explaining hard topics to children."

Every ounce of panic is written in Claire and Scott's body language and facial expressions, and seeing this, and knowing that my Fae life is to blame for it, almost makes me lose my shit right then and there. My mate senses this and takes my hand, entwining my fingers with his. *"Have faith and let Beck handle this, Love. The man is vera', vera' good at what he does. I've seen him handle worse situations than this. He will protect yar' family as if it were his own, while keepin' everyone on an even keel. I promise ya', Lass, Beck and Kevin will keep them safe, sane, and cheerful. They are a vera' efficient team."*

I watch as the Black Knight calmly lays out the situation at hand and his plans to keep the family of four secure and free from as much worry as possible. His voice is authoritative, but kind, and his way of speaking seems to instill a sense of hope and confidence in my big sis and her husband. I can also feel the tiniest hum of energy vibrations under my feet, a sign that there's undoubtedly some glamour magic being tossed around. Normally, I would take issue with my poor family being "fairy-rolled," but this is the calmest I've seen my beloved Mundane family since we've knocked on their door, with Scott even laughing at one of Fr. Kevin's corny jokes, so for tonight I'm joining the "whatever works on their behalf" club.

"Do all four of you have up-to-date passports?" Beck asks.

"We do," Scott replies. "We all went to Cancun last fall, so they're not even a year old."

"Excellent. Getting new ones would take more time than I'd prefer to spend right now. The quicker we get you settled in your vacation home, the better for everyone. Your boys are going to love the coast of Wales," the Black Knight said.

"Wales?" Claire asks. "When? How?" she questions. "We're not even packed. There are responsibilities to consider. I mean…the boys are out of school for summer break, but the two of us have fulltime jobs."

"As of now, the Kelloggs are on extended vacation. You can trust me. I'll take care of everything. Your employers, your house, your finances. Even your mail. Everything," Beck explained.

"When do you have us leaving?" Scott asked.

"I was hoping this evening if I'm able to file a flight plan. Otherwise, first thing in the morning," our Boss said.

"Flight plan?" my brother-in-law questioned.

"Yes. You will be flying my family's corporate jet to the UK. Hennington Industries," the Black Knight explained.

"I think I've seen that jet," Scott says. "On the runway at Logan. It's the one with that crazy grocery chain chicken painted on the side, right? Henny Penny?"

"That's the one," Beck replies.

"She's a beauty. For all the times I've flown for business, I've never had the opportunity to travel by private jet. It should be an interesting experience."

"It's about an eight-hour flight from Logan. You should be very comfortable. There's even sleeping quarters on board if you can get your boys to settle down, though something tells me they will be running on pure excitement," the Queen's Hand of Justice teased with a confident smile.

At the mention of her sons, my sister's face registers concern. She turns to Scott and asks, "Jeesh…how are we ever going to explain this to Sean and Patrick?"

"Oh, we have that all figured out," Fr. Kevin interjects. "Leave it to us," he adds with a grin.

Claire retrieves my nephews from their beds. Dressed in pajamas and looking thoroughly confused, Patrick notices Declan and I first. "Aunt Rosie…Uncle Declan…what are you doing here so late at night. Is Dylan here too?"

"Not this time, Honey. This is a special visit," I stammer, not sure what to say next as I haven't a clue as to what crazy story the Queen's associates have in mind.

Thankfully, I don't have to figure it out. Beck addresses the boys. "I'm Sheriff Beckett, boys, and this is Fr. Kevin

O'Kenney from Holy Family Catholic Church. I know it's late at night to be visiting your house, but Fr. Kevin and I have such amazing news for all of you that we just couldn't wait until tomorrow to tell you."

Sean chimes in. "I know who you are, Sheriff. You came to our school a few months ago to talk about online safety. Do you remember? Hawthorne Elementary?"

"I do remember. Such a smart bunch of boys and girls. But tonight, I'm here at your house for an even better reason. A few weeks back, your mom and dad bought a raffle ticket for a fundraiser for Fr. Kevin's church. And guess what? Your family won the grand prize! A free vacation to England! To Wales, specifically," Beck said with more enthusiasm than I ever expected him to have with children.

"We're going to England to see whales?" Patrick asked, his confusion causing the adults in the room to smile.

"Not exactly," our Boss explains. "Wales is a country that's part of the United Kingdom. The location you and your family are going for your vacation is near the coast, so you'll be right by the beach. You guys can go swimming, sailing, and snorkeling every single day. Plus, there's some old castles you can explore nearby, and some great hiking paths. I'm not sure about seeing whales, but I know for a fact there's plenty of dolphins."

"Oh boy!" Patrick replied. "That sounds awesome."

"It sure is," Fr. Kevin added. "There's a small tide pool on the beach that's full of crabs and starfish for you to catch and explore. Plus, I bet the little stream behind the house would make the perfect spot for remote controlled boat races."

I have to admit, Kevin and Beck were working hard to sell the idea to the kids. The way they were describing it, a trip to coastal Wales sounded like quite the adventure even to my adult ears.

Sean looked up at his mother. "Mom, are we really going to Wales?

"Yes, baby. We really are," she says with a smile that doesn't reach her eyes.

"When?"

"Tonight, I think," the child's mother replies.

"Wow! C'mon, Patrick" the older of the twins says. "We better hurry up and get dressed."

As the boys scamper back upstairs, completely oblivious to the strangeness of leaving home at bedtime, I wonder again just how much fairy glamour is being tossed around here. Claire looks at Beck and Fr. Kevin. "I don't know what I'm supposed to do next? Do I pack? What the hell do I bring? I don't even know how long we'll be away. I'm really out of my league here, gentlemen."

Though I am grateful for the considerate and tender touches the Black Knight and the Prince of *I Idir* are using with my family, my heart is breaking over the trouble I've literally dropped on their doorstep. I know when this whole ordeal is over, I will have a lot to make up for.

"Pack one large bag for all of you. Take a change of clothes for each of you so that you have something clean and fresh to put on before you land. The weather in Wales right now is similar to the East Coast here in the US. Also, include any medications or personal items you feel you can't live without; for example, any stuffed toys or blankets your sons might sleep with, daily vitamins, allergy creams, etc. The sort of stuff that might be harder to replace. If I may add, I would suggest packing your own beach wear and some sun screen. If your sons are anything like my daughter, they'll want to hit the water as soon as you arrive, and sometimes it takes the house a day or two to get your preferences exactly right," Beck offered.

Scott crinkled his forehead. "The house?"

Beckett grinned, and for the first time in a long time, I didn't see the usual "shark teeth" in his mouth. Yes, indeedy. Fairy glamour was working overtime. "The property in Wales is considered a *"Sedd Myrdynn,"* the junior wizard explained. "A Merlin Seat. It's owned by my father and he sometimes spends time there. His personal magic spills over into the building and property. It's the reason you'll be safe there. It's impenetrable to outsiders no matter who attempts to thwart the magic attached to it. Being the Otherworld's 'Number One Wizard' trumps everything else, except, perhaps, for a handful of powerful monarchs, none of whom have any reason to fuss with a Merlin Seat," he joked. "Whatever you need or want, the house will provide it for you, just like that," he said, snapping his fingers.

"Well, hell!" Claire swore. "How are we ever going to explain a "magic" house to our kids?"

"Or keep them from having a 'free for all' with it," her husband added.

"Fr. Kevin can help you with that as well. Like I said earlier, he's great with kids," the Black Knight stated.

"I've got twelve nieces and nephews, plus another one on the way," Fr. Kevin interjected. "I've had plenty of practice with all kinds of weird topics."

"Fr. Kevin will be traveling with you for the first few days and helping you get settled in. He'll show you around and explain how to work with the house. Unfortunately, I'm going to have to ask for your cell phones and tablets while you're gone. Too easy to track. Before you board, Fr. Kevin will give each of you a burner-style phone so you can contact family, but you won't be able to get incoming calls or have use of the internet. Technology and magic just don't mix. If for any reason you need one of us, the house can contact us and let us know to pop in." Beckett paused to let the couple try and make sense of everything crazy he was telling them.

"Why don't you two go and get your one bag ready and check on your boys. As soon as you're ready, Fr. Kevin will drive all of you to Logan to pick up the company jet."

There was no denying that this situation was more than most Mundane folks could handle, but like me, Claire was a Parker girl, and Edmund and *Aine* didn't raise any shrinking violets. "Alright, if this is what we have to do to keep our kids safe, then this is what we'll absolutely do, weird as the whole thing sounds. It shouldn't take us too long to pack that one bag. Can I get anyone anything before I go upstairs? Coffee? Tea, perhaps? Rosie says you guys drink a lot of tea."

"We're fine, Mrs. Kellogg. You go do what you have to do. We'll wait here for you," Beckett says.

Once my sister and her husband are out of hearing distance, Fr. Kevin says, "I'm sorry this tragedy has fallen upon your family, Rosie. They seem like really good people who surely don't deserve to have their life upended this way."

"Thank you, Fr. Kevin, but we all know sometimes the Universe throws boulders in your path. I'm just grateful they'll be safe from my father-in-law's treachery," I said, meaning every word.

"I'll take great care of them," the princely priest vowed. "I bet your nephews will be talking about this trip for the rest of their lives. And don't worry, I'll help your sister and her husband explain that magic is real to Sean and Patrick. You'd be surprised how resilient and logical kids are today."

"I really do appreciate that, Kevin," I reply.

"Aye," my husband chimed in. "House *Nuada* owes you a huge debt of gratitude, ma' Lord. Someday I hope ta' return the favor."

Back to being his usual impatient self, the Black Knight changed the subject. "I hear you and Robyn made some definite progress with that information this afternoon. I look forward to getting caught up."

"I apologize in advance if I sound whiny and ungrateful, Lord Knight, but I've had about all I can handle for one day. I need to go back to *Dun Siorai*, take a very long, very hot shower, and fall into bed. I really hope any discussions regarding the mission info can wait until tomorrow," I pleaded.

"Absolutely. Herself will undoubtedly have to be included, though I need to speak to her before I can designate any logistics. I'm guessing she'll want us to gather at *Crann Bethad*, but I will let you know," my Boss replied.

Great, I think to myself. Another high protocol meeting with the Queen tomorrow. This day just kept rolling on. Sensing the tension in the room, Fr. Kevin spent the next half hour regaling us with amusing stories, mostly at the expense of his brother-in-law, about the time he and Beck first visited the property in Wales, incognito as a newly engaged couple, before the property became a "Merlin Seat" and was still a honeymoon B and B. It was a pretty funny story, making the awkward time in the parlor waiting for my family to come back downstairs fly by quickly. So quickly, that I was surprised when Scott, Claire, and my nephews, trooped downstairs with their single piece of luggage.

"Got everything?" Beck asked. "Passports?"

Scott held them up. "Yup. We only took the passports and our driver's license. No credit cards and very limited cash as you advised."

"Great," the Black Knight said before turning to my nephews. "You boys ready for the biggest adventure ever?" he asked them.

"We sure are, Sheriff. Wait until all my friends at school hear about my prize-winning vacation," Patrick said, and I wondered to myself how the Powers That Be were going to keep those kids from blabbing once they returned home.

Beck shook hands with each member of the family and I

noted how he wrapped his thumb over theirs. Under my feet, I felt the pull of spell energy and I knew the 27th Merlin was warding my family into the magic of the *Sedd Myrdynn*. Afterwards, he handed Scott a file folder.

"What's this," my brother-in-law asked, his eyes widening over the information he was reading.

"It's a scholarship guarantee for both of your sons, from the Queen of *I Idir*. She regrets the interruption to your lives and is very grateful for your loyal cooperation. When the time comes, Patrick and Sean can attend any school or university they have their hearts set on. Full ride, including post graduate work as well."

My stunned brother-in-law put a hand to his forehead in shock. "This is far too generous. Please tell your Queen that though Claire and I very much appreciate her generosity, this is truly not necessary. We fully support Rosie's Fae heritage. Anything that affects Rosie and Declan, affects us as well."

Fr. Kevin and Beck looked at each other and smiled. "I'm afraid neither of us wants to be the one to tell my great grandmother anything she doesn't want to hear. How about we just put this to the side for now, and you can think on it. College is a long way off yet," the Raven Queen's great grandson suggested.

While the three of them discussed the monumental gift for my nephews, Claire turned and hugged me. "You take care while I'm gone, Honey. Don't be getting into any more trouble with Declan's father. I'll call you if I'm able," she said with tears forming in the corners of her eyes. "I love you, Rosie Posie."

"I love you too, Claire." My throat burned with unshed tears. "Be safe."

"We will," she replied. "I think the Sheriff has done everything he can to make that happen." Then, as my big sis headed toward the front door, undoubtedly spell veiled, she turned to me and said, "Strangely enough, Rosie, I've been thinking of Mama a lot over the past few days. Feeling her presence. I wonder what she'd make of all this."

"I think she'd say she was proud of us," I answered, "and that no matter what happens in our lives, we should always love one another."

"I think you're right, Rosie," she agreed.

And then, Claire, the only living family member left who knew me before I ever became Lady *Nuada*, was out the front door and on her way to the safety of Wales. I didn't know when I'd see her again, or how this all would work out. Sitting in that too quiet living room on the night my sister and her family were forced into hiding by Callum Fitzpatrick, I was thinking about our Mama as well. *Aine Fiacail* Parker had been front and center at the beginning of this whole sordid tale, and I knew, sure as my heart was still beating, that my Mama would be at the very end of it as well.

TOOTHLESS 32

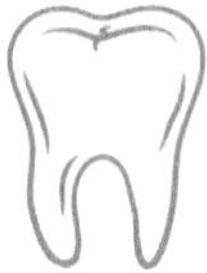

YOU DO WHAT YOU CAN

Going home to my children was a soothing balm to my heavy heart, but even their happy little smiles could do little to douse the burning rage I felt over the injustice done to my sister and her family by one mentally twisted and morally depraved monster of a man. Claire never asked to be the physical image of our deceased mother. Just as I had inherited my tooth fairy heritage through a random mix of DNA, my elder sister was bestowed by the will of the Universe with all the trappings of *Aine* Parker's traditional beauty. Callum Fitzpatrick's crazed obsession with his past love had brought nothing but heartache and suffering to the people who had the misfortune to be drawn up in his circle of madness, and I, for one, had definitely had enough of his cruel interference in our lives.

It was with this anger-fueled mindset that I headed toward *Crann Bethadh*. My worried Eternal Mate did his best to lower my elevated emotions, going so far as to plead with the Black Knight to allow Claire to phone me on her burner once she reached the *Sedd Myrdynn* in Wales. My big sis had sounded calm during our brief conversation, describing how her boys had been filled with excitement when they saw the wide span of private beach that would be theirs to enjoy, and how much Scott was enjoying the "magic" of the house. She didn't, however, mention one word regarding her own feelings about the place, and that spoke volumes to me regarding her continued apprehension.

"Ya' need to put yar'self in the right frame of mind far' this meetin', Rosie Lass. Herself does not hold ta' emotional tirades when the security of har' kingdom is at risk. Surely ya' still remember when Connor Dell was banished ta' Antarctica far' several hours ta' 'cool his temper' after his outburst regardin' the murder of his nephew. She may sympathize with the plight of yar' sister, but it will not keep ya' from a show of displeasure if she believes ya' ar' actin' inappropriately in yar' role."

I understood my husband's preaching was the honest truth, and though I wanted to rail at someone, I was smart enough to realize it couldn't be The Morrigan, goddess of war and destruction. And I can't dump on Declan either. He's already carrying enough shame and sorrow over his sire's actions than one man should have to bear. Universe knows, he suffered terribly at the hands of the North Koreans, and though the physical scars have all faded from his body, minus, of course, the tampering within his brain, there are plenty of nights he still wakes up in a cold sweat over recurring nightmares of the torture he endured. One truth is evident: If I am to be of any help to both my Mundane and Otherworldly families, I need to replace my rage with unshakeable resolve.

Declan and I have been to *Crann Bethadh* enough times in the past several years that the jaw-dropping awe I once had over the Royal Seat of Her Majesty Queen Maeve has waned.

Nor am I impressed when we are met at the hidden back entrance by a contingent of heavily armed troll guards. The oversized tree is home to over one hundred different rooms, so one is never quite sure where you might be taken. Tonight, we are led to the fourteenth floor to a handsome room constructed as a library or study with heavy masculine touches and an impressive collection of antique weaponry upon its walls. It's a room I haven't yet seen before tonight, but it doesn't take me long to guess that it belongs to the Raven Queen's consort, the legendary Celtic warrior, *Cú Chulainn*. The man himself is in attendance next to his queen, the two of them seated in the only single-person seating in the room, though I note few people are sitting.

It is the same group that is usually in attendance at these clandestine gatherings. Doctor Brannigan waves to me from across the room and I wave back, but I notice very little socializing or general chit chat is going on among the somber group, and in a shocking break with Fae tradition, there is no spread of refreshments save for a tray with a single bottle of Dragon's Fire, and a collection of finely etched stemware. When he is sure everyone has arrived, the Black Knight gives an update about the threat against my sister and the plans to keep her secure. He explains that the *Prionsa* of *I Idir* is the contact for that safe house mission and any further questions regarding it should be referred to him.

Beck then called upon Robyn to give a thorough update about our findings regarding the biological samples and documents taken from the terrorist locations. Though the doctor is very complimentary about my help with the research, I am glad that no one asks me to speak. Truthfully, I'm not sure I could have gotten through a neutral report without all my personal vitriol and emotions spilling out.

The tension in the room intensifies as Robyn unwraps more of the horrifying terrorist plot to infect Fae folk with this deadly virus. A few people ask questions, but most of those present have muddy red auras shimmering with rage and fury. The Lord Warrior's current expression is the stuff of nightmares. The Morrigan is the only person in the room showing absolutely no emotion, her aura unreadable, of course. A few times I think I feel her eyes upon me, but there is no voice in my head, no magical presence floating around my brain.

When the doc finishes his presentation, the room was silent except for our Raven Queen. "So, they would have us all dead while they continue their breach of the Veil?" Her dark eyes narrow, and in her expression, there is no denying her standing as the goddess of destruction. "'Tis an affront to the Universe that such wretchedness is able to walk among us." Then she spoke to the doctor. "Is it your belief that you can create a vaccine of your own, Robyn?"

"Recombinant, conjugate, polysaccharide, and inactivated vaccines would all take far too long for us to develop, Your Majesty," Brannigan explained. "At least eighteen months to two years at the very minimum. From our research of the materials brought from the locations in Algeria and Switzerland, I believe the terror groups are much closer to a viable vaccine than we would want, perhaps another month or two. We have no data from the Poland and Spain clinics, so that time line is just an educated guess. Our best bet would be to develop a live-attenuation vaccine similar to their own, though to do it quickly enough we would need to find human hosts who have already been given both the genetic Fae material and the altered *Caliviridea* virus. The test patients would have to be housed in the Mundane world, as they don't carry enough Fae DNA to pass through the Veil and remain alive on this side of it."

The Morrigan thought on it for a moment, then asked the

doctor, "How many live human donors do you think you would need to make your development successful, Robyn?"

"I could probably make do with one hundred donors, Your Majesty. Each virus sample could be replicated in large numbers using 10 to 12 day-old embryonated chicken eggs," Dr. Brannigan replied.

The Queen turned her attention to Beckett. "Do you think you could round up that many human subjects without raising an alarm, Lord Knight?"

"I'm confident we can, Your Majesty. The Algiers and Switzerland locations were large operations. I don't believe every patient that was part of this project was present on the day we took these locations out, and I doubt the locals involved had the resources to leave their homeland. Getting people from the Poland and Spain locations would be more difficult, but altogether, I'm confident we can locate and extract a good majority of them," Beck replied. "However, be aware that if this comes back to us there will undoubtedly be blow back from the countries involved."

The Morrigan waved her hand in a show of indifference. "Nothing that a well-placed bribe can't fix. Most Mundane government leaders don't concern themselves with the disappearance of their teeming masses." Deep in thought for a moment, she remained silent before stating, "Make it so, then, Lord Knight. Round up our virus donors. While they are in our care, they are to be treated with proper consideration. We are not animals like the folk that created this treasonous situation. That being said, whatever you need to proceed with your work, Robyn, is yours for the asking. Set up your lab in a location that is most convenient for you and purchase whatever you need to outfit it to your satisfaction. My Lord Knight will see to your funds."

I am relieved that Herself is going ahead with plans to protect the Fae from the ravages of the disease that killed

Declan's sister, and I am anxious to work with Robyn to help develop that vaccine. Unfortunately, I'm having a difficult time controlling the frustration and rage I feel over Callum Fitzpatrick's continued ability to work in the shadows to wreak havoc on so many innocent lives. It's been nearly seven years since he lured Declan to his near death in North Korea. Seven long years of looking over our shoulders while trying to do what we could to correct the evil deeds he'd left behind. I'd had enough, reaching the point to where every day that man continued to live and breathe was an affront to everything good, and kind and blessed in the Universe.

I also believed myself to be properly shielding all of these thoughts. Thus, I am red-faced embarrassed when Her Majesty looks directly at me and says, "I agree, Lady *Nuada*. I am frustrated as well that our enemy continues to escape our capture. I understand that he's been exceptionally elusive, all the while knowing full well that my hands are tied by sacred law regarding the hunting and killing of a *Tuatha de Danann*. Though the fiend no longer holds the title of Lord, the others within the Ruling Council would be uneasy at my taking the law into my own hands. My Hand of Justice, however, is justifiably allowed to actively stop a threat to the security of *I Idir*, and, with a modicum of sensitivity towards Lord and Lady *Nuada*, execute the traitor on the spot for his crimes against the Kingdom of *I Idir*."

The Morrigan paused to let her words sink in. Next to me, Declan is quiet and still, his head a locked box allowing for no transfer of thoughts between the two of us. "That being said," the Raven Queen continues, "I am told, Black Knight, that you have recently come up with a plan you believe will succeed where all others have failed."

"That is correct, my Queen. Shall I explain the plan of action I believe will be highly successful?" Beckett asked.

"Please do, Lord Knight. No doubt your team is anxious to hear the workings of it," The Morrigan ordered.

That was an understatement. Every eye and ear in the room was turned to the Black Knight, many of whom had their own axe to grind with Callum Fitzpatrick. "To date, our target has been extremely difficult to pin down. Every time we get close, he seems to vanish into thin air just as we make our approach. We believe he is using a combination of *Sidhe* and *Jotun* magic, that as of yet, we've been unable to thwart. Part of the problem is he is gone before we can set up a strong enough snare to entrap him. What we need is a distraction of such large proportions that he won't be tempted toward instant flight mode. It needs to be something that the man won't be able to resist and will allow us enough time to set up a secure hold on him so we can take him in or take him down, depending on the situation. As we mentioned earlier, the target had plans to kidnap Lady *Nuada's* sister, Claire Kellogg, who bears an uncanny resemblance to her late mother, *Aine* Parker, a woman the target believes should have been his true One and Only. This obsession is a sure sign of the man's growing mental instability which we can use to our advantage. His mind-altering desire to forge some kind of Otherworldly relationship with Mrs. Kellogg will undoubtedly keep him distracted long enough to allow for unimpeded action on our part. If *Aine* Parker is who he wants, then we give him *Aine* Parker."

I immediately sense where this is going and see it as a terrible plan. One I absolutely need to shut down, pronto. "With all due respect, Lord Knight, have you lost your ever freaking mind?" I ask, not caring in the least that I'm breaking every ounce of royal protocol. "There is no way in *Dubnos* I will ever allow you to use my totally Mundane, innocent sister as your bait to reel in Callum Fitzpatrick, a man who is already known to have murdered at least two, possibly three, women. You can just forget about this ridiculous idea, Black Knight. It's not gonna' happen. My sister is off limits!"

The Queen's Second looks much too calm to have been offended by my violent outburst, and suddenly, I'm confused and more than a little concerned by his staid emotions. "I agree with you one hundred percent, Rosie," he says, breaking protocol by using my first name rather than my title in such a public forum. "I would never, ever, risk the life of your sister. Under my command, we don't involve innocent civilians in covert intelligence missions. As I said before, if Callum wants *Aine* Parker, we give him the woman he's pined over for so many years. That woman would be you, Lady *Nuada*, taking on the role for us."

TOOTHLESS 33

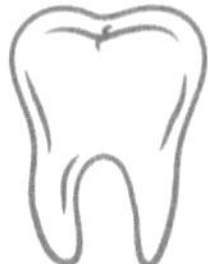

A BITTERSWEET END

BEFORE I CAN EVEN REACT to that ludicrous statement, my Tax Man is up and out of his seat. "With all due respect, Lord Knight, I ken' no sit here and allow ya' to gamble with ma' Lady's life. She is my *Mo Shiorghra*, my Eternal Mate, as well as House *Nuada's* reigning Lady, and therefore allowed certain protections under sacred law. To suggest that she take on the role as yar' baited hook is shocking along with disrespectful."

"I mean no disrespect, Lord *Nuada*. You should know better than most the amount of admiration I hold for the loyalty of your House to The Throne, especially under such difficult circumstances. But Lady *Nuada* is an active member of this intelligence team, duly sworn and professionally trained. Like every other asset, she has the right to turn down a mission she feels she cannot be successful at. Nothing about this mission changes that tenet. If Lady *Nuada* wishes to turn down this commission, it is her right to do so.

But I must hear it directly from the Lady herself, though I would hope she would offer the courtesy of hearing me out before making her decision."

Now, every eye in the room is on me, including my Beloved who is about to go ballistic over holding his tongue. The etched glasses on the tray rattle, along with the glass bowls on the wall sconces, but none of them explode with Declan's fury, proof that he has learned to control his rage magic. What the Black Knight is suggesting is obviously ridiculous. There are one hundred reasons why his plan won't work. "I'm grateful you feel that I can offer service to this important work, Lord Knight. Truly I do. But anyone with eyes in their head can see I look nothing like my mother or older sister. Without doubt, no intelligent person would be fooled into thinking I was either of them, especially not my Lord's sire who, for a handful of years, has had almost daily contact with me. Therefore, I'm assuming you are planning on using some type of glamour spell to help me take on that visage, a plan that is doomed to failure because even after sundown, I can't hold 'glamour' for even a handful of minutes."

I'm sure this is not what my Eternal Mate wants to hear from me. I have little doubt Declan wants me to flat out tell the Black Knight "thanks but no thanks." On the other hand, Ole' Mr. Shark Teeth has immediately picked up on my wavering, so he continues his big sell. "We perfectly understand that, Lady *Nuada*. In this case, we wouldn't use a regular glamour spell. Given the target's current magical abilities, he would instantly pick up on any simple *Sidhe* attempt to hide your true identity. If we decide to go ahead with this plan, it would require you to work one on one with Her Majesty and our Merlin to provide you with a cover realistic enough to fool your father-in-law."

The fact that Beck mentions both Herself and his own father tells me that this whole thing has already been discussed and decided upon. Sure. I could say no and they would begrudgingly accept it. But where would that leave my sister and her family? They can't hide in Wales forever. Their lives are in Swampscott, and even if they did eventually come home, how long would it be before Callum Fitzpatrick tried again? And what about *Oisin*? The truth that he's been the one behind the mysterious raven-gram and letter tells me that he is not completely under his evil father's direction and could possibly want to return home. In my eyes, he's still a child. Part of our family. How could I say no to a chance of freeing him from the clutches of that crazy villain?" I am at a loss for words. It's a crazy plan. That much is true. But might it actually work?

"Even if ya' could help ma' Lady manage the subterfuge, ya' have given no direction as ta' how ya' plan on keepin' ma' Eternal Mate safe while ya' take ma' sire inta' custody," Declan protests.

"Do you really think I would have presented this to the team if I didn't have all aspects of it worked out? C'mon, Fitz. We've done at least fifty top-level missions together. You know how I operate. There's a way of adding a veiling spell on the members of her security team to Rosie's enchantment. Not in my bag of tricks, but one Her Majesty believes you yourself are more than capable of holding. I'd make you squad leader and Duncan your point man. You'd call the shots. If at any time you think your Lady is in danger, you say it and we'll extract her in less than a blink of an eye."

"As much as I want to see Callum Fitzpatrick apprehended," I say before someone speaks for me, "I'll need some time to think this over. Get the nitty gritty details on what's actually involved and what risks I might be taking. I owe it to my

Mo Shirghra and my children to know exactly what I'm getting myself into and how it will affect them before I can give you a definitive answer."

"You make perfect sense, Lady *Nuada*. A wise soul doesn't rush into anything without having all the facts," the Queen states. "The three of us shall meet together; you, Ambrose and myself to discuss this grand adventure you will be undertaking, without the loud input of my opinionated Knight or your worried mate. 'Tis the best way to handle this," she says before up and disappearing

* * *

My husband is angry. Not necessarily at me. Just in general. I know this already because of the Bond between us, but even if we didn't share this intimate form of communication, I'd still be aware by the firm set of his jaw, the curt responses to any and all comments, and the obviously stiff body language, as if he were walking around with a stick up his ass.

I am not much looking forward to a near silent carriage ride back to *Dun Siorai* with Cranky Declan, and that's even before Robyn Brannigan asks if he can ride with us. The Doc has no reason to head back to our estate, so warning bells go off in my head over what's behind this usual request. If he intends to try and plead the case of either my husband or the Black Knight regarding the planned mission that involves me, then I wish I had the nerve to tell him I just wasn't interested in any more debates tonight. My Tax Man doesn't seem thrilled with the man's request either, but general politeness doesn't let him turn the doctor down, so the three of us set off for our Otherworldly home.

Any assumptions regarding Robyn's odd request go right out the carriage window when he states, "I have the results from the blood we drew the other day. I thought this ride would give me an opportunity to share them with you while I have you both together. Dr. Parker, I realize you may not feel my including your husband in this discussion is the most professional way to go about it, but in this case, I think it's for the best as what I have to share involves you both. However, if you prefer, you and I can meet alone when we arrive at *Dun Sorai*."

My heart just about stops in my chest. There's no way I can stand the suspense of waiting. Next to me on the carriage bench, Declan grabs my hand and squeezes it, any feelings of annoyance he might have harbored evaporating like rain on a hot summer day. "No. It's okay for you to speak to both of us at the same time. What's going on, Doc?" I ask, trying to get a take on his body language. Does he seem upset? Relieved? He's a difficult person to read, keeping his feelings close to the vest.

He opens the file folder he's holding on his lap, and hands it to me. "I'm happy to tell you that your white blood cell count is perfectly normal. I see no indication that you're suffering from the onset of 'Wasting DIsease.' Your metabolic panel numbers look fine as well. No anemia that I can see."

Relief fills every cell in my body. I don't have wasting disease like my mother. I'm not going to be gone from this life before my children grow up. Declan reaches out and shakes Robyn's hand. "I ken' no tell ya' how much I appreciate you lettin' us know, Robyn. 'Tis the best news ever."

Another thought comes to my mind. "So, why am I feeling like this, Doc?"

"As you suspected, Dr. Parker, your estrogen levels are very low. Lower than what is the accepted norm for peri-menopause, but not quite in the menopausal stage. It's most likely the reason for your symptoms; the night sweats, poor sleep habits, thinning hair, and such."

"I see," I mumble, watching the door close on my child-bearing years. My case is not uncommon. Fae women go into menopause earlier than their Mundane counterparts, and I was nearly forty. "Well, it's not like I wasn't half expecting this, Dr. Brannigan. But you have put my mind at rest about something entirely more serious. I appreciate that."

"I understand that the two of you were hoping for another baby. While I would say it's not impossible, the Universe having a mind of its own, from a medical view point, I think it's not very likely," he says with a flicker of sympathy in his eyes. "That's actually the reason I wanted to speak to you both. Because you have added the Eternal aspect to your bond, should something happen to you Dr. Parker, Fitz would have to undertake the *Bás Beo*, as we've recently seen happen to Lord *Mac Badh*. But there is a caveat in the contract that allows for the negation of that codicil once the women in the Bond reaches crone status. There's some paperwork I need to fill out and certify, and the Queen, as well as the two of you, must sign off on it, but I don't see Herself denying your request. Plus, it's all done very quietly and privately, so it's no one's business but your own." He stops a moment before adding, "I just felt with everything going on, these being difficult times and all, you might want to guarantee that your children are never left without the guardianship of at least one of their parents."

Declan brings the hand he's holding up to his mouth to kiss it, then asks, "What do ya' think, Rosie Lass. Is this somethin' ya' wish us ta' pursue?"

In my head, I see *Cillian* at Meghan's cremation, his eyes, dark and dead, his once auburn hair the color of old pewter. I consider Lord and Lady *Badh*, cheated out of the presence of their eldest son in their lives, and finally I think about little *Féchín* growing up without the love of either his *athair* or his *mathair*.

"Of course, we'll go ahead with the necessary paperwork,

Dr. Brannigan," I say, my voice only hitching with emotion one time. "I truly appreciate your handling this for us. I think, as you've said, in these dangerous times we're all living in, it's the wisest course of action." And with that said, in the dark of a moonless night, I move onward in my sacred life cycle from Maiden, to Mother, and now to Crone.

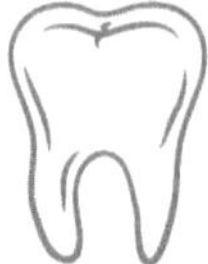

LET'S NOT PRETEND

ONCE BACK AT *DUN SIORAI* , Declan and I celebrate, in the very best way, the wonderful news that we are alive and in love, and that I don't have the dreaded Fae "Wasting Disease." Afterwards, I cry in his arms over all the beautiful babies we'll never have together. My beloved Tax Man lets me shed every last tear before gently telling me his feelings on the subject.

"I understand, more than anyone, yar' deep feelins' on the subject, *Rós mo Chroí* (Ros of my Heart). I also felt the little stab of sadness in ma' heart over Robyn's news. I love the sound of our children happily runnin' through the halls of *Dun Siorai*. Their laughter fills ma' par' weary heart with such gladness I ken' no describe it ta' ya' with the right words. 'Twad have been a generous blessin' ta' have yet another, perhaps a wee *iníon* (daughter) with yar' lovely eyes and perfect smile. But if it is no to be, then I accept the news with much gratitude towards the Universe far' blessin' us as it has. Yar' lookin' at a man who, at one time not too long ago in the past, thought he'd never find his One and Only and who could not have imagined bringing three healthy children to the line of his House. I ken' no stay sad when I have been given mar' gifts in this lifetime than I cad' ever deserve.

That is not ta' say ya' should gage yar' own feelins' on ma' timeline, Love. Ya' take as long as ya' need ta' come ta' terms with this new role in yar' life cycle. I will do ma' vera' best ta' support and comfort ya'. And if ya' wish ta' hold off adding that new codicil ta' our Eternal Bond, then we shall wait as long as necessary."

"Oh no, Sweetie!" I say, as I pull away to wipe my eyes and blow my nose. "We need to get that done sooner than later. I'm not risking going into the Afterlife and leaving you to wander alone until the Universe decides you should join me. If the unthinkable happens, I want to go knowing our children still have you in their lives. No. We can't put something this important on the back burner. We need to get this sorted out as soon as possible."

He must sense something in my tone, or perhaps I'm not shielding my thoughts from him. The Bond makes keeping secrets a full-time job and frankly, I'm not up to such heavy-duty mental activity in the wee hours of the morning. "So, you have decided against all better judgement ta' accept this ridiculously dangerous mission Beck has put together," he complains, his mouth turning down into a fierce frown.

"I haven't decided anything yet, Declan. I want to keep an open mind until I get all the facts. You know darn well that there's no way I can refuse a private meeting ordered by Herself. At the least, I will have to go and hear them out," I rationalized.

"Ya' know she will just bully ya' into her way of thinking using subtle threats and a great deal of guilt," my husband replied. "It is how she has managed to keep her Throne all these years. I admire what she has done far' the people of *I*

Idir, but she is first and foremost the goddess of war and destruction and an empathetic monarch second. She does not play by the same rules as the rest of us."

"I'm well aware, Sweetie. She's been in my head for years since she helped pull you out of North Korea. I know perfectly well what she's capable of. She is the ultimate puppet master of the people around her. I get that. But surely you understand better than anyone else that we can't continue on this same path. For too long, we have allowed your father to travel both worlds spreading his evil any way he pleases with no repercussions. Too many poor souls have suffered because of that man, and it's time to finally put an end to his reign of terror. If I can help stop him, how can I possibly say no? You're the one always preaching that we must follow the path the Universe has laid out for each of us. What if this is my path, Declan? The one I'm called to walk."

He lies down on his back and closes his eyes, not speaking for the longest time. So long that I wonder if he hasn't gone ahead and fallen asleep. After several minutes, he turns over to face me with eyes dark and troubled. "I am afraid, Rosie Love. Vera' afraid that if something happens ta' take ya' out of ma' life, I will be unable ta' continue on ma' path without ya'. Either with the *Bás Beo* or without. It would make no difference. Ya' would still be lost ta' me and I would be totally alone, much like the Ritual years that came befar' I met ya'. I accept the burden that by tellin' ya' all this that ya' might be disgusted, thinkin' that yar' One and Only was nothing but a weak coward, and maybe that is exactly what I am. But the truth is, even with yar' disappointment in ma' lack of courage, I would still hope that ya' wad' not take on this challenge, ma' sire be damned, if there be any chance of a life without ya'.

However, yar' correct. I have always been a believer in the Old Ways and it seems vera' wrong of me ta' now disregard ma' faith because I might have ta' face the unthinkable. That is worse than being a coward. Therefore, if like ya' have said, that this be the path you must walk, then we will walk it together until the day comes when the Universe make the decree that we should no longer share the same road. This I say and this I believe. Mote it be."

TOOTHLESS 35

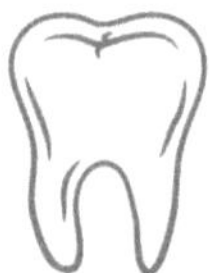

THE WEIRD STUFF GETS STRANGER

I ATTEND the ordered meeting with Her Majesty and our Merlin believing I know exactly what I am getting myself into. After all, I had already negotiated a deal with The Morrigan and lived to tell about it with my sanity still intact. I assumed that this time I would also be able to handle whatever type of ancient *Sidhe* and wizard magic my two superiors planned on throwing my way. Sadly, like most of my assumptions, I was dead wrong. Okay. Maybe "dead" is the wrong word to use in cases like this. Manifestation and all that. Still, my preconceived notions of what I might expect didn't hold a candle to the reality of the whole situation.

Despite his promise to support my decision regarding undertaking this mission, my beloved Tax Man argued up to the very last minute about partaking in this meeting completely on my own. He petitioned the Black Knight using several tenets of *I Idirian* law which supposedly stated that my mate had the right to accompany me. His legal attempts fell on deaf ears. According to the Black Knight, who himself had a legal background in the Mundane world and was a leading authority on the Otherworldly kingdom's sacred and civil laws, in this particular case, Herself had declared the right of *Riail na Banríona* (the Queen's Rule), overruling any objections on her word alone, much in the same manner Declan had overruled Duncan's parent's request to stop him from marrying Mel. Truth be told, Beck wasn't very happy either about being kept out of the loop and was quite testy about the whole discussion.

I will admit the Queen's dictate about meeting me alone scared the shit out of me. Herself was going to an awful lot of trouble to keep me away from the influence of others and that caused all kinds of red flags to pop up in my mind about what I was actually getting myself into.

I was met at *Crann Bethadh's* secret back entrance not by troll guards, but by the Merlin himself, Ambrose Myrdynn, who had always been pleasant enough towards me. "Good day, Lady *Nuada*. I am so pleased that you've decided to join Her Majesty and I today. I believe what we propose will be very intriguing to you." The entryway seemingly disappeared as we walked through it, turning back to what I could swear was a solid wall. The wizard led me to an elevator located further down a narrow hall. Once we stepped inside, there were no buttons to push, the lift moving on its own, and because the ride was longer than previous ones I had taken, I guessed that we were traveling to the upper boughs of the gigantic oak.

When the doors opened up, Ambrose let me alight first, but two steps forward, I immediately stopped, my eyes and brain trying to make sense of what I was seeing. The elevator doors had opened directly into a room that didn't seem to have any…well…walls. Or glass windows. Or anything to determine the size or the shape of the physical space within. Instead of the bright light of sunshine I had just left outside my carriage, I was surrounded by a cavalcade of shifting colors in a sea of inky black, bands of purple, green, red and gold moving in what seemed to be a rhythmic pattern. I tried to look away because the movement was making me dizzy and more than a little disorientated, but as hard as I tried, I couldn't keep my eyes from following those color bands.

"Take your time, dear Lady. Breathe normally. This place does take a while to get used to," the Merlin said.

"Where in the world are we?" I ask. "Are we still inside *Crann Bethadh?*"

The Merlin smiled in a gentle way. "Yes and no. We are everywhere and nowhere. Don't try so hard to understand it. Relax and try to be in the moment."

"I know you're only trying to help, Lord Merlin, but when you say crazy things like that, relaxing seems out of the question," I comment.

"You're probably right about that, Rosie," he says, switching to my given name instead of my title. "You go ahead and mentally process this place any way you can. Just know you are completely safe here. No harm will come to you. This is The Morrigan's personal space. Not the Queen who sits on the very real Throne of *I Idir*, but the goddess whose magic we'll need if we are to succeed in our plan without causing unnecessary death and destruction. 'Tis a very special magical space you stand in, one created long before either the Mundane or the Otherworld."

I felt like my knees were turning to jelly and I started to sway. I noticed a thick, comfortable arm chair suddenly appearing out of air while the Merlin took my arm and helped me to settle myself down. He handed me a tea cup and saucer. "Have a few sips of this, dear Lady. It will help with the vertigo."

I do as he asks because the movement is starting to make me queasy. The tea tastes of black licorice and rose hip and after a few mouthfuls I begin to feel less "ungrounded," for lack of a better word. I find that I am able to take my focus off of the moving color bands and it helps settle my stomach. As expected, I have a million questions, but somehow, I can't seem to make the words go from my brain to my mouth. I'm not sure how long I just sit there, sipping my tea while trying to put words into some kind of sensible order, but when I look up from my tea cup, The Morrigan is standing in front of me, dressed completely in black with raven feathers trailing down her gown.

"So, you have found your courage, little tooth fairy mama. I knew you would. If only *Aine* had done as much, we might not find ourselves on this particular path. Time and hearts always move as they like, though in this case we must push time along at a quicker pace. Too many lives are in jeopardy to let nature take its course. Has our Merlin explained to you where you are?" the Raven asked.

"A bit, Your Majesty. He told me this is your goddess space. I'm not sure what exactly that means, but I believe it's entirely different from your home at *Crann Bethadh*."

"Aye. That it is. The magical energy we will need for your transformation requires more than I can gather in the sacred oak of *I Idir*. Here in my goddess space, my magical gifts exceed the bounds of the Otherworld. Do you understand what I'm telling you, little rose?"

"I think so, Your Majesty." I stammered.

"Good. I will try and explain what I must do to make you a convincing double of your *mathair*. You share DNA with both your sister and your late mother. I will manipulate those strands so that they will overwhelm the ones that make you 'Rosalinda.' It is not especially painful, but you may feel your bones shifting, much like your mate feels when he shifts into his fox form."

"I don't mean to contradict you, Your Majesty, but his

Lordship has told me on multiple occasions that his shifting is more than a bit uncomfortable. I want to be completely honest with you. When it comes to things that hurt, I'm rather a big baby."

The Morrigan smiled. "You have birthed three children, little tooth fairy. I think you underestimate your endurance of pain, but we can try to manipulate your reaction to it as much as possible. Magic always requires something in return, you understand. Now, I would like to start the process if you're willing to take this duty upon your shoulders. Not only for the kingdom, but for the ones you love the most. Callum Fitzpatrick will not stop in his attempts to change his unrighteous path. We must take him off of it, once and for all. Do you have any other questions, little rose?"

"Just one. How long will I look like my sister?" I ask, wondering if her image will linger like The Morrigan did in my head. To my mind, that would be super creepy.

"The spell has a limit of 3 rotations around the sun. 86 hours in Otherworldly time, 72 hours in Mundane time. It will leave us with a very small window to do what we must do. Once the spell dissolves, you will return to the physical form you now possess. Ambrose is here to see to your safety and comfort, as well as your mental clarity. No one is better in that role than a pure Merlin Druid." Then, the goddess of war and destruction put out her hand for me to take. "Come, child. Let us change the course of destiny together."

TOOTHLESS 36

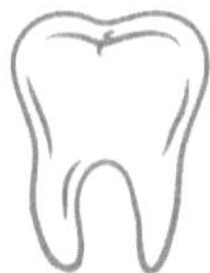

WALKING INTO DANGER

WHEN CONSCIOUSNESS finally returned to my brain, I found myself lying in my Salem bedroom, dressed in my tatty, old bathrobe with several concerned faces swimming fuzzily above me. "Rosie, Love, how are ya' feelin'?" I recognized the voice as belonging to my beloved Tax Man, but I couldn't seem to focus my eyes well enough to look directly at the face attached to the sounds.

"Weird," I said. "I feel all woozy and discombobulated, as if I'm seeing, hearing and thinking through a fog. Wait. Am I in Salem?" I asked, noticing the space around me and thoroughly confused as to why I'm here and not in the Otherworld.

"Aye. After yar' transformation, we brought ya' back here. We thought ya' would be able to recover more comfortably," Declan said, then quickly added, "plus, we obviously couldn't return ya' ta' *Dun Siorai*. Not lookin' the way ya' do."

I blink over and over again trying to bring the world into focus. "Mirror," I reply. I need a mirror."

"Give yar'self a few minutes to wake more fully, Love. Then we will answer all yar' concerns," my husband says.

"No. Not later. Now," I argue. "I need to see."

There is a flurry of voices in the background discussing my request, but finally, Declan hands me the small hand mirror from my dressing table. I struggle a bit with holding the glass up in front of my face, my arm feeling all floppy and out of control. My Eternal Mate offers to help keep the mirror steady, but I ignore him. Instead, I bring the mirror as close to my face as I dare, not wanting to bop myself in the nose with it. Then, I focus my eyes on the reflection. "Oh feckin' hell," I blurted out, a favorite obscenity I've picked up from my husband over the years.

The face looking back at me in the mirror is not the one I saw this morning as I dressed for my meeting with Herself. It's my mother's face staring back at me, looking as she did from my earliest recollections. This *Aine* is young, vibrant and beautiful with her heart-shaped face, long lashes, rose bud mouth, and captivating dimples. I can see bits of my sister in this face, but it's mainly my mother's reflection, returned from the dead and appearing years younger than my mind remembered.

"Shit," I mumble. It's the best I can do at the moment, overwhelmed as I feel. As my clarity returns, I notice for the first time the IV in my left hand. "What's this about?" I ask as I raise that arm off the bed.

"It's just some saline, dextrose and electrolytes, Dr. Parker," Robyn Brannigan answered from somewhere in the background. "Just to keep you hydrated. We weren't sure how long you'd be unconscious."

"Just how long have I been out of it?" I question.

"About seven hours," the Doc replied. "All things considered it wasn't very long at all."

That's easy for Robyn to say. He's not the one that just

lost seven hours of his life, I think to myself. "So, I assume Her Majesty's magic went as planned?"

This time, it was the Merlin who answered me. "'Twas very much a success, Lady *Nuada*. You handled everything better than we could have hoped. Her Majesty sends her appreciation for your loyal service to the kingdom and relays that she will speak with you when your mission is completed."

I try to recall any of what preceded this drastic change in my appearance, yet everything that happened after I stepped out of the carriage is a blur. I hope my lack of memory regarding the experience is a temporary thing due to the magic involved. I sure as hell wouldn't like to think that I've permanently lost chunks of time.

"What happens now?" I ask

"As soon as you feel up to it, Rosie, we'll get started. As you may be aware, there's a limited amount of time attached to this spell and a slew of logistics to put in place beforehand; 72 hours of which we now have about 60 left. Not to rush you or anything," says the Black Knight's voice from somewhere in the background. Buttons to banjos! How many people are in this space? My bedroom has become Grand Central Station!

"I need details," I argue. "How is this going down?"

"We can catch you up when you're feeling better," the Black Knight answered. "Just concentrate on your physical and mental well-being right now.

"Not good enough," I counter. "I don't like 'surprises.' My husband can attest to that. I like to know in advance exactly what's coming down the road so I can properly prepare myself. It's how I function. I'll need you to explain things now."

There's more quiet murmuring amongst my uninvited guests. Finally, Beck's face comes into view hovering over me. "When you are ready, we'll move you to your sister's home in Swampscott. Ambrose is capable of physically moving the two of you in the Mundane dimension, but the rest of us will have to jump back to *I Idir*, and then to your sister's house. We have reliable intel that the house is being watched, so there's no going in or out the physical entrances. Once we're all assembled, we'll glamourize four of our team members to appear as your sister, her husband, and the two children. It will look to anyone watching that your brother-in-law and the two boys are going on a fishing trip, something they've been known to do in the past. It will seem to the observer that your sister is home alone. We believe this information will be easily relayed to the target. If all goes as planned, we expect the target to attempt his abduction. When he does, we'll be ready for him."

"So, what do I do during all of this?" I ask.

"Your job is to act the part. Be Claire. Be your mother. We were concerned that your voice would give you away, but Herself has given us information on how to circumvent that problem with a very simple house spell. When you speak, the house will automatically match the voice to the face. Unfortunately, none of us can tell you exactly how the confrontation will go down. The target has shown himself to be highly unstable, both mentally and emotionally. That's where your skill comes in, Rosie. You're terrific at thinking on your feet, so we're very confident you can play along with whatever scenario is presented. However, I want you to know that no matter how this plays out, our first priority is your safety. If anything feels wrong, we will instantly extract you to a safe location. You have my word on that," the Black Knight explained.

"I appreciate that. Overall, it sounds like a pretty solid plan," I replied.

There was a slight pause from the Black Knight, which

I've come to learn over the years, means there's more to come. Something I won't particularly like. And as sure as the sun sets in the west, he adds, "There's one more thing you need to know, Rosie. We have positive identification that the person that has been watching your sister's house is Fitz's half-brother, *Oisin*. Truthfully, we currently aren't absolutely sure which side he's playing for. He sometimes proves helpful, but we can't get a solid lock on what role he might have in this abduction. That's a red flag as far as I'm concerned. We aren't even sure if he'll enter the house with the target, or stay completely out of this interaction. I just wanted to give you the head's up on that, because if he attempts to cause any harm, we'll have to neutralize the threat."

Neutralize? What the hell did that mean? The kid was barely sixteen years old. "I know you'll think my opinion is slanted, but I believe he's trying to help us. He sent us those locations and it's only because he warned me about the danger that Claire was in that we even have this opportunity. It wouldn't make sense for him to do all these things if he wasn't on our side," I argued.

The men in the room all look at each other in that condescending, patriarchal way I can't stand. As if I'm just talking silly, female nonsense. They all eyeball my husband. Apparently, he's been the one chosen to publicly contradict me. "I want ta' believe that theory as much as you, Rosie Love. It is painful far' me ta' believe ma' own brother, the boy I think of as blood family, would betray us. But Beck is right. We have ta' prepare for a variety of outcomes. All of this…help from the boy cad' be a trap. Or, it could be that perhaps like our sire, he's lost his soul spiritually and magically. We need ta' consider those possibilities."

"I think you're all being ridiculous. You can't deny that every bit of the information *Oisin* sent us turned out to be helpful. You were able to take down the Algiers and Switzerland locations without them knowing in advance you were coming. There's no way that would be possible if it always was meant to be a trap. That would make no sense at all. But hey, what do I know? I'm only your feminine bait, right." I swung my legs over the side of the bed, careful how I did it because I have an audience and I'm pretty sure I wasn't wearing anything underneath this robe. The thought made me consider something else. "How did I come to be wearing this?" I asked. "And what happened to the clothes I was wearing when I went to *Crann Bethadh?*"

No one answers me, a sign that I probably don't want to know and no one wants to tell me. "Whatever," I answered with more vitriol than I should probably use as a lower ranking team member. I was an asset of Her Majesty's Intelligence Organization. This is a mission I fully accepted on my own. My modesty or my missing garments shouldn't matter when so many lives were at stake. "I believe, gentlemen, that it's time to get this damn show on the road. I need a long, hot shower, a change of clothes and then we can go."

* * *

In truth, it's not the shower I need, but the privacy. Although I've already had a quick look at my new "face" when Declan handed me the mirror, I'm guessing by the way my favorite cozy bathrobe is hanging on me that my face wasn't the only thing that has changed. Initially, I made sure my back was turned toward the mirror when I walked into the bathroom suite so the first thing I saw when I entered wasn't my reflection in the large mirror that hangs over our double sinks. I needed to do this in my own sweet time. At my own pace.

Honestly, I'm wasn't sure what it was that I was afraid of seeing. The whole idea of this plan was based on the necessity that I would look like my late mother and my elder sister in order to fool Declan's father. I knew this going into this mission. But knowing and actually seeing are two entirely different things. Seeing a different face in that tiny hand mirror had been hard enough. But now, in the quiet privacy of my bathroom suite, there was no hiding the fact that, appearance wise, Rosie Parker was gone, replaced by a magical, AI-style duplication of two people who meant the world to me.

Slowly, I turned around so that my whole body was now visible in the mirror and slid the bathrobe off my shoulders. I choked back a sob, sticking my fist into my mouth to stifle the sound. It wouldn't do to let the others hear my emotions get the better of me, especially my Eternal Mate who would surely call the whole thing off, then and there, to save me the emotional distress. That wasn't what I wanted. I gave my word I'd go through with this, and I was determined to do so.

It wasn't that the body reflected back at me was in any way terrible. It was, in fact, perfect, especially when judged against both Mundane and Fae standards of traditional beauty. I was now thin and lithe with an actual waistline for the first time in forever. I had the tiny B-cup, perky breasts I'd always envied in my sister, and collar bones that stuck out in an aesthetically pleasing way. My neck was long and swan like, my hips narrow, and my legs long and shapely. It was the body I had desired for most of my life; the body that for so long I'd anguished over, dieted and exercised trying to achieve, all the while punishing myself mentally when I didn't meet culture's fashion standards.

All the curves my Tax Man swore over and over again he loved were gone, along with the stretch marks and belly pouf that were the earned badges of three amazing children. I finally had the body of my dreams but it wasn't the one that truly belonged to Rosie Parker Fitzpatrick, and I never wanted anything more than to have that old one back.

TOOTHLESS 37

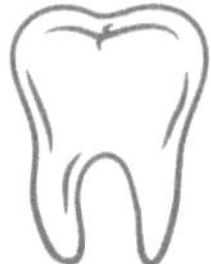

BECOMING CLAIRE

WHEN I LEAVE the comfort of my shower, I see three different outfits hanging on the towel warming bar. I don't recognize any of them but assume they have come from my sister's closet. Underneath the clothes is a complete set of teeny-tiny, lacy undergarments, making me wonder how Claire would feel about strangers poking around in her things. I tell myself that my big sis would be one hundred percent okay with it all if it meant she could finally have this whole damn nightmare behind her.

I slide on the bra and panties; a wispy little set in a melon color I'd never choose as a red-head, in a size I can't ever remember wearing. It's while I'm putting on my big sister's undies that I notice it for the first time; a small dark smudge on my lower back, a few inches above my sacrum. I back up closer to the mirror, thinking what I'm seeing is some kind of bad bruise. That's when I can tell that my so-called bruise has a definite shape. It takes a lot of angling and body maneuvers with the hand mirror before I see clearly that the smudge is body ink in the shape of a bird. More specifically, a raven.

For a second, panic sets in, my heart racing. Magical ink is always considered permanent. Does having this mark mean that I am now forever tied to The Morrigan? It took over five years before traces of Herself evaporated from my head. What does wearing her ink mean to my life going forward? Am I some kind of blood slave now? A female Renfield to the goddess of war and destruction?

"Calm yourself down, Rosie," I think to myself. *"You're letting your imagination run away with you. Maybe it was just some ritual magic required for the spell. Most likely it will fade in 72 hours just like Claire's face and body. You need to focus on the mission ahead. People are counting on you. This new ink dilemma has to go on the mental back burner until Callum Fitzpatrick is safely in custody.*

I turn my attention back to the process of dressing in my "costume." I'm not sure who selected these pieces, but all of them are reflective of my sister's contemporary fashion style. I eyeball each outfit and eventually decide on pale gray, form-fitting pants and a blue pin-stripe linen shirt that I tie up at the waist, something I've seen my sister do countless times. The outfit shows off a fit and trim, athletic body; flat tummy, toned calves and shapely, little breasts. The effect is startling. I can almost believe that even my Eternal Mate would be fooled into thinking I was my sister if he wasn't privy to the truth. I add a little color to my cheeks and lips from a selection in my sister's make-up bag, then comb my shoulder-length, strawberry blonde hair into a bouncy ponytail at the back of my head, Claire Kellogg style.

Taking a deep breath, I leave the bathroom and present myself to my fellow team members. I am greeted with absolute silence, causing me to ask, "Okay, what's wrong. Do I not look convincing enough? I can try a different outfit if you think it would help."

"'Tis just the opposite, Lass. Ya' look so much like yar' beloved sister that it's…remarkable. If I didna' know it was really you who went into the bathroom, I'd think Claire had suddenly materialized here in Salem. The resemblance is uncanny. I didna' know yar' *mathair*, but from the pictures ya' have shared with me, 'tis no wonder ma' sire was obsessed with yar' sister the moment he saw her at our Mundane wedding. They look vera' much alike."

"Herself's magic is clearly wondrous," Duncan adds. "Ya' look a whole different person, Cousin Rosie. 'Tis so much better…mar' realistic than a common Fae glamour spell. I know in my soul this plan will work."

"If it does, then this will all be worth it, Duncan," I reply. Turning to the Black Knight, who as of yet hadn't said a word, I ask, "Will this do, Boss?"

"You look the part of a perfect undercover asset, Rosie," the Black Knight replies. "Unless the target has somehow gotten more magically powerful than Herself, which I highly doubt, he will be totally convinced that you are your sister, some type of birthed reincarnation of the woman he lost years ago. Well done, Lady *Nuada*."

"I appreciate everyone's confidence. If you're all ready to go, then let's get to it," I say with more bravado than I actually feel. Though I may look the part, I wonder if I have the acting skills needed to convince that evil bastard father-in-law of mine that I'm truly his beloved *Aine*.

Now that I am ready, everyone except the 26th Merlin and I jump back to the Otherworld. Because of the physics of the Mundane world, almost all Fae are unable to transport magically within the boundaries of the human dimension. They are forced to use the same forms of transportations as their counterparts while in the Mundane world. Tooth fairies, all members of House *Ficail*, are the only folk of the Otherworld who can jump from one Mundane location to another, and only after sunset. It's why they have the job of collecting teeth that they do. With this in mind, I've always believed the reason the other *Sidhe* looked down on tooth fairies had more to do with their jealousy over we "lowly Fae" having this transporting ability than with any so-called bloodline nonsense. After all, many of them, like my husband, had a strong dose of human DNA which gave them the capability to easily cross back and forth while existing safely in the Mundane world. I can't fathom any other reason for their long-held animosity towards the tooth fairies.

With the rest of the team gone, the Merlin drew a chalk circle around us. "Before we leave Lady *Nuada,*I just want to tell you how honored I am to be part of this very important mission, and how confident I am of your success," Ambrose said. "Despite everything thrown your way over these past years, you have proved yourself to be a woman of courage and honor. I have seen no other tooth fairy in my lifetime walk her path as spiritually committed as you have walked yours. *I Idir* is better because of you and I know I speak for the goddess as well when I say this. The Morrigan believes in you, dear Lady, and that is no small thing. She is very selective about who she allows in her tight inner circle."

I know better than to share that I could have lived my life quite happily without the notice of the goddess of war and destruction, thank you very much. Maybe someday I'll have a different perspective, but it won't be today. "I appreciate your kind comments, Lord Merlin. And the Queen's…benevolence toward me. Though I will admit it's a little overwhelming."

"That it is, dear Lady. The Raven Queen is a force you can never take for granted." The wizard took my hands in his. "If you are ready, I will move us both to Swampscott now."

"Ready as I'll ever be," I think to myself. "I'm good, my Lord. We can move."

* * *

Jumping locations within the Mundane world provides a different physical reaction in me then it does when crossing through the Veil, similar to the way riding a bike feels different than riding a motorcycle. Both modes of transportation have two wheels and while you can certainly feel forward motion in both, the energy behind the magic in a Veil jump vibrates at a much higher frequency than a local jump. In my position as a tooth fairy, I've jumped locations more than a thousand times. The East Coast headquarters for the Tooth Fairy Corps is actually located in Boston, with satellite offices in New York, Philadelphia, and Annapolis. I've jumped to all of them, especially these past few years in my role as a supervisor. In addition, there have been the countless visits to human homes that I've been sent to for the retrieval of baby teeth. Those inter-dimensional moves, even when they are miles apart, are usually over in a blink of an eye with the only noticeable sensation being a slight buzzing sound that seems to focus on the inner ear.

On the other hand, a jump through the Veil into the Otherworld on my own always reminds me of being on a motorcycle; I can feel every vibration from my feet on upward, with a whistling sound and a loud "pop" at the very end. When I travel with Declan, his far superior magical skills make it feel more like I'm flying through clouds; I can feel the momentum along with the sensation of wind on my face, while the popping sound at the end is less pronounced. Jumping locally with the Otherworld's current Merlin, however, is best described as a hiccup. There is a minor spasm in my diaphragm, and, before I can register anything else, POOF, I'm standing in the middle of Claire's living room four and a half miles away.

There's a lot of activity going on, both magical and tactical; sigils and what looks like a Solomon's Key drawn under my sister's large Oriental rug, black salt sprinkled underneath as well, and small round malachite pieces hidden around the room in certain obscure places to create an invisible pentagram. "Won't my father-in-law be able to sense all this warding?" I ask Ambrose.

"I believe I will be able to veil the wards as well as the team's presence and then immediately drop the spell when we have him in position," the wizard explains. "He won't be aware of any of it."

"That's a pretty neat trick," I tease.

"It does come in handy for this line of work," the Merlin laughed. "Though in all seriousness, dear Lady, if there is any sign of threat towards your person, I will move you myself directly to *Crann Bethadh*. It is the safest location, as we believe that despite his increased skill, Callum still does not have the ability to cross the Queen's magical defenses, nor the wherewithal to fight the line of trolls that would be waiting for him. I tell you this now because if and when that time comes, there will be no way to let you know in advance. It will be a last-minute call based on a number of factors and you will likely be caught off guard. Be aware that a Veil crossing like I would cast, situated in a space so heavily warded, could be a mite uncomfortable, like tumbling in a clothes dryer. I do not want you to be unduly frightened."

"I understand," I reply. "Frankly, when I first started crossing the Veil on my own, I rarely arrived standing up, so I'm already used to a less than stellar 'landing.'"

Our conversation is interrupted by my Tax Man who, like everyone else on the team, is in his usual head-to-toe, black mission get-up with an AK 47 slung over his shoulder. In fact, there is a large collection of human weaponry amassed in the room. "That's a lot of fire power for a magical take-down," I commented. "I didn't think you could take out *Tuatha de Danann* types with rifles."

"It won' put them down permanently," he says, avoiding the word "kill." "But it will slow them down long enough to attempt an easier capture. We also can't be sure he won't bring back-up team with him, most likely human thugs." He patted the rifle. "In that case, this works vera' well."

It's nearly impossible for me to wrap my head around the idea that this may all come down to a shoot-out in my big sister's living room, so I ignore my husband's comment. "It looks like we're almost ready to get on with this charade," I say, gladly changing the subject of deadly weapons and permanent "take downs."

"Aye, Love. Beck has already let us know he's sending out the glamour team out in T minus 20. Once that happens, it is hoped that our target will take the bait and attempt to breach the home. Has the Black Knight explained the logistics of your placement in the room, Lass?"

"Not yet. But I'm sure he will very soon. I think he's avoiding me for as long as he can so as not to get me all 'nerved' up too early in the game," I replied.

Declan doesn't answer. Instead, he turns towards Merlin and asks, "If ya' ken' give us a moment of privacy, Ambrose?"

"Absolutely," the wizard agrees before stepping away to talk to his son.

My husband leans in to embrace me, but then hesitates. Instead, he takes both my hands in his. "There is still time to change yar' mind, Rosie Love. No one would think less of ya' if ya' did. We ken' find another way that does no make you the bait."

It wasn't like I didn't expect him to give it one more try. He's a fighter, a need-to-have-the-last- word kind of guy, especially when it comes to his thinking he's right and I'm wrong. But I've come too far to give this up now. Still, despite my strong conviction, I feel immensely sad that I can't give him this one thing he's begging for. He's asked for so little from me over the years. "I'm sorry, Declan. I just can't. We'll never be free of him if we don't take this opportunity. I have to do this. For all of us. For Claire and Scott and the boys. For *Oisin*. And for all the innocent victims he's destroyed in his reign of terror. It's my path, Sweetie. And I have to walk it."

As I finish my little speech, Robyn Brannigan comes up behind us. I'm surprised to see him here as he almost never takes part in nitty-gritty action like this, preferring to be on hand afterwards to take care of any casualties. Also odd is the fact that he's dressed in the same tactical gear Declan's wearing. I almost always see him in his "doctor uniform" of dress pants, collared shirt and tie and with an immaculate white lab coat covering them. This all-black, body-hugging get-up seems like more of a costume on him. "I apologize for interrupting, Lord and Lady *Nuada*. If I could have a moment of your time before chaos reigns?" he asks.

"Sure, Doc," I reply, not anxious to go back to the conversation at hand. "What do you need?" I asked while noticing for the first time the stack of official-looking papers in his left hand.

He holds them up. "I have the documents for the codicil to your Eternal Mate contract. The one specifically freeing the two of you from the *Beó Bás* tenet of the requirements. Her Majesty has gone ahead and signed them, so now all we need is a signature from the both of you. The Black Knight can witness them and then it'll become official." My face must give away my unwillingness to close the door on this phase of my life, to finally give up my dreams about having any more children. "I realize this might not be the most comforting time and place for such a thing, Dr. Parker. But as your physician as well as loyal friend to both of you, and in consideration of the inherent risks involved in this mission, I believed that you would want to protect your husband from taking on such a difficult and permanent mantle should the…unthinkable happen," the doctor explained.

"Ya' don' have ta' sign this now if yar' not ready, Love. I know ya' still have hope in yar' heart," my Eternal Mate offered.

I can't help notice the mix of sadness and fear in my mate's eyes. Allowing me to make this decision on my own without pulling "rank" as Lord of House *Nuada* has been extremely difficult for him. And I sure as hell don't want the love of my life to end up like Cillian *Mac Badh*, wandering around like a ghost, not to mention the idea of my children having to deal with the loss of both of their parents. Of course, I'd sign those damn papers. How could I do anything less? "Thank you for that option, my Lord. You are very sweet and loving to offer it, but I'm ready to move on according to my path. Things will be as they will be."

Then, with two scribbled names across the bottom of the page by both Declan and I, while the Black Knight of *I Idir* stands witness, my beloved husband was officially free from the horrors of facing the "Living Death" should anything happen to pre-maturely end my life. Which, all things considered regarding today's mission, was a distinct possibility.

TOOTHLESS 38

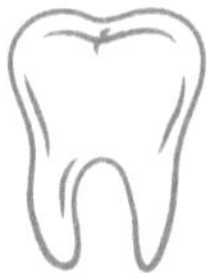

NOT PLAYING FAIR

AT PRECISELY 10:45 AM Swampscott time, I find myself pushing Claire's expensive vacuum around that classic Oriental rug; the one with all the magical sigils and black salt under it. Strangely enough, I don't feel even the slightest hum from all that energy. Music is playing softly in the background. Some 1980's station my sister loves. There are ten sets of invisible eyes on me and I can't stop wondering if I look as goofy as I feel vacuuming the same small area over and over again.

As expected, the Black Knight went over every detail of the plan with me, patiently and calmly, before sending the three team members out the door, glamourized to look like my brother-in-law, Scott, and my two nephews. The house's original wards, set by Declan years ago, were purposely left in place, lest the target find the complete removal of them suspicious. Because of those wards, a Fae person wishing to enter the house would need to get specific permission to do so depending on the perimeters of the spell.

Based on past history, his psychological profile, and the target's believed "relationship" between himself and Claire, the consensus was that Callum Fitzpatrick would try and abduct me on his own as to cause the least amount of fearful retaliation from his "beloved." It was assumed he'd try gaining entry by using a glamourized disguise of someone who my sister would willingly let inside her home. It would then be my job to convince that "person" to come in, get myself firmly situated on that rug as close to the center as I could, and then somehow draw him towards me. Beck and I had gone over several scenarios that could be used to gain his trust, but it would be ultimately up to me to decide which one had the most chance of success based on the personae the target had selected.

Though I didn't say this to anyone else, I wondered what possible role *Oisin* would play in this scenario. Would his wretched father include him in my take-down? How was I going to react if the child I lovingly raised as my own for so many years played an active role in my "sister's" abduction. This was only one of a million worries that ran through my head as I vacuumed that damn rug over and over while I waited for my would-be-kidnapper.

Even though I knew to expect it, when the doorbell actually rang, I gave a startled jump, my pulse beating widely in my throat. *"This is it, Rosie,"* said a familiar voice in my head that did not belong to my husband. *"Nice and easy. Don't spook him,"* the Black Knight ordered. With a prayer to all the goddesses I knew to be benevolent, I shut the vacuum off and headed toward the foyer to answer the bell's call. I forced myself to look through the side glass to see who it was, an action common to most people answering the door. The person standing in my line of view was a male who I guessed to be in his mid 30's, bland of appearance in a nondescript kind of way: Someone you probably wouldn't think of again if you saw him on the street. He had a large water jug on his shoulder, a match to the one in Claire's kitchen, and was wearing some type of delivery uniform. Seeing me through the glass he smiled and waved. "Carrigan Quench delivery," he said loud enough for me to hear through the glass.

I forced myself to smile back and gave him a thumbs up signal, then went to unlock and open the door. "Haw' are ya' this mornin', Mrs. Kellogg," the man said in a typical Boston accent.

Without giving myself away, I smiled sweetly while getting a good look at the name tag on his shirt. "I'm great, Jimmy. How 'bout yourself?" I ask.

"Can't complain, Mrs. K. May I come in?" he asked.

"Of course," I replied, smiling so hard my teeth hurt. "Look's like it's going to be unseasonably warm, today, huh?"

For a second, the delivery man hesitated and I worried that perhaps something seemed amiss to him. I wondered if he may have felt something akin to magic under his feet. Then, he seemingly brushed off his hesitation and asked me, "That's what I hear, Mrs. K. Do you want the water in the same spot?" he questioned.

"Yes, Jimmy. That would be perfect," I said still smiling. *Jeez, Rosie. You must look like an idiot clown with all that grinning,* I thought to myself.

I followed him into the kitchen and watched as he set the jug on the floor. "Looks like ya' didn't finish this last one, Mrs. K. Will your husband be able to replace it when needed?" he asked, casually looking around for who or what I'm not sure.

"Oh, I'm sure Scott can handle it," I replied. "We've been away from the house a lot these past two weeks with the kids out of school now. I'm sorry. I probably should have cancelled this week's delivery."

"No worries, Mrs. K. If you think you need help replacing

the jug, give the office a call. I can pop in and take care of it for you," the fake delivery guy offered. "So, you said your kids were out of school for summer break? It's so quiet here this morning. Where are those two little guys?"

"Out fishing with their dad today. They're planning on spending the afternoon at Red Rock Park," I stated, still trying to scratch up a plan to get him out the kitchen and onto that blasted rug in the living room.

That's when I remember seeing one of Claire's expensive handbags left open on the dining room table. Undoubtedly, my sister would offer a delivery person a tip. She was known to be very generous that way, so I had no worries "Jimmy" would find the suggestion a reason for alarm. The scam regarding a tip would also provide a solid reason for us both to cross the living room rug to get to the table where the purse was located. Or so I'd hoped. "I appreciate your understanding about a second trip, Jimmy. Let me get you a little something extra," I suggest, still grinning like a hyena and speaking loud enough for my veiled team members to hear and react because it would be awkward if Claire hadn't left any cash in that purse.

I started to move from the kitchen back towards the living and dining room. "Jimmy," aka my father-in-law, followed behind me. Knowing I had my back turned to that monster didn't fill me with a whole lot of confidence, but I couldn't very well insist he walk in front of me without raising any red flags. My plan centered on me removing some cash, then heading toward the living room where I would casually stop in the center of the carpet to hand the target the money, thus allowing the rest of the team to do whatever it was they planned to do in order to take Callum Fitzpatrick into custody.

That was the plan anyway. And it might have worked if

my husband's father wasn't such a vile, horny bastard. As I reached into the purse to grab a magically produced twenty-dollar bill, the creep came up behind me and wrapped his disgusting arms around my waist. I'll admit that I wasn't expecting sexual assault to be part of this plan. I wrenched away from his grasp, giving him a hard shove. "What the hell do you think you're doing?" I holler in Claire's higher-pitched voice. "Get away from me before I call the police."

The figure of Jimmy shimmered a bit before fading altogether. The man before me resembled my father-in-law, Callum Fitzpatrick, but his skin was so drawn, so tightly pulled away from his face, it looked like the head of a grotesque Halloween skeleton. His flesh was an unnatural, sickly gray color and his once, thick red hair, the same color as my husband's, was now hanging in limp, pewter strands down the sides of his head. The transformation was horrifying, and that was before I saw the large, grayish-brown rat poke its pointy-nosed head out of the pocket of Callum's stained, shabby lab coat, its ratty, coal black eyes staring straight at me.

"Come now, *Mo Ghrá Go Deo* (My Forever Love), surely in yar' heart ya' recognize yar' One and Only? 'Tis I, Finbarr Lally, come ta' make good on ma' promise ta' ya'," my father-in-law said as he reached out to grab me again.

The whole rat thing got to me. I don't do rats. Or mice. Period. They have always creeped me out and it took every bit of whatever self-control I still possessed not to let out a scream. Under my feet, I begin to feel the tiniest zing of magical energy that I assumed was the Merlin getting ready to pull me out. But I wasn't ready to give up. "No! Not yet! I need more time. To think!" I yelled, intending my words to reach the ears of the hidden wizard without the kook in front of me being any wiser.

"What is there to think about? We have waited long enough, *Cailín Milis* (Sweet Girl)," the man said. "Take my hand, *Aine*. We will return to *I Idir* and rule the Otherworld. Not just *I Idir*, but Avalon and *Asgard* as well. No one will stop me. Not with you by my side as ma' *Banríon* (Queen).

"You know I'm not *Aine*, right? You're confused, Callum. *Aine* was my mother. She's dead. I'm her daughter, Claire. I'm not Fae. Not one little bit. There's no way I can go to the Otherworld." I babbled, all the while considering if a dash to the living room was remotely possible. If I could just get him to follow me to the center of that rug, we could still do this.

The truth was obviously not what he wanted to hear. His eyes narrowed and he grimaced. "You are *Aine* reborn. All these years spent among the Mundanes have caused you to forget your true nature, that you are my everlasting *Mo Shiorghra*. But once we cross the Veil, I have faith our love will come back to you."

I decide it's now or ever. Pushing off the dining table for momentum, I sprint across the room, past the man with the rat and toward that rug in the living room. I would have made it too, if I hadn't caught my foot on the edge of the ornate grandfather clock that stood as a marker separating the two rooms. The klutzy gene in me that kept me out of most athletic activities caused me to lose my balance and I found myself sprawled out on the hardwood, at least a half foot away from the edge of the Oriental.

At this point, I would have expected to find myself some-where safe in *Crann Bethadh,* courtesy of the Merlin's magic. However, something apparently was drastically wrong in the save-Rosie's-ass department. My wretched father-in-law was across the room in mere seconds. He leaned over and tried to roughly help me up, but I used my basic training to kick myself free as I crawled toward that damn rug. In return, he reached down and grabbed the edge of my shirt to use as leverage to pull me up and toward him. Because it's tied at the waist, the shirt fits more snugly and instead of using it to pull me up, the bottom of it rode further upward, exposing the skin on my back as well as that crazy black raven ink left by The Morrigan.

TOOTHLESS 39

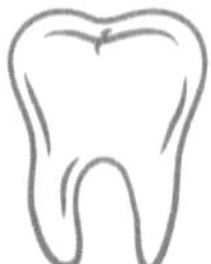

IT ALL ENDS HERE

"Wʜᴀᴛ ᴛʀᴇᴀᴄʜᴇʀʏ ɪs ᴛʜɪs?" Callum shouted, his anger physically present as a hazy shadow around his body. Without warning, I find myself helplessly levitating several inches off the hardwood floor with my back to this fiend who I once called family. I seemed to have no control over my body, as if I were some rag doll, puppet flopping around at his whim. At this point, I will admit to being absolutely terrified. I could feel my mate's rage like hot liquid fire inside my head, but at the same time, there appeared to be some type of magical wall between us, solid and foreboding. "This be the mark of that Raven sorceress. How does my One and Only come to wear her dark magic?"

"I already told you. I am not *Aine*. I'm her daughter," I plead, kicking my still dangling feet in protest. I am suddenly flipped around so I'm now facing my husband's father. He peers intently into my eyes while placing two gray-skinned hands at my temples. "You speak the truth, lying whore. You are *Aine's* daughter, but not the one who is my love reborn.

You are that dog-faced abomination my worthless son has attached himself to. That low-born tooth fairy changeling." Callum Fitzpatrick wrapped his large hands around my throat. "Where is your sister?" he growled.

"Nowhere you can reach her," I squeaked.

Straight away, I find myself slammed to the floor, hard enough to knock the wind out of me. As I struggled to catch my breath, Callum spoke out loud. "Boy. Bind her."

The rat clambered out of his pocket and landed on the floor next to me, a twist that added a whole other level of "ick-factor" to my present situation. Like I may have mentioned before, I don't care much for rodents. But a mere second later it wasn't a rat I was looking at. In its place stood my husband's half-brother, *Oisin*. He was taller and more muscular than I remembered. Older, with a light graze of ginger-colored facial hair across his chain and bearing a great resemblance to the portrait of my husband at that age which hung in the great hall at *Dun Siorai*. "*Oisin*. Sweetheart. It's so good to see you," I blabber. "It's me. Rosie."

He didn't answer. Nor did he seem to take notice of the fact that though I looked and sounded like my sister, I was admitting to being his "Lady Sister," the woman who once upon a time kissed him goodnight and taught him to read. My heart sank at the thought that perhaps I had been wrong all along about him being on our side. Plus, the fact that he had been able to easily shift from Fae form to rat indicated a high level of magical skill and I wondered if that meant he, like his father, had crossed into the dark *Jotun* magic of the *Dökálfar* people. I let him bind my hands and feet with some type of hemp rope that vibrated with magical energy, though I took heart that he had left the knots around my wrists very loose.

When the boy finished his binding, he helped me to a standing position and I let myself believe that he was being as gentle as he dared. "Shall I take her to the *Myrkiborg* (Dark Fortress), *Faðir* (Father)?" *Oisin* asked.

"That won't be necessary, Boy. I have a feeling fate is already in motion." My father-in-law said as he grabbed me roughly and pulled me towards him. He removed a small black case from his pocket and took a filled syringe from it, then mumbled a few strange words. Before my eyes, the entire "mission team" materialized with weapons aimed directly at the three of us.

"Let her go, *Athair*, or I will kill ya' where ya' stand," my husband said, sounding ridiculously calm for the situation at hand.

"Such blustering, *Deaglan*. Ya' war' always more comfortable with threats than actions," Declan's father replied. "We both know ya' won't risk a hair on yar' whore's head, so bewitched as ya' are with what lies between her legs. Though, I will say I am mildly impressed ta' see that ya' have been able ta' seed in her three strappin' sons. Pity ya' won't live long enough ta' see them stand behind ma' throne."

"There's nowhere for you to go, Fitzpatrick. In the name of Her Majesty, Queen Maeve of *I Idir*, I arrest you for multiple counts of treason and murder. As per the just laws of the kingdom, you'll be allowed a chance to plead your case before Her Majesty and the Ruling Council," the Black Knight stated.

"What a ridiculous notion, Black Knight. We both know there will be no fair trial. The Dark Raven will always demand her blood sacrifice. Of course, that is only if you can stop what's coming. I think you will not be as successful as you imagine. So let us save time and just give me the sister. A trade. One for the other. And then we can go back to fighting our same little war, one the *Sidhe* ken' in no way win," my husband's father predicted.

"There will be no trade," my Tax Man replied. "You will

let Rosie go or ya' will die where ya' stand." My husband took a step forward, a rifle still pointed at his father's head.

"I think not, traitorous heir." Callum lifted the syringe and placed it near my neck. "Ya' already know that this is a death sentence. A slow, painful one at that. You have seen first-hand what it can do. You will bring my *Aine* to me. Now. Once we are all safely away, I will send this wretched tooth fairy back to you."

The Black Knight laughed, a cold, mirthless sound. "All that fucking black magic must have rotted your brain, old man. The only way you're leaving this room is in brass cuffs or dead. I'll be a nice guy and let you choose."

"As you wish then, Black Knight," Fitzpatrick muttered as he turned his attention to the syringe at my neck. "You lose, tooth…"

My loathsome father-in-law never finished his words as he went down under the ambush of a five-hundred-pound lion, while the deadly syringe dropped to the floor and rolled away. Yes. That's correct. A genuine full grown, bushy-maned, teeth-barred, snarling lion. The kind I'd seen maybe once or twice at the Franklin Park Zoo in Boston. The beast was in a complete frenzy, ripping and tearing at the older man's flesh. At one point, the animal stopped and looked up at me with a pair of gray-green eyes I immediately recognized. "This wad' be a good time ta' get out of the way, Lady Sister," the lion said, then went back to his attack on the screaming man, who despite possessing a high level of magical skill, seemed unable to parry any of the animal's bites.

I managed to stumble over to Declan where I completely lost any sense of courageous decorum, sobbing and burying my face in his chest while sounds of continued carnage went on behind me. At some point, the screams turned into gurgles and groans. I forced myself to take a peek at the scene I helped to create. The lion had padded off to the corner of my sister's living room. It sat down and began cleaning its bloody paws with a long pink tongue in the way of a common house cat. The idea that it was actually our *Oisin* under all that fur, muscle and bloody teeth made the bile from my stomach rise up into my throat. "I think I'm going to be sick," I said to no one in particular.

Someone handed me a plastic bag and for a few moments, all I focused on was emptying my gut of every bit of horror and grief that had built up inside of me. By the time I finished, Callum Fitzpatrick, the one-time Lord of House *Nuada* and my beloved mate's father, was begging in a whimpering voice for *Trócaire Naofa* (Sacred Mercy) according to the sacred tenets of *I Idir*. I watched the Black Knight remove the ancient sword of the Otherworld, *Caladbolg*, from its plain dark bag. "Best ya' look away, Love," my *Mo Shiorghra* said in a voice strained with its own grief and suffering. "'Tis a vera' gory sight."

"No. We'll go through this together," I said, weaving my fingers through his, and turning around to face the inevitable.

The Black Knight stepped up to the man, the gleaming blade raised over his head "Callum Fitzpatrick, be it your desire to call for the ancient rite of *Trócaire Naofa?*"

"Aye," the man groaned in a weak voice. "I gladly welcome the next life, for this one has been a grand disappointment."

"Then in the name of The Morrigan, goddess of war and destruction, I offer you the gift of *Trócaire Naofa*. So, mote it be." In one smooth swing, the Queen's Hand of Justice brought down the sword upon my father-in-law's neck. And for years afterward, I had a hard time spending any time in that particular room within my dear sister's home without recalling Callum Fitzpatrick's empty eyes staring up at me from his severed head.

TOOTHLESS 40

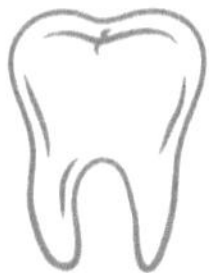

SHAKING OFF THE FEAR

I SPENT 43 additional hours in Swampscott awaiting the transformation of myself back to normal physical standards. The process was slow, piece-meal, and more than a little uncomfortable. Unlike my initial change, I didn't have the Merlin's superior skill keeping me in a magical stasis while it took place, as additional hocus-pocus supposedly delayed the natural DNA from regrouping. Therefore, during this time I was physically miserable, extremely weepy, highly emotional, and unusually cranky, refusing to see visitors, eating myself silly, and missing my kids something awful. My Tax Man was a real trooper, always trying to keep me upbeat and never taking offense at all the nasty comments I threw at him.

He didn't say as much, but I knew Declan was secretly concerned that I wouldn't be completely the "same" as I was before The Morrigan's magic. All *Sidhe* believe in the concept that magic, no matter how big or little, has a "price" set by the Universe. In addition, he'd always been very superstitious and was rightfully concerned that our Beltane "bad luck' would linger indefinitely despite his sire's demise. I was aware that Lord *Nuada* had formally petitioned Her Majesty for permission to allow *Oisin* to retrieve the missing fox cup from wherever it might be and return it to *Dunn Siorai*, but as of yet, we'd gotten no response to that request from The Throne.

In fact, we had absolutely no information whatsoever regarding the boy's whereabouts or his current situation. The recall of those minutes after Callum Fitzpatrick's death is, for me, a blur of emotional chaos and lingering disbelief. The horror of it was so overwhelming I secretly wished memories of it would dissipate along with the remnants of this face and body that wasn't mine, though, in truth, I believed the odds of ever forgetting those terrifying images was highly unlikely.

Still, certain elements of my recollection were very clear. Once my father-in-law's head had been removed from his shoulders, *Oisin* reverted from his lion form to his *Sidhe* one. At that moment, I remember thinking how wrong *Siobhan* Donnely had been about Declan's shifting ability coming from her family's bloodline. I also noted that the boy was able to shift back wearing his clothes instead of being naked, a useful facet of that particular magic that my unfortunate husband had yet to master. I realized these were strange things to ponder in the midst of wild death and destruction. It just went to show how crazy the mind worked to save one's sanity in the midst of something truly insane.

Oisin offered no resistance when he was approached and brass cuffed by the Black Knight. The two of them engaged in quiet conversation, but with my head buried in Declan's shoulder, I couldn't make out any of the specific words. However, as he was led past his sire's body, the teenager stopped and said in a voice loud enough for the entire room to hear, *"Tá sé déanta, a Mathair. Tá díoltas déanta agam ardo bhás* (It is done, Mother. I have avenged your death)." In truth, every hair on my arms stood straight up at those eerie words.

It didn't surprise Declan or myself that *Oisin* had been taken into "official custody." His behavior over the past eighteen months had been contradictory, and it would take slow and careful dissection to determine what had actually been in play the whole time he'd gone missing. Plus, even though Callum Fitzpatrick was dead, there was still a whole band of other bad actors out there in the Mundane world, along with a deadly virus to be concerned about. No doubt Beck would want to derive as much information from the kid as he possibly could on those subjects. Ultimately, his future would rest in the Powers That Be, and what that would involve, or how long it would take to reach that decision, was anyone's guess.

In the meantime, I counted the hours and the minutes I could be done with the after effects of this "mission" and back home with my family. Duncan was the only person I consented to see other than my husband, and that was because he brought me news from *Dun Siorai* about my children and their nannies. His stories about Liam's general mischief, Dylan's determination to train his falcon, and Ronin's new found philosophy that he was a dog instead of a boy lifted my spirits during the hours when pieces of me changed at what I considered a snail's pace.

On the third morning, when I awoke to find every part of the real me in its rightful place, I cried tears of joy. My Tax Man was quite emotional as well. Pulling me to him, he said with eyes watery with unshed tears, "I want ya' to know, Sweet Rosie Lass, that I wad' have loved ya' faithfully forever had ya' not fully returned in appearance ta' the woman I pledged ma' life ta'. But ta' have all of ya' back…the face and body I have adored from the vera' first time I saw ya' seven years ago, that last vision I see every night befar' I close ma' eyes, and the first thing I see when the new day dawns, is a gift I ken'no be thankful enough far'. I love every part of ya', *Ghrá Mo Chroí* (Love of My Heart)...now and always." Then, he spent the next several hours showing me just how much he loved all those individual parts in a way only the Tax Man could, and in his arms on that final third day after, I truly believed I was as beautiful as he claimed.

* * *

Despite the fate of *Oisin* heavy on our minds, our return home to *Dun Siorai* was a joyous one. Our children believed that both of their parents were forced to return to the Mundane world for "an important meeting their Da had in Boston" and that Mama went along "to keep him company." Obviously, they knew little of the constant threats against the Fae from humans in the Mundane world, nor did they understand the important roles both of us play in keeping their Otherworld heritage safe. Both Declan and I understood that at some point we might be forced to explain this all to them when they were old enough to understand, but for the time being, "ignorance was bliss."

Gossip being what it is in *I Idir*, we note the quiet whispers and quizzical looks behind our backs by the staff, no doubt regarding what was going on with our missing half-brother, but not a single one of them would think to question us about anything they'd heard. Not even Cook, who has known the child since he was brought to the estate as a new born infant. I liked to believe that everyone who was part of House *Nuada* genuinely respected and admired their Lord and Lady, and would never utter a single word against us.

The weeks of summer continued to pass uneventfully. I tried to take advantage of the precious free time with my children before we once again needed to return to Salem for the new school year. This September, Liam would attend *Cerridwen Prep's* new pre-school program, leaving only Ronin at home with *Brigit* and *Niamh*. I suppose some would say it was unnecessary to have two full-time *scathach* nannies with only one toddler still at home, but the Fae women have become like family to us and the thought of them not being around is…well…unthinkable.

On a day sunny and clear with the most beautiful blue June sky, the seven of us planned to spend the day at *Tir na Fathach* to check on the final aspects of the cottage build, followed by a family day complete with camp-fire cooking. His Lordship had a rare day free of estate and business responsibilities and he and the boys were looking forward to some afternoon fishing that hopefully would be successful enough to become the centerpiece of our meal. It's why the unexpected visit by the Black Knight was so unwelcome.

Declan sent the children and the nannies out to hunt for bait worms with the promise that the trip would not be long delayed. We met in my husband's study, the most heavily warded room in the entire estate, as a visit from Beck is almost never a social call.

Today was no different. The Queen's Hand of Justice came bearing the news that Declan and I had been waiting for in the aftermath of our last mission.

Beck began with an update on Robyn's progress in the development of a reliable vaccine to neutralize the deadly mutated Norovirus designed by the Mundane terrorists to weaken and kill Otherworldly residents. Most of what he told us was information I already know, as Robyn had kept me in the loop on his progress. Though recent tests of the new vaccine on laboratory mice had shown some positive results, the overall rate of death by the disease was still too high at thirty-eight percent to call the vaccine a complete success, but the doctor was optimistic that he would eventually find the key to better results.

All the clinics in Algiers, Spain, Poland and Switzerland had been completely annihilated. However, attempts at breaching the Veil border continued to be a problem, signaling that not all parties involved had given up on trying to produce a viable process to alter human DNA for safe passage into the Otherworld dimension. Intelligence teams were working to find where these secret labs might have been rebuilt which caused he and Declan to go on at length about the best method to discover them while I sat there tapping my foot.

By the time ole' Mr. Shark Teeth got to the topic of *Oisin*, I was beyond frustrated. "Lastly, I wanted to give you an update on what's going on with your half-brother," he said.

"Please do. We've had no information for over four weeks now," I say, not bothering to hide my exasperation. "Nothing. Nada."

This makes Ted Beckett smile, as he always seems to find my annoyance humorous. "It was a very unusual situation, Rosie," he explained, not bothering with the protocol of titles. "The boy's interactions with Callum Fitzpatrick were a mixed bag. On one hand he appeared to be offering inside information that helped our cause. On another, he did things that adversely harmed the Fae community. He was unclear on why that was, only going as far as saying he needed to gain his father's trust in order for the man to impart to the boy his extensive knowledge of *Jotun* magic. *Oisin* still holds to the claim that the murder of his *Tuatha de Danann* sire was based on the ancient Elven law of *Hefnd* (Vengeance). We've checked into the *Dökkálafar* sacred tenets, and such a law exists and does offer permission for revenge to be taken, including the murder of a family member. Their culture holds strongly to the 'an eye for an eye, a tooth for a tooth,' concept, and because we know by DNA testing that the boy is of half Dark Elven heritage, Her Majesty believes we are bound to accept their sacred laws regarding this unfortunate situation."

"So, he's free to come home then?" I ask.

"Unfortunately, that's a 'no-can-do.' Both you and Fitz saw the high level of the kid's magical ability. To say that it's in the extreme capacity is putting it mildly. He admits to being able to shift into over a dozen different forms. He can jump locations in both the Otherworld as well as the Mundane, and has claimed to have personal contact with the Elven goddess, *Frejya*. Within the Otherworld pantheon, *Frejya* is in the same divination category as our own Morrigan. They have similar roles in each tradition. Her Majesty thinks it is highly unwise to let him continue that relationship and has offered him a different option, one which, as of yet, I have not been made privy to. But I can assure you that this new option will be one that benefits Herself and the Kingdom of *I Idir*.

For the time being, *Oisin* is safely ensconced at *Crann Bethadh*, under Her Majesty's protection and guidance. I'm aware that my father visits with him daily to offer spiritual and magical assistance. He is healthy and calm for the time being, and being kept from the clutches of the Ruling Council, who we all know would be less than understanding of the boy's actions. As you can imagine, the Lords get a little worked up over the idea of patricide."

"Has he said anything at all about what caused ma' sister's death by that insidious virus? Was it by ma' wretched sire's hand?" my husband asked. It's a question that has been haunting him since the day Meghan's body was found.

"That was an interesting twist," Beck replies. "He told me that Lady *Mac Badh* actually died a hero. He swore on Balor's Eye that your sister was trying to save a handful of Fae prisoners Callum was using as test subjects when she accidentally exposed herself to the virus. Since no successful vaccine had yet been created, she succumbed to the disease and her father had her body dumped at the Veil border. I mean no disrespect, Fitz, but I have to admit that I never found your sister to be the altruistic type, nor did she strike me as martyr material. Still, the kid was steadfast in his story and Herself intends to award your sister some kind of hero's medal posthumously. I'm sure some recognition of her sacrifice won't hurt our intelligence network's relationship with House *Mac Badh*."

"I agree 'twas not in Meghan's nature ta' sacrifice far' the greater good, but perhaps her path ta' motherhood changed something in har' soul. I know this information might offer ma' Lady *Mathair* some balm far' her grief."

As far as I was concerned, I would take to believing that my murderous sister-in-law died a hero when the Christian version of Hell froze over. Something about *Oisin's* story regarding Meghan's sacrifice didn't ring true, though I couldn't pinpoint exactly what it was I found "fishy." Nevertheless, because this information seemed to lift my Eternal Mate's spirits, I didn't offer my negative opinions on the subject. Instead, I changed the conversation to a topic heavily on my mind. "Now that you've officially interviewed him, may we see him? A short visit, at the least? Please?" I ask, trying hard not to sound like I'm begging.

"I think we're going to have to hold off on any family visits for now, Rosie," Beck said to me. "The kid is confused and seeing the both of you right now would probably make things worse according to Herself and my father. They believe he needs time to reflect on his new path without the burden of old emotions clouding his thinking. He carries a heavy weight for a kid so young. I promise you, though, as soon as they give the okay, I will personally set that meeting up. Even here at *Dun Siorai*, if that's what you wish."

It was the best we were going to get from the Black Knight. Despite my disappointment at his answer, I wondered if we had been anybody else would he have been as forthcoming as he'd been. It was obvious that Ted and Maureen Beckett considered us friends, and because of that relationship, we were being allowed more leeway than perhaps other Ruling Council members. Thus, it looked like for the time being we would have to trust our beloved family member to the ever-changing whims of the Raven Queen.

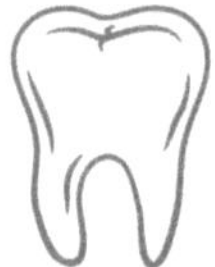

A GODDESS WITH A GIFT
TWO MONTHS LATER

IT WAS A DEJA VU MOMENT, one full of so many memories: Me cooking in my old kitchen, a kitchen that looked almost exactly like the one seven years ago in those oh-so-special first days the Tax Man and I shared as a brand new couple. Declan and I had worked hard these past few months to recreate the original cozy atmosphere of our first home together before it had become the sprawling conglomerate of Fitzpatrick's Folly. Using old photographs, original pieces long tucked away in storage, and a sprinkling of Declan's magical know-how, the new cottage on *Tir na Fathach* was a very realistic copy of our honeymoon home.

As I chopped garlic and rosemary for the rack of lamb, I tried to remember when I'd last prepared a meal from start to finish. Between life and professional responsibilities in both worlds, I found myself with little time to putter in the kitchen. Cook had been besides herself when I had handed her a list of pantry items and stated that I intended to do all the cooking myself directly in the new build. Hauling the extensive collection of necessary groceries, poor Master Tuck was forced to make at least a half dozen jumps back and forth from *Dun Siorai*, a protocol "no-no" he appeared excited to break in the way of a kid purposely ignoring the rules.

Cooking, it seemed, was just like riding a bike. I easily stepped back into the rhythm of getting a whole, complicated meal on the table as if it were something I did everyday. The dough for the rolls was rising nicely, the fresh scallops were cleaned and waiting for the pan, and the pastry for the fresh fruit tart was chilling in the fridge. This meal was important to me and I wanted everything to be perfect for the small group of friends I expected later that evening.

It had been Declan's idea to host a gathering here at the new cottage instead of *Dun Siorai*. It was meant to be a housewarming of sorts as well as a celebration of our handfast anniversary, an apropos suggestion considering the two of us had spent the night on this very spot seven years ago. We were expecting three other couples sans children; Mel and Duncan, Robyn and Roxanne, and of course the Becketts, who were happy to shed both their royal and parental roles for a limited opportunity to just socialize as friends.

As I returned the lamb back to the fridge to marinate, from the windows over the sink I caught a glimpse of a large red fox trotting off into the underbrush on the east side of the house. Undoubtedly my husband, off for a carefree run in his favorite woods. Truthfully, I was relieved to have him out of the house. He was beginning to get on my last nerve, fussing over the Mundane-style plumbing in the bathrooms, re-arranging the couch's throw pillows, and worrying whether Robyn or Ted would get called away at the last moment. A four-legged run always did him a world of good, and I hoped he'd enjoy the woods long enough for me to set the table without his re-aligning all the silverware.

No sooner had I turned back around when I found myself face to face with a very large black raven perched on my island in the same spot the rack of lamb had occupied thirty seconds earlier. It was obvious to me this was no ordinary raven, appearing to me out of nowhere and staring at me with un-bird-like, green eyes. I dropped a formal curtsy, which is no easy thing to do in Mundane yoga pants, as I had changed out of Otherworld attire in keeping with the throwback theme of the evening. "Good Morrow, Your Majesty. To what do I owe this honor?" I asked.

The bird hopped from the island to the tall chair next to it, and in an instance, feathers and beak were replaced with the Fae form of The Morrigan, an appearance I was far more comfortable with. "A special day for you, little tooth fairy mama?" she commented as she took in the Mundane vibe of the cottage.

"Yes, Your Majesty. Today is the anniversary of our handfast. His Lordship and mine. Seven years ago on this very day," I stutter as I worried that perhaps Declan and I had committed some type of protocol faux pas by not inviting the Queen to our little celebration.

"The *Banphrionsa* is looking forward to her evening out, as is her mate. 'Tis good for them to be free of responsibilities for a few hours. As it will be for all your little circle." the Raven Queen replied. "These are trying times. A few hours of good cheer among friends is the perfect cure for troubled souls." A steaming tea cup on a saucer appeared in front of The Morrigan and now I was in a sweat over the fact that I hadn't immediately seen to my formal hostess duties. "And you, Lady *Nuada*…how do you yourself fare after the intense events of your last mission," she asked as she sipped her cup of tea.

It made no sense to lie to her. She'd see right through it and call me out. Instead, I went the route of complete honesty. "I will admit to still having nightmares, Your Majesty. It was rather gruesome."

"You don't believe Callum Fitzpatrick was deserving of such an end?"

"Oh no, Your Majesty. I believe he was most deserving of it, and truthfully, I am not sad that he is gone from this plane of existence. My husband and our children are much safer in his absence. He was an evil man," I admitted. "However, witnessing a lion eating someone's face off, followed by a full-on beheading, is something one tends not to easily forget."

"I suppose some would find the spectacle distasteful," The Morrigan stated. "To my mind, Callum Fitzpatrick is lucky my Black Knight is a firm believer in the sacred laws. The Knight before him would have likely ignored the man's pleas for *Trócaire Naofa* (Sacred Mercy) and let the bastard suffer. There should be no regrets by all involved. That evil man got better than he deserved." She paused and looked at me pointedly. "And your Lord mate? How does he fare in the aftermath of his sire's demise?"

I absolutely did not want to talk about Declan's feelings regarding his father's crimes or his dishonorable demise. Anything I'd say could be misconstrued and doing so seemed inherently disloyal to my beloved Eternal Mate. "With all due respect, Your Majesty, I'm afraid it's not my place to discuss my Lord's feelings about such a private topic. I would much prefer if you asked him yourself so he could answer you in his own voice. He is currently out on a run, but I expect he will be back soon," I blustered.

I was expecting to get the stink eye over my refusal to answer her question, but she laughed instead. "Well done, Lady *Nuada*. What a loyal mate you are. I have always thought the Universe matched the two of you well, and your three sons are visible proof of your strong physical bond."

"Thank you, Your Majesty. I am more blessed than I surely deserve," I blushed. Then, in for a penny, in for a pound, I framed my own question. "If it pleases, Your Majesty, I would be most interested to know how my husband's brother, *Oisin*, fares. I admit to having much concern over his well-being."

"Always the little mama, aren't you tooth fairy? In that way, you remind me of my *Banphrionsa*. She is more maternal than is natural for someone Raven born. I can tell you that the boy sorcerer is healthy of body, but suffers from a past that has shaped him against his true nature. My Merlin believes that he can bring the boy's soul to rest, but that it will take time. I share the wizard's confidence that the young sorcerer can be turned from his dark side. Until then, you and your Lord must trust us to do what is best for both the boy and *I Idir*."

I couldn't help but think that what was best for *I Idir* far outweighed what was best for *Oisin*, but I didn't bother expressing that opinion. No doubt she already knew how I felt on the subject. Shifting topics, the Queen surprised me in a way I'm not expecting. "I do have a specific reason for meeting with you today, little tooth fairy. I have come to present you a boon in return for your recent work on my Black Knight's team."

I knew better than to consider accepting any reward from Herself, as they always came with lots of strings attached. "That's a very generous offer, Your Majesty, but a reward is completely unnecessary. I did what I did for the good of *I Idir*. For my Kingdom and its people," I stated.

The Morrigan threw her head back and laughed. Like I mean…she really guffawed. Loudly. Somehow, I got the impression that she was laughing at me, not with me. When she finished, she said, "Oh little mama, you may be a tooth fairy by blood, but you think like just a *Sidhe*. You've learned quite a bit regarding how the game is played here in *I Idir*. Let me phrase it another way. I've come this morning to give you a gift."

"A gift, Your Majesty?"

"Aye. For the 'anniversary' celebration of your handfasting," she replied.

Now her Raven Self had me slyly backed into a tight corner. Claiming it was a "gift" instead of reward changed everything. The Fae were very sensitive about the etiquette of gift giving. Here in the Otherworld, there was none of the self depreciation often practiced by the Mundanes with their false pronouncements of "you-shouldn't-have." A "gift" was always to be received in a grateful and polite manner no matter the size or usefulness of it. I must have mentally debated a few seconds too long before answering, because she sarcastically added, "You have my word there are 'no strings attached,' as you so amusingly believe. I am feeling very generous today and want to allow you to have this one-time experience."

"What might that experience be, Your Majesty," I ask as my mouth goes dry and my palms begin to sweat.

"How would you like to run with your mate this morning, little one, on this, your special day?" she asked with a knowing smile on her face.

"Your Majesty should be advised that I am, unfortunately, not much of a runner, and the few times I've accompanied my husband on his fox runs, I believe I have ruined the experience for him by moving too slow. He looks forward to the speed his shifted form gives him. I just hold him back." I explained.

"Silly girl. I didn't mean you should run beside him on

two legs, but rather four," she clarified, while I swore I could see some kind of magical twinkle in her eye.

"Are you suggesting I should shift physical form, Your Majesty? Into a fox?" I asked, not working too hard to hide my shock at the suggestion.

"Exactly," she said. "Before the last remnants of my ink fades from your body, I can give you this opportunity to share something unique and special with your Eternal Mate. Just this one time."

I couldn't but help to think that the goddess of war and destruction had, perhaps, lost her ever loving mind. "That's quite a fantastical offer, my beloved Queen, and a very generous one as well, but as a tooth fairy, I have no magical power of my own during the daylight hours. It would be impossible for me to hold your spell."

"As impossible as changing you into your sister? 'Twas a feat that allowed even the magically experienced Callum Fitzpatrick to be fooled. You insult me with your disbelief, little mama. 'Tis nothing for me to spell cast a short-termed shift," she said with a pout.

"I don't mean to doubt your power, Your Majesty. If you say you can do this, then I wholly believe you." I paused to think about the ramifications. I'd always envied Declan's sense of free joy when he was in fox form. To share those emotions with him, on the anniversary of the day we pledged our lives to each other, would be a grand gift. It was a lot better token of love than the new boots I'd planned on giving him. Could I really let myself be changed again? Into an animal this time? "How long would this spell last?" I ask, not willing to be stuck with fur and paws when my guests arrived. That one would be hard to explain.

"Two hours at the very most. A very limited time span, but plenty long enough," she said, again with that half smile that always made me nervous: As if she was holding on to some inside joke.

After seven years as part of the *Sidhe* elite, I knew better than to trust one of the ancient ones. They moved on an entirely different morality system. Still, the chance to share this bond with my beloved Tax Man was a once in a lifetime opportunity. I could just imagine the surprise and excitement on his pointy, muzzled face when I came bounding through the woods and he recognized that the lady fox was me. "And I'd change back to exactly this form in two hours?" I asked again, just to be sure I had all the facts.

"Aye. I have already said you would," she answered testily.

"Then I'll do it," I hear myself say all the while thinking I must be out of my ever freaking mind.

"Wise decision, tooth fairy. You will not regret accepting this gift, I promise. Now, come here child, and close your eyes."

* * *

The transformation was quick and, for the most part, painless. Plus, there was the added benefit of not having to get naked in front of The Morrigan. She was able to cast her spell while I was fully clothed, though I probably should have asked if I'd return that way as well. For a few seconds afterward, I worried that I wouldn't know what to do, how to act, or even how to locate my foxy Tax Man amongst the expanse of the woods. But instinct soon took over, and I found myself in an all-fire hurry to be out the door and on my way.

The goddess of war and destruction opened the back screen door and almost immediately, by scent, I presume, I knew exactly where to find my beloved. As I scampered off, I could hear the Raven Queen in my head. *"Off you go, Lady*

Fox. Find Lord Sionnach Rua and tie the final knot in your long-lasting legacy."

EPILOGUE

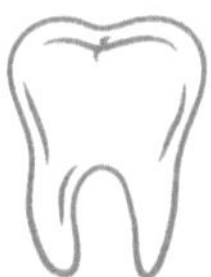

8 MONTHS, 28 DAYS AND NINE HOURS LATER

According to Fae mystical philosophy, the first cries of a new born child are divine in nature. Among believers, it is said that those initial wails are the Universe announcing that a miracle of great proportions has taken place and that an untethered soul has begun its newest journey. The Fae also believed that the stronger the cries, the more impact that particular soul will have on the people the child calls their own. If that is truly the case, then undoubtedly, our daughter will treat our family to one hell of a ride.

Sionna Rose Fitzpatrick *Nuada* entered the world red-faced and screaming nearly nine months to the date her father and I shared a once in a lifetime experience on our seventh handfast anniversary. It's no coincidence that she bears the name of the ancient Celtic fox goddess. Our daughter bears a great resemblance to her father and her eldest brother. She has the same high forehead, strong chin, and moss green eyes, but with one very large difference. Our

Sionna will never shape-shift into his beloved fox form as she falls decidedly on the tooth fairy side of the bloodline fence, taking after my maternal bloodline.

I suppose that anyone with a magical background should never say "never." In my case, I could never have expected to share this marvel of shape-shifting magic with my One and Only, nor the monumental gift that resulted from it, if it were not for the generous benevolence of The Morrigan. Declan and I have no doubt that our daughter was conceived while both of us were in magical fox form, the magic enabling us to break the physical boundaries of my crone status and human menopause. This was and is a goddess level gift I couldn't possibly explain the science behind, and one I remind my husband that Herself will undoubtedly never let us forget.

When Robyn gave us the news in my fifth month that early blood tests showed our fourth child, a girl, was most likely not *Sidhe*, I worried how she would fare in a world where everyone was judged specifically on their magical heritage. I looked for disappointment over the news in the face of my Eternal Mate. But as it usually goes with my weak assumptions, I was dead wrong. Declan was delighted that he'd "been blessed with another beautiful tooth fairy garl' in his life," and had insisted then and there that the baby's name must include some version of "Rose."

We'd explained to our boys in advance that their soon-to-be baby sister, like their mother, wouldn't always be able to use magic during the day. Any thoughts that they might be embarrassed over having a less magically gifted sibling were put to rest by Liam, who announced that "his baby sister didn't need extra magic because between her three brothers they had plenty to share and anyone who said different would answer to him." Afterwards, I hugged him while sobbing at the sweetness of his comment until he pushed me away, in Liam style, and told me with a series of eye rolls that I was getting his favorite T-shirt wet.

I also had not expected to have my fourth baby here in the Otherworld. All three boys had been born in a Mundane hospital setting with the modern technology it offered, along with the coveted, legal Mundane birth certificate. That had been the plan for this baby as well but our *Sionna* decided otherwise. Because of Declan's position on the Ruling Council, the whole family was required to travel back to *Dun Siorai* for the *Ostara* (Spring Equinox) and the traditional Druid service celebrating *Alban Eilir* (Light of the Earth). Despite my advanced pregnancy, I decided I needed to attend in my role as Lady *Nuada*. I'd felt absolutely fine with no early signs of labor and swore to my doctor that I could handle the back and forth through the Veil with no problem. Thus, Robyn had given half-hearted permission for me to go with a stern warning to let him know if anything at all changed.

The morning of the Druid service I awoke in our bedroom at *Dun Siorai* with a scattering of lower back pressure while making the amateur mistake of mentioning it to my husband. Declan promptly called for the doctor, refusing to return to Salem until he had Robyn's advice. Before our physician friend even arrived at the estate, my water broke and I began having definite contractions. By the time the doc showed up at my bedside even I knew I was in active labor. Because this was a fourth baby who could arrive in a very short time, it was far safer to deliver in the Otherworld rather than crossing the Veil in my condition.

It had been the right call. Less than two hours later, our baby girl entered the world, at least the Fae half of it. Now, as we awaited a first meeting between the siblings, I watched as my husband swaddled our daughter after changing her diaper, a pro after four children. "She is a wee bitty beauty, don' ya think, Love? I no look forward ta' the day when the lads start comin' 'round ta' call on her. I shall have ta' be vera' guarded."

He looked so serious, I found myself laughing. "We have a long time until we have to worry about that, Sweetie. Although something tells me that our daughter might be more than capable of taking care of herself. I'm sure you didn't miss her yowling at the indignity of being forced to leave her safe space."

"I dunna' believe anyone at *Dun Siorai* missed her entrance song," he joked. "She has a fine set of lungs, that's for sure."

It was I who reluctantly changed the tone of the celebratory moment. "I'm just relieved that she wasn't born in the chaos of the past several months. Without Callum's presence hanging over us like a storm cloud, I feel as if we are all a whole lot safer." When my mate didn't answer, I added, "We ARE safer now, right?"

"Aye, ta' some extent," he replied as he laid the baby in the family cradle. "My *athair* was surely the head of the snake, the 'go to" guy far' a cabal composed of terrorist bodies from several different Mundane countries. He apparently had promised each one of the groups' leaders that when the Veil was breached and *I Idir* invaded, they alone would join him as part of its new ruling class. How he managed ta' convince them of such a falsehood, I do not know. He had long spent the money he'd stolen from our House's treasury, but was still managin' ta' live like a king, with residences in all of the various countries. Callum made sure no one member of the group held all the pieces ta' the puzzle. It made them all dependent on him far' their next move. Intel we've gathered seemed ta' prove that it was his idea to create the mutated norovirus, a fact I will never be able ta' wrap ma' head around. How he held so much hate far' his own kind…his own bloodline… is beyond ma' understandin'.'"

Callum Fitzpatrick was a vile enigma I don't even want to ponder. Honestly, I believe some people are simply evil, added to the mix of the cosmos by the Universe itself for reasons I can't begin to comprehend. To my mind, at the end of it all, Callum Fitzpatrick got what he truly deserved. Which, of course, I don't say out loud to my Eternal Mate. It would just hurt him more and make him question his own DNA. "Do you know for sure which Mundane countries were part of the original cabal?" I asked, changing the topic off of my wretched father-in-law.

"So far, we've found proof for North Korea, Russia, India, China and Afghanistan," Declan stated. "Beck has his suspicions that the US and Germany are involved as well, but those two factions have done a much better job at hidin' their interests. We had hoped that once we had cut the head off of the treacherous snake I once called ma' sire, the group would splinter, destroying any cohesive measure between them that could produce success in their goal ta' take over *I Idir*. Unfortunately, we are still seein' daily multiple attempts ta' cross the Veil border, though now the ones that do come through seem ta' remain healthy longer than the earlier invaders."

My face must have shown deep concern because my *Mo Shiorghra* quickly added. "Don' despair, Love. We have made some positive progress. With Robyn's new vaccine and inoculation program, we no longer have ta' worry that we will all die from that evil ragin' stomach virus. Plus, even though the humans last longer, eventually they still all sicken and die. Sadly, I have no doubt that keepin' the Mundanes out of the Otherworld will be an ongoin' fight. But I am confident in the work of our team is keepin' our people safe. And now that we have the *Sciathán an Díoltais* (The Wings of Vengeance), I am certain more of these corrupted bastards will find themselves gone from the land of the livin'.'"

I pursed my lips in disgust. "I hate that you call him that. *Cillian Mac Badh* is a living person. Someone's son. Someone's father. You've all just reduced him to being a hateful weapon…an unfeeling assassin living in the shadows. It's cruel and unjust and almost as bad as requiring him to live as a ghost."

Chin out, my husband countered my argument. "He no longer wears the title of heir, Love. 'Twas his choice alone to take on this mantle. The Queen offered him a way around the *Bás Beo* and he took it. What would ya' have the man do? Live in a cave as a hermit? Become a silent Druid lost in mind-alterin' drugs and prayer? *Cillian* is Raven born. The blood of ancient kings runs in his veins. He's been trained from birth ta' serve his House and his Queen. He cad' do no less. If it had been me that was offered such a chance, I hope ya' know me well enough ta' realize I wad' do the vera' same thing."

I don't have time to shudder over that possibility, interrupted as we were by a knock to our bedroom door. *Birgit* poked her head inside. "Is it a good time far' us to visit?" she asked.

Before I could reply, our family dog, Seamus, ran through *Birgit's* legs and leaped on the bed to check on my well-being, gently licking my hand in a polite "hello." He tilted his head and looked at me quizzically. "I'm perfectly fine, boy," I say to the pup as I pat his furry, little head. "We have a new member of the family. Her name is *Sionna* and I wager she'll have you wrapped around her little finger in no time." The terrier licked me again as he wagged his tail. Then, he jumped off the bed and parked himself next to the cradle in guard dog mode, just as he had done with each of our other children when they were babies. I looked up and finally answered *Birgit's* query. "You all can come in for a 'meet and greet.' She's just been fed and changed, so she's content at the moment."

Our little man clan trooped in, accompanied by both *scathachs*, and, as an added surprise, *Oisin* with them. We hadn't seen our brother in several weeks, and to have him come to *Dun Siorai*, a place he had carefully avoided since his return to the Otherworld, just to see his newborn niece warmed my maternal heart. He was dressed in the plain linen robes of a Druid novitiate, a decision he'd made a few months after the tragic events in Swampscott.

The boys clambered around the cradle in solemn quiet that wasn't part of their normal behavior. "Boys, I wad' like far' ya' ta' meet yar' new sister and niece, *Sionna* Rose," their father announced.

Ronin looked toward me and said, "She has the same name as you, Mama."

"Yes, Honey, she does. Your Da thought it would be a nice thing to do."

Looking up at Declan, our youngest son said, "I think it 'twas a good idea, Da. It will make Mama happy."

"Aye, son. And we always want Mama to be happy, right?" he joked.

Oisin smiled at his half-brother. "Ya' always were a wise man, ma' Lord," he teased. Turning his attention to me, he asked, "How fare you, Lady Sister. Ya' look well and no worse far' the experience."

"I'm feeling great, *Oisin*. Four times is the charm, I guess," I replied with a smile. "How is life at *Cloch Chroí* (Heart Stone)?"

"Exactly what is meant far' me, dearest Lady Sister. 'Tis a vera' peaceful place," he said without much emotion.

Everyone took turns holding the baby, joking and

laughing until the noise level exceeded the newborn's comfort level and she began to wail. *Birgit* and *Niamh* gathered up their charges, tempting them away from their parents' room with promises of Cook's home-churned ice cream. Liam took his father's hand and asked, "Can you come too, Da? Cook makes the vera' best frozen cream."

Dylan seconded the request. "Please, Da? I want ta' tell ya' about how well I' doin' with ma' ridin' lessons. *Toirneach* and I will surely take the first prize away from the Princess this year at *Beltane*."

My Eternal Mate pondered my reaction, torn between fatherly duty and husbandly loyalty. "Go ahead," I encouraged. "I'll be fine. The baby is probably going to sleep for a few hours before her next feeding and I could use the rest."

"If yar' sure ya' don't need me here, Lass," he said.

"No. You go. Spend a little time with our boys," I replied.

He leaned down to kiss me goodbye, promising to return later that evening, and ushering our family out the door. *Oisin* began to follow them, when I suddenly asked him to stay a few extra moments. He appeared hesitant to be left alone with me, but took a chair next to the bed. "What is it ya' need of me, Lady Sister. They will expect me back at *Cloch Chroí* soon for afternoon meditation." The sleeve of his robe rode up and I couldn't help but see the magical sigils inked on his forearm, including one that I recognize as belonging specifically to The Morrigan.

"I just want to make sure you're content with the decisions you've made in the past few months. I can't help but feel that you were purposely isolated from your family in an attempt to sway your thinking," I said bluntly to the boy I'd raised from childhood.

"Truly I am content, Rosie. It is the first peace I have felt in…well…years. I know you and ma' Lord Brother have always tried ta' make me feel a part of yar' family, but until I could come ta' terms of ma' own cursed birth, I felt as if I belonged nowhere and to no one. But ma' soul is mendin' and I am grateful ta' Her Majesty and the Lord Merlin far' their confidence in me. I have not felt the urge ta' shift to violent form for many months now, and my mentors see that as a good sign."

I reached over and squeezed his hand. "Declan and I just want the best for you, *Oisin*. We support whatever that might be. But please know, you always have a place with us. In Salem and *Dun Siorai*."

The teenager squeezed my own hand in return. "I am grateful far' that knowledge, Dear Sister. You and yours mean the world ta' me."

He got up to leave, but I held firm to his hand. "Before you go, *Oisin*, there's one thing I really need to know."

A flash of concern marked his face. "What be that, Rosie?"

"Why did you lie to the Black Knight and the Ruling Council about Meghan being a hero," I asked. He blinked several times, a sign I'd caught him off guard. "Please don't lie to me, *Oisin*. I've been part of your life since you've been eight years old. If anyone can tell when you're not telling the truth, it's me."

Seemingly resigned, he asked, "How did ya' know I was lyin' about Lady *Mac Badh*?"

"The Black Knight revealed to us that when you told him Meghan died a hero, you swore on the Eye of Baylor. You and I both know that you regarded the old monster as a 'big deceiver,' a figure from Fae myth that you immensely disliked. I must have scolded you dozens of times for cursing using the monster's name. I just can't believe you would swear an oath on something you held no respect for," I explained, "if you were speaking the actual truth. What really happened with Meghan, *Oisin*?

His demeanor was heavy-hearted, with him shifting from

foot to foot as he did as a child when faced with an uncomfortable situation, and for a moment, I considered dropping the whole thing. But for me to put everything that happened in those eighteen months he was missing behind me, I needed to know the truth. "I will tell ya', Rosie, but you must swear to me that ya' will not reveal the truth ta' anyone. Ta' do so would just cause more unnecessary pain."

"I swear to you, *Oisin,* that whatever you tell me will remain between you and I."

He looked away while speaking. "My half-sister was no different than our sire. She took great pleasure in the sufferin' of those caught up in our sire's evil plan, be they human or Fae. Meghan was especially horrid to those with partial Fae bloodlines, even though she and I both shared human DNA. She called them worthless "half-bloods," and "abominations" and thus volunteered to take part in the administerin' of the virus to them. One day, as she was goin' to inject her subjects, a Fae man of good size loosened his bindings and fought her attempts. In the struggle that ensued, the syringe poked through her lab suit and pierced har' skin. She became ill a day later and there was as of yet no viable defense against the disease. When she died, ma' sire had her body dumped at the Veil Border. He did not seem at all moved by her sufferin' and death, and in that moment, I knew there was nothing of the man worth savin."

I sat chilled to my very marrow at the horror of the story, but not at all surprised that Meghan was as vile as I always thought her to be. I knew, years ago, there was a deep flaw in her moral character, some deep-seated psychosis, that caused her to try and murder me. Though I now feel justified in my beliefs, it doesn't change all the pain that was caused by her abominable behavior, and being right gives me no satisfaction. "If you knew this all along, *Oisin,* why did you lead us all to believe she was a hero? The Queen gave her a posthumous medal she didn't deserve, for Pete's sake!"

"Her Majesty does as she thinks best, Lady Sister. As a goddess, she does not weigh things as we simple Fae do. I don't doubt that she could see through my falsehood regarding Lady *Mac Badh*, but she appeared to be in agreement with my relating of the events."

"But that doesn't explain why you lied in the first place?" I questioned.

He sighed deeply before answering. "Because of the boy, Lady Sister. The son she left behind. No child should have to grow up bearin' the weight of their parent's sins. Believe me when I say I have firsthand experience of the matter. I did not want her innocent boy ta' suffer the same fate. He is, after all, my half nephew. Families need ta' protect one another, even when they are on the wrong path, like you and my Lord brother did far' me. Ya' never stopped standin' behind me despite all the wrong paths I took. I must do the same far' wee *Féchin*. 'Tis part of the legacy we leave behind in the Universe when we move on to another plane."

I kissed the hand of his that I was still holding, this boy considered a man by the folk of the Otherworld, so wise beyond his years. I might have even shed a few tears over what was, what could never be, and what might bloom in the future. *Oisin's* philosophy was at the heart of everything I believed in. Families were a legacy, not only in the bloodlines that made their genetic way through generation after generation; not only in the shape of the face, the form of the body, or the degree of magical strength, but in the dreams and choices made by its many members.

As *Oisin* left *Dun Siorai* that afternoon, set to walk his own path, I looked over to my sleeping daughter in her cradle, a cradle that generations of her family had used before her, and wondered what legacy we Fitzpatricks would continue to leave behind as we all embarked on our own individual journeys. Then, I smiled, peaceful at the thought of what a joyful loving adventure it was sure to be.

* * *

Missing your friends in *I Idir* already?
Join the Black Knight and friends in
The Morrigan Tales

More from Serenade Publishing

Songbird

By Sarah Williams

Songbird

Heartbreak Song

Our Song

Brigadier Station

By Sarah Williams:

The Brothers of Brigadier Station

The Sky over Brigadier Station

The Legacies of Brigadier Station

Christmas at Brigadier Station (An Outback Christmas Novella)

The Outback Governess (A Sweet Outback Novella)

Heart of the Hinterland

By Sarah Williams:

The Dairy Farmer's Daughter

Their Perfect Blend

Beyond the Barre

For more information visit:

www.serenadepublishing.com

About the Author

Victoria Rocus is a retired educator, accomplished miniaturist, and full-time author living near the home of country music, Nashville, Tennessee, USA. When she's not writing new adventures for her imaginary friends, catering beach parties for mermaids, or finding homes for orphaned dragons, she's building and rehabbing one-of-a-kind dollhouses and accessories, just like her favorite character, Dr. Rosie Parker. Many of her multiple miniature buildings are 1/12 scale replicas of settings from her unique fantasy stories.

Victoria started her writing career as a weekly blogger while still teaching middle school language arts. Now retired from the educational field, she's been able to make writing a full-time adventure, penning several fantasy and romance stories she hopes readers will enjoy with both a sigh and a smile.

Find out more at: victoriarocusauthor.com

instagram.com/victoriarocusauthor
tiktok.com/@victoriarocusauthor

Acknowledgments

Finishing this last book in The Tooth Fairy Chronicles was a bittersweet moment for me. Although I'm content over the idea that I was able to take these beloved characters on a seven-book adventure, they have been in my head and part of my writing journey since 2022, so saying goodbye to them as part of a daily writing schedule was sad for me. But, as Henty Wadsworth Longfellow once said, "Great is the art of beginning, but greater is the art of ending." He's not wrong. It's a simple fact that every beginning has an end, and as endings go, I'm proud of this one.

As with all the books in this series, there are many people to thank for the support along the way. First and foremost a heartful *"go raibh maith agat* (thank you)," goes to Sarah Williams, all-around-mentor and publisher extraordinaire, who has been instrumental in getting Rosie and Declan's story out into the world and into readers' hands. I wish for you every ounce of good luck the Universe brings.

Kudos as well to my awesome beta reader team for your genuine feedback and continued support. Whatever the future holds, I know for sure that I will want Carol Peden Fuller, Donna Gentile Ruth, Daniel Caddigan, Kaia Viney, Michele S. Kaspar, and Gail Hoder, along with talented fellow authors and friends, Arla Jones and K.C. Nord, getting my "sneak peeks."

Wishing *"mile beannacht* (a thousand blessings)," to those friends and family that have supported me so wonderfully along the way; Dan and Chris C, Steve and Gail H, Roy and

Denise P, John and Paula D, Shannon and Ryan B, Erin A, Jeannie H, Marcia W, Debbie P, Bill and Carol F, Betty M, Lorraine R, Linda F, Bonnie M, Cindy J, Christine M, and everyone who isn't mentioned here by my fault alone and who I will surely remember right after this book goes to press.

Loads of love to my dear "*teaghlach* (family)," my husband, Victor, my children Steven, Michael, Allison and Kaia, and my sweet, little "peanut," Valerie James. You are there in spirit on each page I write. Love you loads! Kiss, kiss. Hug, hug.

Lastly, a multitude of thanks to my loyal and generous readers who have supported me with each and every book. Words alone can't tell you how grateful I am for your gracious and committed support.

And now, Rosie, Declan and I leave you all with this very heartfelt Irish blessing:

> *May the road rise to meet you, may the wind be*
> *always at your back, may the sun shine warm*
> *upon your face, the rains fall soft upon your*
> *fields, and until we meet again, may God hold*
> *you in the palm of His hand.*

www.ingramcontent.com/pod-product-compliance
Lightning Source LLC
Chambersburg PA
CBHW032218050726
47591CB00001B/167